DESPAIR

A DEADLY SEVEN NOVEL

DESPAIR

LANA
PECHERCZYK

Prism Press, Perth Australia.
Copyright © 2022 Lana Pecherczyk
All rights reserved.
ISBN: 978-0-6454994-5-2

For promotional enquiries please contact Lana Pecherczyk on lp@lanapecherczyk.com

Text copyright © Lana Pecherczyk 2022
Cover design © Lana Pecherczyk 2022
Editor: Ann Harth

www.lanapecherczyk.com

CARDINAL CITY MAP

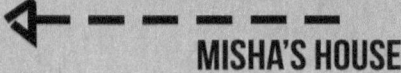 MISHA'S HOUSE

AIRPORT

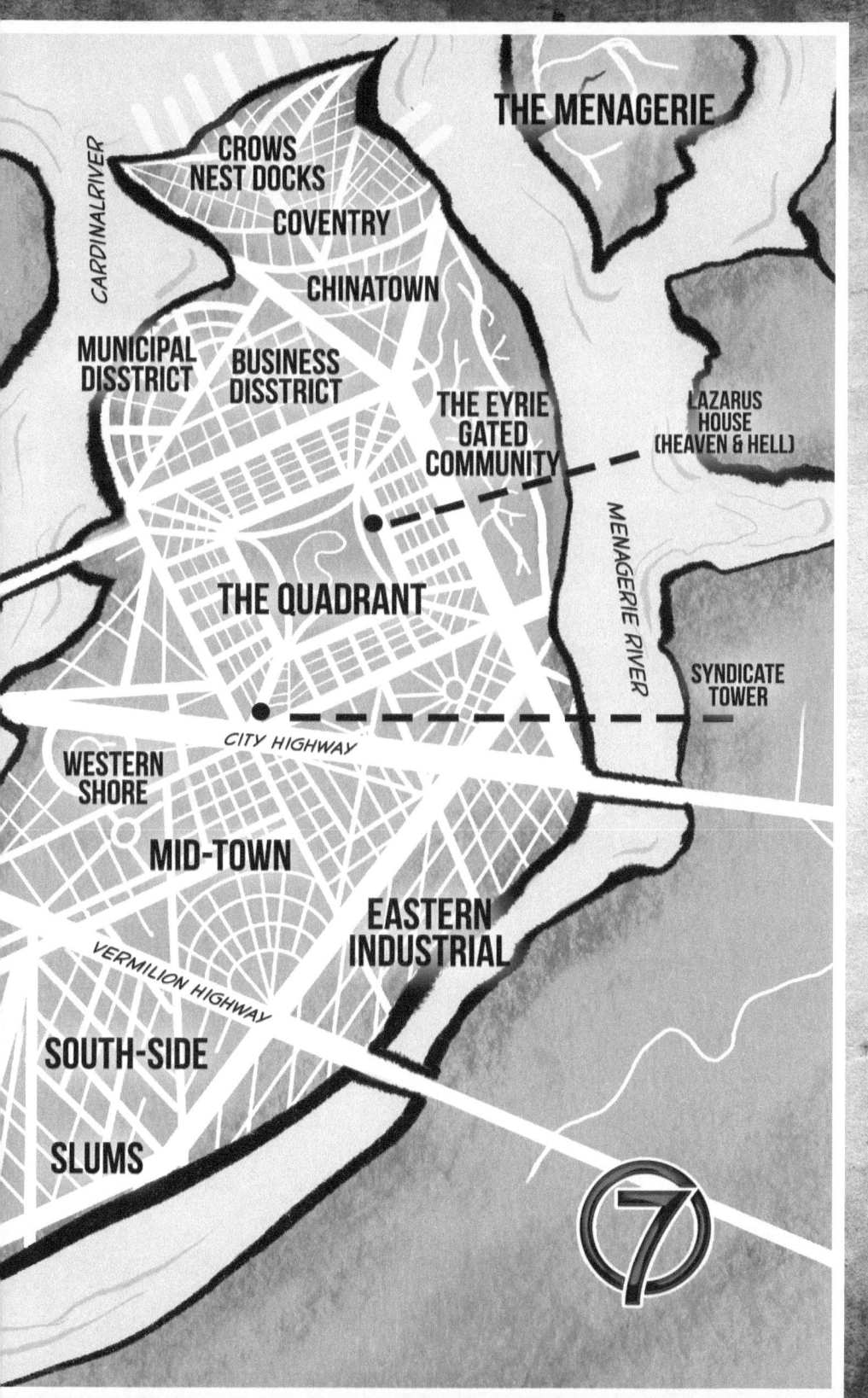

prologue

JULIUS ALLCOTT

IN A DARK, abandoned waste-water facility, Julius Allcott rushed between the computers he'd set up on a rusted metal platform. Cords and wires snaked everywhere and he had to hop to avoid catching his feet. He checked on the status of the replicate tanks he'd positioned around the city. Good to go. He checked on the Faithful teams in place, waiting with detonators at each bridge leading into the city.

"Is it ready?" his wife said to him from over his shoulder. He took a quick glance to reassure himself she was truly there, and smiled.

Incorporeal, and on another physical plane, his wife and daughter looked at him with loving eyes. Lightning flashed in his mind, and for a split second, he thought he caught a glimpse of something *other* beneath their faces. Dark holes for eyes. Skin tearing from flesh. Demonic fear as they seemed to scream and shake their heads in revolt. *Let us go,* they said. But—he shook his head and the strange sight cleared, leaving the smiling faces of his loved ones once again.

He was tired, that was all. He shook his head again to clear the fog and plucked at the chunks of hair on his head.

"Almost, my love," he replied, refocusing on the task at hand. "I've done exactly as you said. The plan is ready to execute."

Kidnap the mates of the Deadly Seven. Destroy the bridges. Lock down Cardinal City so no one can get in or out. Loose the replicates and other weapons. Watch the city burn and destroy itself. Watch sin finally have its day. And then while that was all happening, while the Deadly Seven were distracted or falling into sin themselves, he would be underground, back at that same spot, burrowing deep into the spirit dimension, opening the gateway for his wife and daughter to come back to him.

"Then what are you waiting for?" his wife asked. *"Detonate."*

Julius opened a line of communication with his team and spoke. "It's time."

The city foundations rocked. One by one, each bridge was taken out. It was time for everyone to finally see what Julius had always known—there was no escaping deadly sin.

And he was the father of it.

"Where there is hope... there is life."

– ANNE FRANK

one

DAISY LAZARUS

IN THE BASEMENT headquarters of Lazarus House, a baby's wail added to the chaos surrounding Daisy Lazarus. Like fingernails on a chalkboard, the cry grated down Daisy's spine. Two brothers shouted at each other. A third threw a gadget at the wall, shattering one of the wall-to-wall screens depicting city news. Others argued over intel on a computer at a central table. Daisy covered her ears from the cacophony of sound.

So many people. So much noise. So little she could do.

Her own sin of despair circled the drain of her mind. For years the sin numbed her, as though the fire that stole their mother's life had also charred her emotions. It also stole her feeling, her will to continue with this so-called life. She touched the silvery burn marks on her face. They weren't too obvious thanks to her advanced genetics, but she felt them as though they'd seared her yesterday. The bumpy flaws on her skin brought a new surge of despair. Swiftly, she hid her thoughts by moving her hand to swipe over her smooth, long silver hair.

The heat. The pain. The shame.

Two days ago, her numbness disintegrated, leaving her unprotected—a soft pink embryo. Now she felt too much. Her estranged family had rescued and put their blind faith in her, despite her villainous history. How could she process it all? Where did she fit in with this heroic family—did she fit at all?

Their story about the day she was abandoned was very different to Julius's, the Syndicate leader and their father. But wrap it however they may, the truth remained—for the good of the world, she'd been left behind to die.

Her whole life had been based around that fact.

She'd been stricken from their memories. No one wanted her. No one needed her.

Her recovery from that fateful fire still haunted her. She'd lain bandaged on a hospital bed, her body burning without flames. Phantom tears—her eyes were too damaged for real tears—searing her cheeks because she couldn't save her mother... and she couldn't find her brothers and sisters. A man she'd never met whispered to her, "They left you because they didn't love you. But I do. I'll never leave you. I'm all you've got now." He took her burn-free hand and squeezed it. "It's you and me against the world, my darling."

His palm had been cold and clammy.

"Daisy!"

Her gaze snapped to the right, her body alert and ready to fight, but it was only Mary. The woman who'd made the call to leave Daisy behind and the subsequent adoptive mother of the Deadly Seven. An assassin herself, she had once been a psychic. Somehow knowing that only made Daisy hurt more about her abandonment. Couldn't Mary have predicted Daisy's fate? Shouldn't she have prevented it... if she'd wanted to?

Daisy peeked at her inner wrist tattoo. The yin-yang symbol was unbalanced and more black than white. It meant her internal sin saturation was getting a hold of her. Despair had sneaky hooks. Sometimes she didn't know she was underwater until she was already drowning.

Mary bounced a crying baby in her arms.

"Daisy," she said as she walked over. If the woman asked once more for Daisy to recall information that could help find the missing mates, she would scream.

Mary must have seen the resistance in Daisy's eyes because she paused. She stilled in a way only a predator can, seemed to consider something, but then handed the baby to Daisy.

"Could you hold Amari for a while? I don't think Wyatt is in any state to calm her. We could use your help."

Daisy glanced at her brother, the warrior of wrath. He was one without his mate, and while he'd tried to balance his sin by soaking up the happiness of parenting, it wasn't working anymore. In his Deadly battle suit, hood down and around his shoulders, short black hair askew, he paced the floor. His nostrils flared like a raging bull. Veins popped in his neck and forehead. He'd smashed the television with his furious throw, but still stood before it, staring at his fractured reflection.

Daisy knew well the effects of being out of balance. She'd studied them for the Syndicate when she'd kidnapped Sloan's mate Max. She, herself, had suffered multiple blackouts and come-to with blood on her face and hands knowing in her bones that she'd ended lives. Even now she itched to check her palms.

Mary gave Daisy the baby, then chased Wyatt down before he picked up another gadget Flint had been working on. Flint, Mary's husband, had kept a respectable distance from Daisy. She often saw pity in his kind eyes, but unlike Mary, he wasn't trying to push a parental relationship on Daisy. He thankfully gave her space.

Unlike Julius who'd demanded the world from Daisy, Flint

seemed to be the sort who would gladly support her as she made up her own world.

She liked him for it.

Every cell in Daisy's body froze under the weight of the baby in her arms. From her swaddle, Amari blinked up at Daisy with wet, blue eyes.

"Why has it stopped crying?" Daisy asked anyone within range. "It was making noise and now it's not."

She searched the room for help, but no one paid her attention. The baby cried again and Daisy relaxed, then promptly freaked out because it had *started crying again*. With her heart in her throat, she paced the length of the room, jiggling the bundle in her arms. That's what Mary had done. It should work.

But Amari still cried.

Was she hungry?

But Mary fed her not that long ago, hadn't she?

Maybe she missed her mother. A slice of guilt hit Daisy and she wished she could do more to help her siblings find their kidnapped mates, but the truth was, over the past year Daisy had been included in less of Julius's machinations than at the start. Looking back, she could see that he'd distanced himself from her as much as he could without raising suspicion. Perhaps it had started the moment Daisy realized he'd lied to her. He'd said her siblings had always known she was alive. The distance grew when she discovered Julius had DNA samples of his family—his first wife and daughter—in a locket around his neck, hoping to bring them back as replicates.

But he never included Daisy in that family. He never intended to bring her back, a fact she only learned after years of emotional manipulation. Since Julius's betrayal, Daisy hated him with a passion bordering on psychopathic. He'd manipulated her. He'd kept her real family away. He'd turned her into a monster.

Amari's cry stuttered as they walked past a glass cabinet housing a mannequin wearing a Deadly Seven suit. Amari's joy fluctuated, bringing tingles and effervescent flutters to Daisy's stomach. Backtracking, Daisy used her sense of Amari's joy to locate the object of her desire. There was something about the glass cabinet that held her fancy. Amari's crying stopped all together. Daisy focused on the mannequin and held up the baby.

"You like something in here?" she asked.

Amari cooed and reached out to the shiny glass cabinet. There was nothing but a suit on a mannequin inside. Amari smiled at her reflection and touched the glass.

It took Daisy a moment before she realized all sound in the basement had hushed. Wyatt came over with a frown on his face but a softness to his eyes.

"Her mother plays games with her before the mirror," he murmured, smiled and tapped Amari's reflection. "Is that you, Sweetpea?"

Daisy looked at her brother. Wyatt's blue eyes stood out starkly beneath his black hair. Redness circled them, proving he'd had little sleep. None of them had. Not only were they worried about the fate of their mates, but they'd been battling their internal sin equilibrium while controlling the chaos Julius had unleashed in the city. Like Daisy, unbalanced sin would make her siblings black out and execute anyone with enough sin in their bodies.

Even if that someone was a child.

Daisy may be a murderer, but she'd always drawn the line at children. Now she might not have a choice. None of them might. Nausea rolled in her stomach and suddenly, the weight of all eyes on her was too much. She struggled to breathe under her new emotions. Her palms itched. Inside her body, she was in chaos. Outside, she was a statue.

"Have you thought of anything that can help us?" Wyatt asked her quietly.

Daisy's lips parted. "I…"

"What about your mate?" Griffin stalked over. He'd not removed his battle gear in two days. He only slept to take the edge off his exhaustion and then headed back into the streets to hunt for his pregnant wife. "Have your powers developed? Can they help us?"

"I…"

Evan and Sloan came over. They fired off similar questions. Soon it felt like the world surrounded Daisy and she was drowning. She had no answers, only more questions. With blood roaring in her ears, she handed the baby back to Wyatt and rushed out of there.

SITTING on the roof of Lazarus House, dangling her legs over the multi-story high edge, Daisy finally felt at peace. Or, at least, a semblance of it. Being in the basement had messed with her head. Being here, with a family she'd only dreamed of since she was little, also messed with her head. She knew it wasn't an excuse, and that she had to actively help clean up the mess she'd made, but she had no idea how to start.

How could she clean with dirty hands?

She lifted her face to the sky and closed her eyes. The sun warmed her and the wind brushed her skin. It always struck her as special that, even though the world could be falling apart, the sun still shone, the wind still blew, and the birds still flew.

"Thought I'd find you here."

Daisy startled at Parker's deep voice.

His bionic arm glinted in the fall sun as he squeezed next to her and dangled his legs over the edge. His muscular and virile form dwarfed her pale, lithe frame. Even his auburn hair held warmth, yet her silver hair was cold. To their right and left, a glass balustrade surrounded the pool area and terrace. Less than a week ago, Parker had been up here holding a party, announcing his retirement from Lazarus Tech—a company he'd built from the ground up. And a few months ago, Daisy had been here trying to kidnap Wyatt's pregnant wife. That baby she'd held in the basement—Amari—had almost not been born.

Because of Daisy.

Parker was the sun, and she was the dark side of the moon.

She gulped in fresh air and rubbed her palms on her jeans.

"How did you know I'd be up here?" she asked through a dry mouth.

"Because when we were kids, the lab roof was where we went to feel like we were in control, even if it was of the direction of our dreams." He looked down at her. "You're feeling overwhelmed. I get it."

She wanted to laugh. "You don't get it."

For a moment, he was quiet as he watched his bionic hand open and close. He'd fought with his mate, and his own stubborn refusal to accept her help had been his downfall. At least Daisy had nothing to do with that loss. She felt like everything else was her fault.

He murmured, "Maybe I don't understand completely, but I get some of it. The point is, we're here for you. We can work this out together."

She scoffed and shook her head. "Decades on and you've not changed a bit. Still trying to boss me around—" She clicked her jaw shut, hesitated, then whispered, "Pigeon."

It was her pet name for him when they were children. Saying it felt like coming home. She shot him a side-eye, waiting for his response.

11

"You know I dislike that nickname." His lips curved with a stifled smile and a pointed look at the sky over the cityscape before them. He nudged her shoulder with his. "I hope after all this, you find the freedom you're looking for. It's good to have you here. We need you. We never stopped needing you."

The smile on her lips was slow in coming, but it came. Barely. She couldn't help it. Just spending time with her brother on a roof made her feel... something. The ghost of cherished childish joy trickled back into her heart, but then it was gone with the realization she wasn't a child anymore. Never would be again. Her innocence had been destroyed the moment Julius put a sniper rifle into her eleven-year-old hands and told her to shoot.

They watched the cityscape below. Pockets of smoke rose at intervals. The sirens never ended. Police. Fire trucks. Ambulances. The streets were dangerous for civilians, not only from random replicates roaming but the people rioting and looting. The deadly sin.

"He made me his sniper," she said, surveying the beauty of the heights. "And I would do it willingly because it meant I was up high. I'd convinced myself I was where I belonged. That I was free."

Parker exhaled. "He's a mad man, and he did despicable things to you, but he didn't break you, Daisy."

Daisy felt the fluctuation of his hope in her stomach like butterflies. Sometimes she wished she wasn't the only one out of the Lazarus siblings to sense their sin's opposing virtue. It revealed truths best kept hidden. His hope betrayed his confidence. He wasn't certain she wasn't broken.

She was.

But she didn't have the courage to admit it, so she said, "He came close."

"I know," he agreed. "Normally you would have time to deal with what you're going through. But we don't have time. You need to trigger your powers, and for that, you have to spend time with your mate."

Axel's face flashed in Daisy's mind. Bronzed skin. Sun-kissed and short brown hair. Soft brown eyes that bled compassion. He was a fireman, one of the Faithful, and her mate. A walking oxymoron. He was also dying. She knew because there was no other reason a man would volunteer to become one of the Faithful. They were essentially the Syndicate's suicide mercenaries. They gave their life so they could return as clones in perfect health. But what Julius never told anyone —what *she'd* never told anyone—was that the cloned replicates would be completely controlled by Julius. And they had a shelf life of only a few months before they simply died after outliving their destructive purpose.

Daisy wasn't sure how long Axel had been one of the Faithful. Apparently, she'd conscripted him into the fanatical cult. So much of her time at the Syndicate had been a blur of empty promises. Her sin had taken control of her mind on too many occasions, but she couldn't blame that for her actions. She was lucid for most of it. She was embarrassed to admit she remembered little of Axel, which was surprising. He was eye-catching. Strong. Attractive. Not the usual Faithful lackey.

If she did what was expected of her, then he would be the man she spent the rest of her life with. The very idea of being intimate with someone made her heart palpitate and she wasn't sure if it was nerves, the pressure, or just the fact she'd never been in a relationship. Not an honest one like her siblings had with their mates. Daisy's sexual encounters had been fast and unfulfilling. Her life had been filled with blood, duty and despair.

A noise at the rooftop elevator drew their attention. Alice, Parker's mate and ex-Hildegard Sisterhood assassin came out with a dire expression on her face. Wind whipped her red hair into a tizzy. She located Parker in an instant. Her lips flattened.

"What is it?" He got to his feet faster than a man his size should move.

"A trio of powered replicates have surfaced downtown near a school. Griffin's down there but—" She shook her head, her eyes bleak. "He's on the edge. I think he might black out and I don't want to be the one who must hurt him to stop him."

"It won't come to that." Parker looked down at Daisy. The beast he half morphed into prowled beneath the surface of his composure. If Griffin went dark, his metal manipulation could flatten the city. Alice had been tasked by the Sisterhood to be the last line of defense against the Seven if they went beyond the point of return, but as the Deadly Seven's leader, Parker would be the one to stop Griffin if necessary. Or put him down.

"This might sound harsh," he said to Daisy, "but you need to get on with it. Find your mate, trigger your powers, and then we can bring the rest of our family home. If shit hits the fan, use your watch. One of us will come for you."

two

AXEL ALVARES

AXEL ALVARES SCRUBBED exhaustion from his eyes and then hoisted his backpack over his shoulder. He took a long look around the Cardinal City Fire Station and knew he wouldn't return. The double shift he'd just pulled would be his last and it had nothing to do with the city falling apart.

He rubbed his chest, as if it would help his situation, but nothing helped. His sister Elena was still sick. Julius Allcott had promised a way to save her life... or at the very least replicate it and give her a second chance to live her dreams. All he'd had to do was become one of the Faithful—a henchman for the morally dubious organization— and terrorize the city.

So he had.

For over a year, he'd been a villain by night, and a firefighting hero by day. But even for Elena's sake, Axel found it hard to turn a blind eye to blatant torture. He'd betrayed the Syndicate to save Daisy Lazarus and lost his chance at saving his sister. It seemed no matter what he did, someone ended up losing.

But he wasn't giving up yet.

If there was air in Elena's lungs, there was hope, and his sister's life was more important to him than the city falling apart. If super-humans who shot poison from their mouth could exist, then so could a cure for his sister's mystery illness. She was more important than this firefighting job. More important than anything.

He wouldn't be back to work because he wanted to spend quality time with his neglected sister, and then once he'd regrouped, he'd go all in trying to find another way to save her.

John at the station kitchen had no idea Axel's goodbye wave could be his last. Franny at reception gave her last flirtatious giggle and eyelash bat before she craned her neck to watch his ass wiggle as he walked past. Normally he'd pretend to catch her and wink, but this night, he continued straight through to the garage, past the truck, and into the Cardinal City street now presenting more like a battle-field than metropolis. Desolate during the day, but with the rising moon, so were the undesirables coming out, eager to capitalize on the chaos the Syndicate had wrought.

And Axel had been a part of that destruction.

Had.

He'd put to bed his guilt a long time ago. He'd do it all again if it gave him a chance to save Elena. And Daisy.

As he moved to the sidewalk, Axel pulled his unregistered Glock from his backpack and held it exposed and ready by his side. His brief stint as a Faithful had given him a rare understanding of the other side of sanity. If he wanted to make it home to his sister, then he had to be ready to face anything in his way.

Madness had many faces. It was the whisper of insanity in the ear, the confusion of the moment, or simply the will to survive. It peeled back the skin of humanity and made monsters of them all. Axel Alvares was still trying to figure out which kind of monster he was, if any. Because the sooner he knew, the sooner he could find his way back.

The city was in a strange state. The bridges had all been destroyed, essentially locking the city dwellers in a cage. Replicates were popping up, causing havoc. People were rioting and looting. A curfew had been talked about but was not active, same with Martial Law. The Mayor and the city folk were particularly in denial, or just blindly hopeful that the Deadly Seven would get it under control.

They wouldn't.

Axel had insider information. Most of that deadly family was becoming unhinged because their partners had been kidnapped. As one of the Faithful, Axel had been in a position of trust with Julius, the leader of the Syndicate. If he'd not defected to save Daisy, he'd be out there right now, sowing chaos or being one of the Faithful guarding the kidnapped. He assumed.

He checked his cell phone. No messages. The Faithful group chat had gone dark. He'd been booted out and cut off. Not that it mattered. He was done with them. But he wanted to be helpful to the Seven, make up for some of the shit he'd caused, and he'd thought if he could pass intel back to them, then it was one step in the right direction.

Sure. That's why you want to go back. It had nothing to do with the crush he had on the beautiful, silver-haired, scarred woman. *Nothing at all.*

He shoved his cell inside his pocket and checked his surroundings before heading home. Tall buildings interspersed with smaller, old buildings still kicking, and people going about their lives. No one cared that he wore his CCFD branded shirt. They gave zero fucks that he was someone who put his life on the line to save others. It was this kind of apathy that originally helped him make the choice to become one of the Faithful. He thought about it every time he'd had to do something morally dubious for the Syndicate.

Long-standing denizens refused to believe their city was falling apart. Some walked their dogs. Some went about their nightly duties. Life continued. But for every person ignoring the state of the world, there were two capitalizing on it.

"Hey!" Axel barked at a shady, toothless man watching an elderly lady watering potted plants on her stoop. Something in his eyes said danger. He caught Axel's warning and kept walking on by.

Axel waited for him to completely leave and then turned to the old lady.

"You should stay indoors. It's not safe out here."

"Bah. I've been here for seventy years. Seen a depression. Seen wars. Seen murder in the street. I water these plants every night as the sun goes down. Ain't gonna change nothing now."

Axel's nostrils flared but he got it. He was just as stubborn and so was Elena. If her battle with illness was a matter of will, she'd have kicked it to the curb years ago. He leaned against the building's dusty brick wall and said, "Then it will be a shame to end it all now because of these dark days. I'll stay right here until you're done." Then he added for good measure, "Ma'am."

The old lady grumbled. Axel was grateful to see her hasten her watering. She turned the faucet off and headed back inside. Before she left, she picked up a small pot with sprouting flowers and handed it to Axel. She gave a salute before hobbling back inside.

Huh. Will you look at that. Someone gave a fuck.

As Axel continued the two-block journey home, he noticed most pedestrians had a weapon in their hand. It broke his heart to see the city he'd grown up in, the city he'd fought to keep safe, the city his parents had chosen to realize their dreams of a better life, had fallen apart.

And he'd been instrumental in the state. He frowned at the plant in his hands. His frown deepened when he realized what the flowers were—daisies.

Just like that, he conjured a picture of her face, her *gorgeous* face with violet eyes full of pain he wanted to soothe. And then another memory surfaced. One he hated to think about—Daisy lying naked on a gurney, curled into herself. The room was cold, gray and empty. Spinal fluid extraction had bruised her spine. Her ribs stood out in sharp relief. Her long, silver hair was oily and matted. The Syndicate tortured her endlessly and Axel couldn't find any reason, including Elena's new life, a good enough excuse for that.

Since helping rescue her, the beautiful woman was in his dreams nightly. There was something about her that messed with his plans, his sanity. For her, he'd given up his chance at saving Elena. But he hadn't given up hope. If he had some, there was life.

An explosion somewhere in the distance didn't surprise him. Neither did the new flurry of sirens. His last shift had included a rescue with the jaws of life, two burning buildings, and a chemical situation on Sixth. All of it deliberately started. His grip tightened around his gun and the plant, and he quickened his step.

When Axel arrived at his Brownstone, he vaulted the steps two at a time and let himself in. Elena was on the couch, huddled into her blanket with a beanie on her bald head, watching something on her laptop. A lollypop stick bobbed in her mouth. Axel rolled his eyes and put his Glock and daisies next to the wilted ivy on the table near the door. He frowned at the condition of the ivy. Unlike the old lady's, this one was neglected.

It hurt to see.

Elena used to enjoy taking care of the house plants. Sometime over the past few weeks she'd stopped watering them.

"That better not be your dinner, Ellie," he said as he walked into the kitchen.

The bobbing lollypop froze. She looked at him with guilt written over her face. She seemed to think about apologizing, but then shrugged and went back to her screen and coloring. She probably hadn't moved all day.

She was in her final year of high school, but it had been shut down since the bridges blew. If she wanted to make it to Pre-Med, then she had to do better. She should be studying, or at the very least moving about and eating better. If their mother or father were here, they'd be furious—*muito pistola*.

And they'd blame it all on him.

He strode over and yanked the stick out of her mouth. She drooled when he stole it and wiped her mouth with a scowl.

"For someone who wants to be a doctor, you're making poor health choices," he grumbled.

Something dark flashed in her gaze and she snapped, "You know I'll never get there. Stop saying shit like that. I don't even know if I like medicine, anyway."

"Never say never," he shot back, then strode around the living room to look for her scarf. He couldn't give up, because if he did, then she would give up. "Pack your things, we're going out."

"We are?" Interest sparked in her dull eyes, and she straightened. "But it's dangerous out there."

"We're alive. We're still breathing. It can always be worse, you know that."

"We're really going out?" Her excitement made him realize she'd needed this. While he might be strong and confident enough to walk the streets without getting hurt, she was just a skinny, weak teenager with dark circles under her eyes. She'd needed him home and he'd been so caught up with finding a solution to her illness, that he'd missed the most important thing of all—her.

"You need fresh air," he said. "A walk will do you good. If you've had your meds and feel okay, I'll take care of the rest."

He checked his reflection in the empty oven. Bit tired around the edges but his hair looked good. Always had. He sniffed near his underarms and nodded. Smelled okay. He'd showered before he left the station, and the walk hadn't made him too sweaty.

He should probably grab a bite to eat. He pivoted and came face to face with his sister. She smirked up at him.

"A walk will do me good, eh?" she teased.

He blinked. "Don't know what you're getting at."

"Who are we seeing?"

"No one. I thought we could go to the batting cages."

Stupid, hasty coverup but it worked. They needed a bit of fun to take their mind off the abysmal. He side-stepped her and opened the fridge. Awful. No wonder Elena had deferred to candy. Goddamn it, he knew that double shift would come back to bite him. He slammed the fridge shut. A photograph wobbled on the door. The picture was of his parents the day they journeyed to America. Axel was eight. Elena was just a bump in his mother's stomach. They'd figured if they made it across the border, and Elena was born here, then no one had the right to remove her. And they were right, to a point. For five years they'd lived happily in Cardinal City. No one expected them to fall sick. No one expected Axel to be left as sole guardian to his sister. And no one expected her to get sick too.

Bad luck had followed his family for generations. His mama used to say they were cursed. He kissed his fingers and touched the picture reverently. He didn't believe in curses. He didn't believe in luck. But he did believe the moment you gave up, everything ended.

"It wouldn't happen to be your pretty lady friend, would it?" Elena asked, still smiling. "You know, the one you helped rescue?"

"Ellie…"

Two days ago, he'd spilled the beans to her about Daisy and his misguided time as a Faithful. But he hadn't told her the whole truth. He'd said he worked for extra money to pay her medical bills. She knew nothing about his deal to have her cloned, or the full extent of his dangerous and sometimes cruel nighttime escapades—that he'd killed people, maybe innocent people. He slammed the door on that guilt, and on Elena's questioning gaze.

"Aw, come on, Axel. You're not going to deprive me of this. I could drop dead any day and knowing you've got some lady in the wings will—"

"You're not going to die." He pointed at her face.

The fight left her eyes and he hated it.

"No one knows how to help me," she mumbled. "You know this, Axel. This illness is killing me and eventually you'll have to accept it."

"I'll accept it when you're six feet under and pushing up daisies. Until then, we keep looking for a way out of this. Got it?"

She didn't answer, instead she moped and stared at her feet until she mumbled, "Speaking of daisies…"

"Fine," he sighed. "Let's go pick her up and then I'll take you both on a date."

Her smile brought color to her face. "Does she know about me? Do you think she'll like me?"

He tried not to grin at how quickly her mood had turned over this.

"She's not my girlfriend, Ellie. I just helped rescue her. I do that a lot."

"But you said date. Wait… is she even feeling up to it after what she went through?"

"She's a tough cookie. Much like another pain in my ass." He tugged her beanie down so it covered her ears and then punched her playfully on the shoulder. "Come on. Let's go before the curfew is announced."

"Roger Dodger." She saluted him and collected her coloring supplies and put them in her backpack.

He locked the door behind them and explained the ground rules as they left the building.

"Don't engage with passersby. Don't look anyone in the eye. And if you see one of those powered clones, run. Got it?"

She nodded, eyes wide. "Where do I run?"

"Home, or the place we're picking up Daisy from." He swallowed the lump in his throat. Daisy had no idea he was about to turn up on her door step. If she was feeling better, she was probably out there with her crime-fighting family, doing what they did best. But he had to see her. The need was an itch he couldn't scratch. And despite playing it down to his sister, if putting his heart on his sleeve where Daisy was concerned gave Ellie something to live for, then he'd do it. "Ellie, I want you to know that if you're ever separated from me, or I don't come home one night, this place we're headed is where you go. The people there will always help you."

"Why wouldn't you come home, Axel? Are you still working for them?" she asked, stopping in her tracks and lowering her voice. "You know… the bad ones?"

She was so innocent sometimes that he forgot she was almost an adult. He had to stop sugar coating things, but protecting his little sister was in his DNA. The chaos of the world was evident all around them.

"No, I'm not," he answered with a pointed look around. "But anything can happen. You need to be prepared."

"Will they come after you for defecting? Are you sure we should be heading out?"

"Not many will recognize me. I wore a mask most of the time. Besides, this is our last chance to have fun before the curfew hits. Before you know it, Martial Law will be called and then the National Guard will be here. But don't worry, sis, I'll keep you safe."

She gave him the eye. It was a squinty pirate look she'd claimed when she was little, and they'd reenacted Peter Pan in their living room. She'd been Tinker Bell and he'd been Hook trying to entice her over to his side. She never trusted him, and it showed. Since then, he'd always known what she was thinking when she used 'the eye.' She would push until he told her the truth.

"So then why am I to go to the Lazarus family? You rescued one of them and now they're your best friends?" she said dryly.

"Not exactly."

"They don't know we're coming, do they?"

He smirked. "Can't fool you."

"You're not afraid they'll tell you to leave? I mean... they're important people."

"I'm hard to say no to."

"Tell me about it," she mumbled through a smile.

After a blessedly uneventful walk through the city, they stopped just outside the boarded-up restaurant Heaven.

He glanced up at the apartments above the restaurant where the Lazarus family lived and lost his nerve. Daisy had always been so cool and collected. But after he'd saved her, she'd not asked him to visit. Nor had she given him any vibe that she felt an iota of interest in him, not like he did for her.

Can't exactly flirt when you're about to die, he reminded himself. It was stupid to think she felt interest for him. That's why it was important he showed up and let her know he cared.

Sucking it up, he took a deep breath and plowed onward.

three

DAISY LAZARUS

DAISY SAT on the roof for longer than necessary, but the weight of responsibility tugged at her. More shouts and sirens rended the night. She supposed she should do as Parker said, but while she was up here with a bird's eye view of the mayhem, she couldn't help running scenarios in her mind. It was how her brain was trained. This was a perfect sniper spot. She picked out multiple easy targets on the ground.

Maybe that was how she could be useful—take replicates or criminals down one by one. Still, nothing felt right. Nothing felt enough.

Eventually she forced her legs to walk back to the basement. The baby was gone, but Liza, Flint and Mary were still there. Dressed in her Deadly suit, Liza spotted Daisy and rushed over.

Daisy braced.

"You should be out there helping," Liza said with a bleakness in her eyes. "Not wandering the halls of Lazarus House."

"I would help if I knew how."

Liza shoved a floppy Deadly suit into Daisy's hands. "Just put it on and get out there. Do whatever you think is right to help settle the situation. It's the least you can do."

Daisy stared at the dormant suit and wanted to laugh. Each of her siblings had a different colored face scarf so they could mark each other in the field. They'd given her white. It was a flash of her old life, of the old white leather suit she wore to become the Falcon—the Syndicate's enforcer. It was a reminder that she would fail if they put their trust in her. She stared at it as she spoke.

"My first instinct when I walk into a room isn't to assess the exits and know where to escape. It's to get up high, find a position of power, and put down the weak." She lifted her gaze to her sister. "If you put me out there in the field to help, whatever I think is right is wrong. Dead wrong."

They all gaped at her but it was the truth.

"*Mija*," Mary sighed. "Believe me, I understand a lifetime of training to kill. It takes time, but those instincts can be repurposed."

"Don't call me daughter," Daisy clipped, "in *any* language. You lost the right to that title the day you left me to the fire."

Mary backed up. A sadness entered her eyes and the sensed despair made Daisy sick. She had hurt Mary's feelings and now she felt bad. And that made her angry. Daisy knew what Mary meant to the family, but the truth of it was, Mary would never mean the same to Daisy. The woman was singularly responsible for her fate over the past few decades.

Daisy tossed her challenging gaze to Mary's husband, Flint. She remembered him vaguely from her childhood. She'd felt his sadness through the one-way glass separating them from the scientists in the lab. She supposed he was also to blame for Daisy's lot in life.

"That's not fair," Liza said, eyes flashing. "Mary did what she had to. At least she's trying to make amends. You're so stubborn. You won't let us help you. You're just—"

Daisy stepped toward her younger sister then clenched her fists and stifled her instinct to retaliate. Liza was right, and that pissed Daisy off even more. Liza—the entire family—wanted to help Daisy. And that was the problem. Everything Daisy remembered about being in this family revolved around *her* being the one helping *them*. As the eldest, she'd caught them when they fell, not the other way around.

But right now, Daisy didn't care about the poison in Liza's mouth or the dark circles under her eyes because she feared for her mate. In that moment, Liza was simply an obstacle to Daisy's path out of there. Liza moved to block Daisy, to force her to stay.

"Don't, Liza," Flint warned. "Let Daisy have her feelings. She's entitled to them. She needs time." He turned to Daisy and added, "I know what it's like to be thrust into a new world. It's tough. But don't shut us all out while you're adjusting."

It was the opposite to what Parker had said, and for that Daisy was grateful.

Liza glared but stepped back. "FYI, you need to earn the title of sister, too."

Daisy dumped the suit on the table and stalked out. She wasn't sure where she was going, but knew she needed to leave. Whatever she was doing here wasn't working. The rush of emotions coursing through her body was new. With Julius, she'd blocked everything out until she'd been cold and empty. Now, her brain hurt, and she didn't know how to make sense of it. The worst part of these feelings was that deep down, Daisy wanted the same things as her family. But how could she earn her place as a sister to a family of heroes when she'd never truly been one?

Fuck it. It was all too hard.

"I'm out of here."

No one stopped her this time. She had no idea where she was

going, but away was a good idea. She couldn't stand the pressure. Confusion still whirled in her head as she stormed out of the elevator leading into the ground floor lobby. There used to be a doorman there, but they'd put him on paid leave until the city was safe. He might never come back.

She had a clean path down a dark hallway toward the street exit. The nightclub on the left was dormant, and the restaurant on the right was boarded up. They had extra security at this entrance, a metal door instead of the old glass. It made the lobby feel like the inside of a box at the bottom of the sea.

There was a time when the destruction of this city was all Daisy wanted. It was the gold medal in Julius's race to create a new utopia. Now the madness was here, she knew it had never been something she'd wanted. But it felt too late to stop.

She punched the exit button at the door and burst out into the fresh night air—and slammed into a tall, hard body.

"Whoa." Two hands gripped her shoulders and held her steady.

Daisy froze. It was Axel, the very man Parker had bidden her to get in touch with. Her mate. And he was touching her. He was here.

Looking into his handsome face, with his hands on her, she was instantly transported to the moment he'd pulled her from the storm drain. This man was supposed to be one of the Faithful, one of the wicked and morally destitute desperados who'd terrorized this city. Back then, Julius ordered Axel to hurt her, but instead he'd found a way to feed her and keep her alive while she was a prisoner.

He'd rescued her, a woman who'd given up.

He seemed to realize he was touching her the same moment she did and let go.

"Axel," she greeted, and slid her gaze to the young woman next to him. Inexplicable irritation hit Daisy. The woman was pretty beneath her beanie. A little young for Axel, but then again, Daisy was comparatively old to be his mate. There had to be at least ten years between them. Probably more. Her next words came out harsher than intended. "What are you doing here?"

"Um." He scratched his head. "I'm..."

The more his tongue got tied, the more a blush stained his cheeks. *Amusing.* The young woman next to him answered.

"We're out for ice cream," she said with a genuine smile.

Daisy glanced up and down the street. Every café and restaurant was closed or boarded up. Her brow arched.

"That's not true," Axel laughed nervously. "We came to see you."

"We?"

"Oh," he jolted, and shook his head. "Sorry, I should have introduced you. Daisy, this is my sister Elena. Elena, this is Daisy."

Sister.

The word settled something wild inside of Daisy. She studied Elena more closely. She was skinny and weak looking. A thin layer of despair emanated from her. She would be one of those people Julius said took up valuable breathing space and should be put down. *There's no room in paradise for sin. There's no room for the weak.* Daisy pushed Julius's voice out of her head and forced a tight smile on her face. She should at least try to appear normal and polite.

"Nice to meet you, Elena." That was the correct way to respond, wasn't it?

Elena adjusted her backpack. "So... you worked with my brother for the madman?"

Daisy blinked at her candidness. This was now definitely outside the typical social conventions. Daisy's normal interactions revolved around ordering Faithful to her putting down sinners. Not knowing how to respond, she shrugged. Awkward silence descended.

"Um," Axel said, his voice pleasantly deep and smooth. "I actually brought Elena here to show her where to go if she needed help. Parker and Alice said I could stop by any time. Hope that's okay."

Daisy frowned and fidgeted. "I guess."

More awkward silence.

"I also wanted to see how you were feeling after... you know."

Elena tried to hide her smile, as if Axel had said something humorous. Daisy didn't understand. And she also didn't know why he was checking in on her. She might know he was her mate, but he had no idea. If he worked as a Faithful, then he was probably dying. That's the way the Faithful worked. The sick and the dying traded their current life in return for becoming better replicates. There was probably a tank somewhere with a carbon copy of Axel floating in it, waiting for this version of him to kick the bucket so it could be born.

"So how are you feeling?" he asked.

"Fine."

His brows flinched in the middle. "Are you? Because last I saw, you weren't looking too good."

"Bit tired," she admitted. Her spinal fluid took longer to regenerate than she'd anticipated. And then there were the scars from the exploratory surgery on her stomach. She was stiff, sore, and grumpy. But she wasn't complaining about that. For all her snippy words at her family, she was still grateful to be alive. Today. Tomorrow might be different.

Her palms itched and she wanted to wash the blood away but knew there was none there. It was all in her head.

"So..." Axel said. "You on your way out?"

"I am."

He looked at her expectantly, waiting for her to elaborate but she found herself getting lost in his eyes. They were two dark pools of comfort. Looking into them felt so familiar, like she'd dreamed of him so often that the memory of him had imprinted on her soul. The notion made her squirm. She gestured over her shoulder to where she'd come from and blurted, "They're just so…" She took a breath. Scowled. "And I'm… *not* like that."

"Ahh," he sighed knowingly, a twinkle in his eyes. "I get it."

More spilled out of Daisy, and she didn't know why. "I don't even know what I'm doing here. They expect me to, you know, and I—" She glanced at the sky and shook her head.

"*Totally* get it."

"So I needed some air."

Elena's gaze ping-ponged between them. "Oh my god. You guys already speak your own language."

Axel shoved her playfully and they both grinned, but it wasn't at Daisy's expense. She wasn't sure how she knew that, but some of her nerves settled. She had the sense she could trust Axel, and it was more than the fact he'd pulled her from the storm drain or snuck her food while she'd been tortured. It all came back to that feeling of knowing him.

For some strange reason, a memory from her childhood hit. She'd just arrived at Julius's family home. Every corner of the house was filled with mementos of his dead wife and child. From the photographs on the halls, watching her every move, to his daughter's bedroom—still pristine with frills and dolls. Once, Daisy had been bored and explored. She'd come across the box of dolls she'd found under the bed and, having never had such a plethora of toys in her life, she'd fallen into playing with them.

When Julius found her, it was the first time she'd seen a crack in his caring façade. She supposed she should have known then. But she was too young to understand and could only focus on his deep despair as he snatched the dolls from her hands and said, "I'd rather these be destroyed than played with. They don't belong to you."

Even then, for a moment after Julius had snapped at her, he

followed it up with a swift apology and the promise that, together, they would fix everything wrong in the world.

Hope.

That's the feeling Daisy had with Axel. Hope was the lifting of her soul, the dreams of an orphaned child, and the wings of a bird. But just like Julius's boot on the dolls, hope could be crushed, and when it was, the dark empty despair that replaced it was the worst of all. Daisy wanted to shut herself off but couldn't do it any longer.

Maybe this unyielding resistance she now had to giving up was an effect from the mating bond. And maybe that wasn't so bad. At the very least, she owed it to everyone to figure out Axel's story.

"So," he said, eyes hopeful. "Do you want to come out with us?"

"Now?" Daisy's brows lifted.

"Why not? Curfew has only just been announced, and it doesn't start for another hour or so."

"I'm supposed to be helping."

He thought about it, then cocked his head. "Do you want to be?"

She studied him before answering. "I don't know. But I do know that the right thing to do isn't to take a break."

"You don't strike me as someone who always does what's right."

Elena slapped her hand on Axel's gut and he grunted, annoyed at her.

His words were a tease designed to cause trouble, but they awoke something that had been slumbering inside her. The bird of prey spreading its wings, testing the space.

It was those words that finally sparked Daisy's attraction for her mate. That maybe he had a little monster sitting on his shoulder, whispering daring things to him. She looked at him in a new light and wondered if he would be the perfect cure to her apathy.

"You need to blow off some steam," Axel said perceptively. "So do we. Come on."

"But…" She gestured down the boarded-up street.

He took her hand. "The end of the world can wait."

All the despair she'd been sensing from the neighborhood suddenly winked out of existence. Daisy gaped at their joined hands. Without that squirming churn of sensed sin in her gut, his touch was rough, calloused, yet warm and soft. Not sweaty. It sent little sparks skipping up her arm. He must have thought her wide eyes were offense, because he tried to let go, but she tightened her grip.

She couldn't believe she was considering this. "Where can we go?"

He shared a knowing grin with his sister. "We know a place."

AXEL'S STOMACH fluttered as he led his sister and Daisy away from Lazarus House. Daisy was out of his league and older than him by more than a decade, more experienced in... everything, and she'd been right. This was completely not the time to go on an outing, but as his father, his *pai,* always used to say, the moment you give up is the moment it ends.

Call him stupid. Call him hopelessly optimistic. Call him reckless. He didn't care. Axel's worth was measured by the hopes and dreams realized in the eyes of his loved ones. That's all he cared about.

Paranoid about Daisy's discomfort, he'd let go of her hand but now longed for it back. He spent too much of the short journey internally berating himself for letting go. For most of the walk, they'd escaped stumbling into trouble, but as they approached their destination, he wasn't sure if their luck would hold out. Or Elena's energy.

Three older teenagers in hoodies congregated at a street corner, their heads bowed as they spoke quietly to each other. Each had an obvious gun tucked into baggy jeans. They were plotting something no good.

"Stay close," he said to his sister.

She hugged her jacket and stepped toward him. He was so proud of her. After their parents' death and before her illness, she'd shut herself off. But a trigger had flipped in her since, and she wasn't afraid to take risks or try new things. The sad part about that was that she didn't have enough time to do all the things she now loved. But since his time with the Faithful and CCFD was done, he wanted to give her as many experiences as he could.

A brush at his fingers was the only warning before Daisy stole the gun from him. His mouth opened to protest, but she shut him down with a look. And then there was that split second of physical contact that sent his heart into hyperdrive.

"I'm a better aim," she declared and then checked the rounds. He tried to protest again, but she continued talking over him. "I was trained as a sniper at eleven. I know what you Faithful are like. You have no real finesse or skill. You're babies when it comes to real conflict. It's better I handle protection from here on out."

Babies?

Irritation swarmed in his veins. He was twenty-five, and no runt either. He packed almost one-eighty and could carry a full-grown man out of a burning building. As a Faithful, he'd killed. He'd rescued. He'd seen a hellova lot in his lifetime.

Before he could reply, the trio of youths looked up and noticed them. Axel tensed, ready to fight, but the youths quickly moved on. Daisy trained her gun on them with cold eyes until they turned a corner. Axel forced Daisy's weapon down.

"Not everyone is the enemy," he reminded her.

She frowned at him but acquiesced and, just like that, his earlier irritation was replaced by a surge of masculine satisfaction. She'd listened to him. He liked that. Maybe he could offer something to this strong woman, after all.

"Come on," he said. "It's just through here."

The double doors were locked but a side door would let them in. Down the narrow alley, they stopped at a dumpster with a vented window behind it on the brick wall. Axel slammed the dumpster lid shut and then boosted his sister on top.

"You got it, Ellie?"

She grinned down at him. "Always."

Then she slid out the glass vents until she'd made a gap big enough to squeeze through. She disappeared into the darkness. Daisy was about to hop up to do the same, but he stopped her.

"She'll open the door for us," he explained. Elena needed to feel useful too.

"Oh." Daisy nodded, then checked up and down the alley. He wondered if she was always switched on like that. After sweeping their surroundings, her arresting violet eyes landed back on him. "You do this often?"

He cleared his throat. "I work crazy hours and we always miss opening times. One night, me and Ellie decided to just find our own way in."

"You broke in."

He shrugged. "I guess raising ourselves gave us looser morals than most."

"You raised yourselves?" Her brows lifted as she stepped closer.

Her floral, heady scent stuck to him like glue. God, she was hot. Instant hard-on hot. Instant trouble. So out of his league, but he was going for it. Sooner or later, he'd have Daisy as his woman, in his bed, and he'd give her the world.

"Axel?"

"Sorry, what?" He'd forgotten the question.

"I asked if you and Elena raised yourselves."

"Oh." He scrubbed the back of his neck. He didn't like talking about his past. He shouldn't have brought it up. "Our parents immigrated from Brazil." When he didn't elaborate, she watched him patiently. He had the sense nothing he would say could scare her away. She would keep their secrets to the grave. "They were illegal."

"Have they returned without you?"

"They died," he explained. "Same mystery illness Elena has. I think it had something to do with why we left Brazil, but I guess I'll never know."

"I'm sorry for your loss." Her brows pinched and he must be nuts to think she was adorable like this, but he wanted to tell her every sob story of his life just to see her look at him with compassion again.

Elena opened the door with a broad grin on her tired face.

"Got it," she panted.

"You okay?" he asked.

A chagrinned expression crossed Elena's face moments before her gaze flicked to Daisy then back to him. *Right. Got it.* Don't give Elena special treatment in front of Daisy.

"Let's go." Axel placed his palm on the small of Daisy's back and guided her inside.

His fingers lingered a little too long after they'd shut the door. Daisy turned to him expectantly. The open trust in her eyes hit him squarely in the chest. He cleared his throat and gestured further down the darkened corridor.

"Time to have some fun," he announced.

Elena whooped loudly and he smirked. Daisy's lips twitched and a spark of *something* entered her eyes. It gave him a little boost to keep up the charade that he knew what he was doing. Within moments, he'd taken them through the back hallways like mice in a maze until they emerged in a large shadowy warehouse.

He quickly located the fuse box and triggered the lights. The space illuminated to reveal the city's prime batting cage complex.

"Batter up!" His voice echoed across the empty space. Elena released another whoop and jogged to the nearest netting enclosure where she dumped her backpack and picked up a wooden bat from against a net.

Axel turned to gauge Daisy's reaction and found innocent awe plastered over her face. She ran her fingers idly down her long silver ponytail and spun, taking it all in.

"You ever been to a batting cage?" he asked.

"I've never seen a baseball game." She shook her head, and then mumbled, "I've never been to *any* sports game."

"Fuck that," he grumbled and strolled to where more bats leaned against a net and handed her one. With as much seriousness as he could muster, he promised, "After this mess with the Syndicate, I'm going to take you to your first game."

Doubt flashed in her eyes, and she cocked her head as though her next words were obvious. "The world is supposed to end, Axel, despite what we're trying to do to stop it. There could be no after."

But he only smiled back. "It ain't over until the fat lady sings, Daze."

"Daze?" Her brow arched.

"Don't like it?"

She shrugged.

"Well, stick around. I got plenty more where that came from. Like *Margarida*. Or how about just Gorgeous?" He winked.

Elena cupped her mouth and shouted from the pitch machine, "You gonna be boring all night or we gonna play?"

"Boring?" He tossed the bat over his shoulder. "I'll show you boring."

Within seconds he was tickling the guts out of his sister. She giggled and laughed and wheezed, so he stopped. If he went too hard, she might have an asthma attack, and those were deadlier for her now than they used to be.

"I used to do that to my siblings," Daisy murmured wistfully.

"Used to?" He straightened his hair and shirt.

Sadness entered her eyes and he hated it. "Things happened. We grew up."

"I don't care how old Elena is," he announced with a mock-warning look thrown his sister's way. "You're never too old for a tickle fight."

But Elena was tired, he noticed, as he helped her to her feet. Her eyelids drooped already. She might need a nap before they headed home.

"Come on," he said and went to the pitch machine. "Let's make this interesting. The person with the most hits wins."

"Wins what?" Elena lifted a sardonic single brow. "Because it better not be something dumb."

"Do it for the glory, sis."

"Glory schmory."

"What about ice cream?" Daisy suggested warily.

"*Yess.*" Elena raised her palm to the silver-haired woman for a high five.

Daisy blinked at Elena. Axel jogged in and stage-whispered, "Don't leave her hanging."

Like a stiff robot, Daisy slapped her palm to Elena. The resounding thwack echoed in the room and was the flip of the switch. Time to have fun. But first—he surreptitiously asked Daisy, "Could you do me a favor and stay up at this end to keep flyaway balls from hitting Elena?"

She gave him questioning eyes but nodded.

"Thank you." He watched his sister get herself ready at the plate. "She pretends she has more energy than she does."

Daisy suddenly blinked and jerked. "You're not dying. She is."

five

DAISY LAZARUS

DAISY'S PROCLAMATION hung in the air. She should have realized it was Axel's sister dying, not him. She should have picked up the clues from the moment they'd turned up at her doorstep. She should have investigated him when their bond connected. This changed everything.

He wasn't dying.

But...

She watched him glance at his sister. Pain flittered over his features. He loved her so much. Elena was the reason he'd risked his life for the Syndicate. He'd joined the Faithful for her.

Daisy tried to tug him back after he started for the pitch machine, but a quiet desperation in his eyes asked her not to push the subject. That flitter of pain he'd revealed was squashed so fast that she wondered if it had ever been there. Daisy glanced at Elena and found her watching them.

Axel walked to the end of the cage and stood behind the pitch net. A bucket at his side was filled with baseballs. He flicked on the machine and picked up a ball.

"You ladies ready for a reckoning?"

Elena snorted. "As if. I'll hit every one and then you're paying for ice-cream."

The two of them continued the charade that the world wasn't going to hell in a hand-basket. *The end of the world can wait.*

It was just the sort of thing she used to say to Parker when he would scowl and refuse to go out to the lab roof and play when they were younger. And he'd always end up enjoying himself.

Axel put a ball in the pitch machine and shouted through cupped hands, "Batter up!"

Elena glanced at Daisy.

"After you," Daisy said.

Elena tapped the top of the bat on the plate, then raised it to the ready position and stared down the pitch machine. Axel taunted her with a chant kids probably used in the sandlots. But it didn't irritate Elena. It made her more determined to focus on the coming pitch. Daisy approved of her moxie. And there was something about her sickness, something about the way she faced it headlong, that reminded Daisy of herself after she'd been burned in her youth.

Axel switched the machine on… and… nothing happened.

"Wait!" He peered into the barrel of the machine. "Must be jammed. Two secs."

While he worked at dislodging the stuck ball, Daisy and Elena stood uneasily next to each other. Daisy should probably say something, but she was a terrible conversationalist. She was terrible socially, period. All she could think about was how she'd blurted out that Elena was dying. She stared at Elena and wondered why she sensed so little despair in the young woman when her fate was announced. How? Why?

Normal people are sad when their impending death is pointed out.

"You're looking at me," Elena said with a smirk on her pale lips.

"Yes," Daisy replied.

"So spit it out. I get questions all the time."

"Why do you feel no despair about your pending death?"

"Wow." Elena blinked. "I expected something about the missing hair but not something so deep. Wait a minute… You can *sense* despair. You're really one of the Deadly Seven, aren't you? I can't believe you're here. Oh my God, which brother is Gluttony? Cos he always winks at the camera—swoon. And…" Her eyes lit up with a sudden thought, she checked to see if Axel was looking and then leaned in to whisper, "I made these collectable Deadly Seven cards—don't tell Axel, I was supposed to be studying—but maybe, if you're okay with it, I could get you to sign one for me?"

"The Deadly Seven are my brothers and sisters. Not me." Daisy wasn't sure she'd ever be part of that crime fighting unit. She wasn't sure if she wanted to be, let alone to appear on a set of cards that glorified her. "We'd have to be the Deadly Eight, and that's not going to happen."

Elena nodded to herself and her eyes turned wistful. "Yeah, eight. You'd need a whole new logo. I'm getting ideas already. If Axel wasn't watching, I'd pull them out of my backpack and start drawing."

"Please don't."

But Elena's eyes were already focused inward, her bottom lip drawn into her teeth as she no doubt planned to do exactly what Daisy hoped she'd not.

But she was right. If Daisy did become part of that crime-fighting group, then Parker would need a complete brand overhaul. That would be costly. And then there was the fact Daisy didn't like the idea of dressing up and heading out to fight crime. It reminded her too much of what she did for Julius—just the other side of the same coin.

"You asked why I feel no sadness," Elena said. "It's because I've accepted my fate. It is what it is."

Her brow furrowed and a slice of despair trickled in.

"But now you feel sad," Daisy pointed out and cocked her head. "Why?"

Elena shrugged. "I'm sad because of my brother."

Axel cursed in Portuguese and kicked the machine. Seeing them look his way, he smiled sheepishly and waved at them. "Don't worry, I'll get it sorted."

Elena laughed quietly. The despair was still there. It confused Daisy.

"I don't understand your emotions," she said.

"My brother is a never-ending source of positivity for me. But I'm not the same for him. I'm sad because he soiled his pure heart to help me. He did things he'll regret for the rest of his life and that's not what I want for him. Our parents didn't come to this country for him to get caught up with bad people." Her lips curved and a wistful look filled her eyes as she rested them on Daisy. "But I'm over the moon those bad things brought him to you."

"Me?" Daisy jerked back. "Why?"

She was the worst thing Axel could find.

"Because he won't be alone after I'm gone. I see the way you look at him. You like him. Admit it."

"I…" Heat seared Daisy's cheeks. She forced her emotions down and clenched her jaw. She wasn't even sure she had what it took to *like* someone. "I'm not good for him."

"Because you did bad things too?"

"How did you…?" She glanced again at Axel. He'd removed his scarf and pushed up his sleeves. Somehow, the effort and focus he put into fixing that machine made Daisy see him as someone whose loyalty would never waiver. It was the strangest notion, yet it fit.

"He told me how he found you," Elena murmured. "Plus, I'm a bit of a Deadly Seven junkie. I read all the articles. I pieced together a lot. It's given me something to fixate on when I felt so shitty, you know? I'm sorry you were treated poorly by the person who was supposed to care for you." Her eyes watered and her next words came out a little choked but full of gusto. "You have to know that Axel will *never* do something like that to you. *Ever.*"

"We've only just met," Daisy said, trying to dismiss the gravity of the moment.

"Somehow," she replied. "I don't think that's a factor. Axel has his eye on you. He's hard to deny."

A baseball shot out of the machine and flew at their faces.

Daisy caught it before it hit Elena who squeaked and jerked back. "Oh my God. That almost got me."

"I won't let you get hurt." Daisy dropped the ball.

"Machine's working," Axel said, brow crinkling like he thought he would get in trouble.

Elena wrapped her arms around Daisy in a tight embrace.

"What are you doing?" Daisy asked.

"I'm hugging you." Her voice was muffled against Daisy's front.

Elena's honeyed hope was a warm bath on Daisy's nerves. Hugging was once Daisy's most preferred method of communication. She'd almost forgotten about this part—the surge of dopamine that came with it. Hugging and singing. When Elena pulled away with a sheepish smile, Daisy felt cold and it made her scowl. She rubbed her arms and glanced at Axel watching them intently. He shot a hesitant smile her way, and then popped another ball in the machine.

"Less huggy huggy, more batty batty," he announced.

"All right, brother," Elena warned. "Let's see what you got."

The ball fired. Elena swung. *Crack!* Her bat connected. She shielded her eyes, pretending for a moment she'd hit it out of the field.

"And it's outa here!"

Axel clapped his hands. The hit of warm hope Daisy had felt earlier bloomed to defrost her entire body. She smiled and stood to the side to watch. She even clapped a few times and shouted encouragement when Elena missed a ball. A few rounds later, Elena was swinging and missing more than she was hitting. She was tired. Daisy edged closer, just in case, but found Elena didn't need help. She knew her limits and handed Daisy the bat before saying breathlessly, "Your turn."

"Oh, I don't—" Daisy shook her head.

"That's okay. It's not hard." Elena forced the bat into Daisy's hand and then mumbled something about a quick nap before shuffling to a spot outside the cage. She plumped her backpack, laid her head onto it, and rolled to face a wall with her beanie pulled over her eyes.

"Is she okay?" Daisy asked Axel as he jogged up to the plate.

He shot his sister a concerned look but nodded. "She gets tired fast. A short nap and she'll perk up. Right. Your turn."

Daisy pointed the bat back at him. "I don't play. You have a go."

"Are you shitting me? You've *never* played baseball?" He blinked. "I thought you were exaggerating before."

She lifted her shoulder in a half shrug. "Never had the chance."

"I guess I can see that. What with learning to be a sniper, and all that."

Disapproval turned his voice tight, but it wasn't directed at Daisy. Axel's gaze was turned inward. His distaste was probably aimed at Julius.

He was right. Daisy had been too busy scouting sniper positions and following her psychopathic father around as he machinated and planned. Even after Julius had rescued her from the first lab, he brought her to a second lab. It wasn't until he was sure she was well and truly brainwashed that he brought her to his home. And then she had to live in the attic.

She didn't want to think about that now.

Axel looked like he wanted to ask her a question but held his tongue. Instead, he did something even more uncomfortable. He guided her to the plate and stood behind her, making sure to line up their hips before sliding his hands down her arms until they covered her fingers around the bat.

If Daisy's body liked Elena's embrace, it rejoiced at Axel's. Every nerve ending was on fire. The yin-yang tattoo on her inner wrist itched as the ink changed color to reflect her now balanced internal sin equilibrium. She lost focus and shivered. It had been so long since she'd had human contact like this. Not just the quick embrace of family or required touch like how he'd carried her after pulling her from the storm drain—but affectionate, deliberate, intimate touch.

"You okay?" he asked.

"You set my body on fire," she blurted. Then immediately felt the flush of a blush in her cheeks.

She heard his intake of breath. His pause as he considered his reply, and then… his lips hovered at her ear as he spoke. "I'd like to say I'm good at putting out fires, but I don't want to." He tightened his grip on her hands. "I'd rather control the burn. Would you like that, *minha margarida*? If you're nervous, will you let me help you?"

Why was she out of breath? Why did his words sound so sexual? Were they? Yes. Wait. Were they? And why did he just call her a margarita? That was the part where his tone had dropped to a baritone. It had to be a nickname. She had no idea what was going on, and while she weighed his words, trying to figure out what would be an acceptable response, he gave a breathy grunt that sounded suspiciously like a self-satisfied chuckle.

As if rendering her speechless was his goal all along.

"Hold the bat like this," he said gruffly, all business again. His breath was hot near her ear and sent shivers down her spine. "You have to look at the bat, Daze."

She swallowed the lump in her throat and focused forward.

"Relax," he said. "Drop your shoulders."

Daisy exhaled. With her breath, so went her tension. But then came glaring awareness of the tall, muscular and hot-blooded fireman behind her. He knew full well what he was doing with this position. His intimate tone was deliberate. The closeness of his hips to hers.

"Hands need to be this far apart." Husky. Rich. Deep. "Point the bat at the ceiling. Yes. Like that. Good work, Daze. *Good.*" He kicked her feet apart. "Widen your stance. Perfect."

His praise triggered butterflies in her stomach. Just as quickly as he'd arrived, he gave her ass a friendly swat and then jogged back to the pitch machine. They stared at each other down the length of the cage. Daisy's world shifted on its axis from the force of his attention. The fingerprints he'd left on her body remained. It was a seismic shift in her being. She'd never had someone look at her so piercingly, so full of... longing. Never had she felt an echo of it back.

He smiled and said, "Ready?"

She cleared her throat and nodded.

He flicked on the pitch machine and dropped the ball into the chute. The ball hurtled at her from across the expanse, but all she could do was hold his steady gaze. Brown, striking eyes looking at her as if she was his world. So lost in the trap, she forgot about the ball flying toward her face. Axel, also captive, realized a split second before she did.

"Look out!" he bellowed.

The ball! She closed her eyes, waiting for the hit to her face.

Nothing.

"Holy shit." Axel's voice had her peeling open wary eyes.

The baseball floated in the air an inch before her nose, but the moment she registered what had happened, it dropped. Axel rushed over.

"You saw that, right?" He picked up the ball. "I mean... what the fuck? It stopped in front of your face like it was caught in jelly." He locked eyes with her. "Did you do that?"

Daisy's heart halted. She gasped in a breath. "I don't... I don't know."

"You wanna see if we can do it again?"

We? He acted like he was on her team. He didn't even know he was her mate, or the effect he had on her internal sin equilibrium.

"Axel..." She shook her head and stared anywhere but at him. It was one thing for him to know secret things about her family, but actively helping her in this would turn the tide of their relationship. "I don't know."

"Hey." He dipped to catch her eyes. "That's a good thing, right? If it was you that stopped it, doesn't it mean you're becoming like your siblings? You're leveling up?"

"It means..." She couldn't let it out, because once she did, then it became real.

His long lashes swept down in a slow blink as he waited for her to continue, and when she couldn't, he pushed her further.

"Tell me why you were running out the door when I found you?" His brows pinched in concern. "Is it something to do with your powers? Are your family not treating you well? Because if they aren't, then—"

"How much do you know about us?" she asked. Most Faithful were strategically kept unaware of the grander Syndicate operation. She wasn't sure how much Axel knew. Toward the end, he must have had more security clearance than most if he had access to her in the prison lab.

"I don't know much about you except what I've put together from being a Faithful. I know more about the replicate system than anything else, and even then, I was kept in the dark about most things. You know what it's like for the Faithful."

"So… what do you know about us, specifically?"

"Well, my sister talks incessantly about you all, plus I picked up some things from the Syndicate. You were created in a lab to sense sin. You have powers, except not all of you do. Or—" His brow furrowed as he recollected. "Maybe you do but something happens to unlock them. I know that you each have a special person in your life that balances your sin, and that's why they were kidnapped. Julius wanted your stem cells to help him fix a problem they have with the replicates. I figured that out after he mumbled something he shouldn't have in one of his crazy, talking to himself moments. And he kept you from your brothers and sisters for decades." His eyes locked with her. "You were lied to."

Hearing him say it like that made Julius's version of the truth even more fake. It was *his* fault Gloria set the fire in the first place. It was him who said Daisy's siblings didn't want her. He'd made it look like Daisy was dead, so Mary and Flint *never* came back for her.

She didn't think Axel knew about the mating bond… specifically theirs. And with the way he looked at her, all stars and hope, she knew she'd end up disappointing him. Or, like he did with his sister, he'd end up doing bad things for her and she couldn't be the cause of another stain on his heart.

For some explicable reason, his eternal optimism had survived. She couldn't be the one to finally crush it out. He was a good person at the core. She wasn't.

"I don't know if I can give you what you want, Axel."

He cocked his head, confused, probably at Daisy's sudden turn of the conversation. "You don't know what I want."

"I know I'm not it."

Something shuttered in his eyes and he stepped back. He picked up a bat to study it. When he finally slid his gaze to her, it was with a look that belied his age. Confidence. Determination. Heat. He pointed the bat at her face and said, "I'm going to enjoy correcting that statement."

She snatched the bat from him. "I don't want this."

He tugged it back. "*You* don't know what you want."

"I know there's too much pressure," she blurted. His eyes narrowed. He stared, clearly understanding there was more to this situation than she let on. Each second that ticked by chipped away at her resolve until the rest of her worries tumbled out. "They want me to be like them, but I'm not. I'm not a hero. They expect me to be a savior and I'm not. You saw the kind of work I did for the Syndicate. I'm a bad person, Axel. You don't need that in your life, trust me."

"But you're trying to be good."

She threw up her hands. "A fat load of good that's doing. I can't find their missing mates. The city is falling apart. Your sister is dying. You're—" she cut herself off before she blew it and said he was her mate. She'd already said too much. "I'm over a decade older than you. It's clear you want more than friendship."

"I do," he admitted.

"But I just ran away from my responsibilities, and now my powers are triggering, and I have no fucking clue what to do."

He tossed the bat and stalked closer to cup her nape. That simple touch was like a button to release her tension. She had no idea how he did it. Every time he touched her, she melted for him.

"When I was younger," he said, "my father—*meu pai*—used to help me with school work. Once, I had a science paper due. I'd studied. I knew the subject, but every time I stared at the blank paper before me, I froze. *Meu pai* sat me down and said, '*Não pense no todo. Comece com o que você sabe.*' Don't think about everything. Start with what you know."

"I don't understand." That statement was stupid. There were too many things she knew. Not all of them relevant.

"You know I'm your friend," he said.

"Friend..." Daisy tested the word. It felt nice. But not quite right for him.

Axel continued, "You know Elena thinks the world of you, and you know I want..." His gaze blazed a slow path down her body. He seemed to catch himself admiring her, cleared his throat and met her eyes again. "But what do *you* know for sure, Daisy Lazarus? Tell me one thing."

She opened her mouth but nothing came out. This was the opportunity to reveal he was her mate. He mentioned he understood every Lazarus sibling had a special person that balanced their sin. It would be logical to talk about it now... but everything was loaded with expectations, even the small things.

Something shuffled in the shadows beside the pitch. They whirled toward the sound. A white robed intruder emerged from the shadows. It was impossible to see his identity behind the faceless white mask. Slits for eyes, nose and mouth. *One of the Faithful.* Daisy had been the one to pick those masks from the Halloween shelves when the psychotic henchmen were born. She'd only been fourteen at the time. Julius had paraded her down the store aisles and said to pick the most frightening costume.

To her, the most terrifying mask was a blank canvas—no emotion, no identity, nothing.

Two more Faithful entered the room. Each held knives or a bloody katana sword; standard weapons for them, but after the Seven had destroyed the clubhouses during their hunt for their missing mates, there should have been nothing left.

Clearly, they'd regrouped somewhere. Daisy should have realized. The Faithful were fanatical cockroaches, impossible to eradicate.

Daisy picked up the fallen baseball bat. She checked on Elena sleeping soundly to the side of the net, then shared a glance with Axel. He inched closer to his sister.

Their leader's gaze shifted to Axel then to Daisy. His voice came out muffled through the mask. "Falcon?"

She wasn't surprised they recognized her. With silver hair and violet eyes, she stood out.

"What do you want?" she asked.

They all glanced at each other, confused. The leader shrugged. "We're just sowing chaos like the boss asked. Isn't that what you're doing?"

They had no idea Daisy had defected. Or Axel. The shock of it hit Daisy hard. Had Julius not put the word out that she was public enemy number one as far as they were concerned? Madness must well and truly have a hold of Julius's usually ruthless and strategic mind.

Parker's fiancée used to be a Sinner—one of the Hildegard Sisterhood assassins. They believed Julius was trying to open the gates of hell. Daisy didn't believe in hell. But she was with Parker in his belief there could be other dimensions. She knew Julius too well to believe that even in madness, he'd waste his time on a lost cause.

She was the prime example. The moment she'd betrayed Julius, and he realized she wasn't ever going to be the powered soldier he wanted, he decided she was worth more for her organs and bodily fluids.

Suspicion sparked in the eyes of the Faithful. She wasn't in her Falcon white leather battle uniform. Nor was Axel wearing his Faithful gear. And they had a sleeping teenager nearby. If they were *sowing chaos* like they should be doing, why were they hiding here in the dark?

"Something's not right. Call this in," the leader announced to a Faithful who pulled out his cell phone and dialed. Probably Julius, or whoever had taken over as enforcer.

Axel pitched a baseball and knocked the cell from the Faithful's hands. Each white-robed fanatic turned his plastic-masked face Axel's way.

Cold emptiness bottomed out Daisy's stomach. She hated that they'd ruined the precious moment she'd been carving out for herself. The fizz and light Axel and his sister had given Daisy died with each of their advancing steps.

"This," Daisy said to Axel.

His brows furrowed at her.

"This right here," she said, and pointed to him and Elena with her bat. They'd been kind to her. They'd embraced her as a friend. It was more than anyone had done before. "This is the small thing that I know. I won't let them hurt you."

"Stop her." The Faithful leader pointed his sword at Daisy.

Daisy wanted to be good. But right now, she needed to be bad. Very bad.

She launched at the intruders. Starting with the leader, her bat swung toward his head. He blocked with his sword, but it was sloppy. Weak. He parried like an infant. She booted him in the middle and sent him to the floor. A swift jab to his mask with the heel of her bat and he was out.

The remaining Faithful approached Elena and Axel. Rage exploded inside Daisy. She screamed and went for them as Axel dove for his gun somewhere near Elena's backpack. But there was no need. Daisy was a hurricane of vengeance as she struck each Faithful in the head, then repeated her attack aiming for different body parts. She moved so fast, and with such swift violence, that she shocked everyone.

It was a tactic that had been drilled into her. Give it a hundred and ten percent, shock them, overwhelm them, put them on the back foot.

Don't stop. No mercy.

She used the baseball bat like a hammer to pulverize white-masked faces, giving them anger and hate until the masks cracked. Until her anger lessoned and relief oozed in.

"Don't stop," Julius growled in her ear as she fought her martial arts instructor. She was fifteen. Her instructor was forty. She had him on the ground, face bloody beneath her fist. "Keep going until he's finished. Or he'll finish you. Is that what you want, my darling? Do you want him to take you away from me?"

Her roar came from her gut as she raised the bat a final time—

"Stop." Axel gripped the bloody bat mid swing.

Daisy wheezed in air like she'd forgotten to breathe.

"Daisy, that's enough."

"But..." With wide eyes, she darted a glance between him and her quarry on the floor. Red had splashed over the white. Her face was sticky. "They were going to hurt you and Elena."

Axel nodded calmly. "Now they're not."

Elena hugged her backpack, her eyes as wide as Daisy's. But where Daisy was full of adrenaline, Elena looked full of fear.

Daisy let go of the bat. "I'm sorry. I... I don't know how to be good. I told you."

"It's fine, Daze."

"It's not fine!"

Her vision closed in and all she could hear was Julius's words taunting her on the day Mary left Daisy behind. His evil voice was always there, waiting to test her and push her. She punched her temples.

"*Bad people do bad things,*" Julius said. "*You were created to stop those bad people. The others couldn't handle that, so they left.*"

"*But if I stop them… doesn't that mean I'm doing a bad thing?*" And if she was doing bad things, then she was a bad person.

"*You're my darling.*"

Axel pulled Daisy into his arms and crushed her with his embrace, still looking down at her with something decidedly *not* hate.

"How can you look at me like that?" she blurted through the burn in her throat.

"Like you're the most incredible woman in the world?" he asked. "Because you are. You saved our lives."

"But…" The Faithful were a bloody, pulverized mess. "I don't know how to…"

"Be good?" He surveyed the destruction with a grave look, but then landed on his sister, trembling and shaking. She offered them a hesitant smile, and Daisy didn't see hate there either. She would have at least expected that fear to transfer to Daisy. But the two Alvares siblings looked a little shell-shocked, but grateful. Relieved. Axel shifted his hands to Daisy's waist. "Yeah, you keep saying that. I don't buy it."

"You don't know anything," she whispered, but her words had lost their power as they locked eyes and held.

Elena gave a shaky laugh then groaned dramatically. "Are you guys going to kiss? Because, ew. There are still bloody, masked fanatics on the floor. And… maybe I want to go home now."

"Search the bodies first," Daisy said.

"We can go home." Axel shot Daisy an unabashed wink and then went to assist his sister. As if none of this ruffled his feathers. As if this was just an ordinary Tuesday for him. Heat flushed Daisy's cheeks.

When the heat didn't leave, she realized she was blushing. Because Axel had *winked* at her.

She supposed he had seen a lot of violence as one of the Faithful himself... even in his job as a firefighter he'd seen this kind of gore. And Elena, Daisy's gaze shifted to them as Axel lifted her up and steadied her on her feet. Elena was okay. Daisy was glad she could protect the girl. She cleared her throat and then helped Axel with the search before covering the bodies with some canvas they found. She didn't want a poor staff member discovering the mess the next time they were in.

These Faithful wouldn't be the last Daisy crossed paths with. If Julius's madness abated for long enough to put the word out about her defection, then she'd have a whole horde of fanatics after her.

Unless she got to him first.

"YOU HAVEN'T RELEASED ENOUGH REPLICATES," the voices of his loves hissed from the darkness in the rear of his car.

"I know," Julius replied and checked the rearview mirror. The ghostly visage of his wife stared back at him. It flickered. He thought he saw her scream. Then it was gone again. He returned his gaze to the road, to the journey home.

"But we need more to open the gate."

"Shut up. I *must* do this slowly. If they're all out now before the Deadly Seven turn, they'll be destroyed, and then, my loves, who will bring you back?"

Julius tugged at his mangey hair. His mind raced as fast as the car he drove. He had this all planned. He had it sorted. But if his loves kept hounding him to go faster, he'd never bring them back to this world.

"We have to time this properly. Patience," he said, realizing he'd let go of the steering wheel. He quickly gripped it again and brought the car back into his lane.

When he'd started the Syndicate decades ago, and helped create the Deadly Seven, his original plan had been to turn them dark so they would ruthlessly hunt down every sinner in the world and bring about utopia for his replicated family to enjoy, sin free. But then the Hildegard Sisterhood happened. Then he found out Gloria, the Seven's creator, had built in a failsafe into their DNA to stop them from going dark.

For years he'd stewed over the betrayal, only to have a solution drop into his lap. *Kidnap the mates.* Even after he lost the ability to replicate his wife and daughter, he never gave up. He didn't see Despair's betrayal as the gift it was. He never wanted clones of his family. He wanted them—the originals—back. The ones that mattered.

To do that, he had to complete the rituals needed to open the twin gates to the afterlife. One went to the dark place, one went to the light. But with the Deadly Seven and the Hildegard Sisterhood protecting this magical spot where he'd glimpsed his loves for the first time, he needed a distraction to gain access.

And Julius had backup plans for his backup plans. There would be no failing him this time. He could taste victory on his tongue. He could smell the scent of his wife's perfume.

He'd blown up the bridges leading into the city, trapping the sinners of Cardinal City inside like pigs waiting for slaughter. Without their mates, the Seven were dancing with darkness. It won't be long before the rest would follow. He had half a mind to tease them with a video recording of their mates in captivity.

Let them watch their loved ones from afar, just like he was separated from his.

No.

He shook his head.

Focus. He would get to the mates in good time. Destroying them at the optimal time would drive the nail in their coffin. He wanted to crush their hope when it was highest.

First, he needed to collect the items for the ritual, and then he would release more weapons on the city to grow the chaos. Sinners would destroy each other, and the Deadly Seven would destroy them, and then he would destroy the Deadly Seven by destroying their mates.

A hysterical laugh bubbled up inside of him at his own genius and he accidentally planted his foot on the gas. The burst in speed only made him laugh harder. His wife and daughter behind him also laughed.

With the city in chaos, and those ungrateful menaces undone, there would be nothing standing in his way to access the gates. He could complete the ritual his loves had whispered to him overnight.

They said if he opened one gate, then their gate would also open. The afterlife was two sides to the same coin. A yin and a yang. Once open, he could pull them through, and the dark Deadly Seven would systematically take care of any sinning souls hitching a ride at the same time. Then he would close the gates. His wife and daughter would be by his side, and the sinners in the city would be gone. It would finally be safe for his wife and daughter to come back.

"What's taking so long to open the gates?"

Julius tugged his hair again as he met the black eyes of his wife in the rearview. They looked disturbed. Hollow. "Soon, my loves, soon," he placated. "I haven't got all the tools. I need your personal items."

"And then?"

"And then all hell breaks loose."

His cackling laughter echoed against the windows.

seven

AXEL ALVARES

WHEN THEY ARRIVED at Lazarus House, Daisy acted differently to how she'd been when Axel had picked her up. Then, she'd been reserved and uncomfortable. So upset, in fact, that she'd left her family—in the middle of a citywide catastrophe—to blow off steam with him and Elena. But now, after doing just that, she stood taller. She walked with confidence. With purpose.

Her version of blowing off steam had been to take down a few Faithful. But he liked to think he had a little something to do with it. He hoped.

Elena trailed after Daisy as they entered the lobby, asking questions about the power stats of Daisy's siblings. She wanted to know who was the strongest in a fight. Axel was happy to see her post-battle shock had worn off. The fact she chatted like this meant she felt safe. Daisy called herself a monster, but she'd protected the innocent.

"So?" Elena asked Daisy, hugging her backpack. "Envy or Greed. I think Greed, right? Or… wait. I just thought of something. What if there was no metal in the area? Oooh. That would be a handicap.

Okay, I change my mind. Pride. Nope! Lust. Oh shit... I don't know. Come on. You have to give me something."

"I don't know," Daisy mumbled as they entered the elevator. She rubbed her forehead with the back of the hand still holding the baseball bat. He offered to hold it for her, but she refused. Axel caught the amusement in her eyes as they faced the closing doors.

"Hello, Daisy Lazarus. You have guests." The female voice came from a speaker within the elevator car.

Axel put his arm around his sister. She leaned against him. There must be a camera marking their movements. This all felt very high tech.

"They are..." Daisy appeared flummoxed for a moment.

"Axel," he reminded her with a smirk.

"I know that," she grumbled back. "That's not why I... never mind." Louder she said, "This is Axel and his sister Elena. They're... friends."

"Nice to meet you Axel and Elena. I am AIMI."

"Hi AIMI," Elena replied.

"Hello, Elena. May I ask your surname?"

"Don't—" Daisy started saying, but Elena answered.

"Alvares," she said.

"Aah. Yes. I have you in our database. Elena and Axel Alvares. You are already on the approved list."

"We are?" Axel asked. He'd hoped, but never expected to be welcomed so soon. "Why?"

"Axel Alvares, as Daisy's m—"

"That's enough, AIMI!" Daisy snapped, then shot Axel a nervous smile before explaining. "She's a computer. You don't need all that extra information."

Right. Of course the Deadly Seven would have computer-run security. It was still odd that they had been put on a safe list. Was it simply because he'd helped rescue Daisy, or was she hiding something? He found it odd the entire family had trusted him so swiftly after knowing he'd worked for the enemy.

Elena got a look on her face Axel could only construe as nosy. Her lips parted as she looked up at the speaker but before she could ask AIMI questions about which Deadly Seven heroes were more dangerous, he tightened his grip on her arm and shook his head. *Next time,* he said with his eyes.

She nodded and looked at her feet.

The elevator doors closed. When they opened again, it was to a long hallway with two doors at the end.

"Parker is out," AIMI said. *"Mary is in Wyatt's apartment with Misha's family. The door is unlocked."*

Daisy steeled her spine and beckoned them out.

"I'll leave you two here with Mary," she said as she walked. "You'll be safe until this mayhem ends."

"Hold up." Axel stopped Daisy by the shoulder as she arrived at an apartment door. "What do you mean, leave me here?"

Daisy scratched her palm with a thumb. Alarm bells went off when she wouldn't meet his eyes.

"No," he said. "Nah-uh."

Her violet gaze snapped to his. "No?"

"You heard me."

"I need to go back out there and fight. You don't. Simple as that."

She dismissed him by opening the door. A baby's squeal and conversation filtered out as Daisy strode through like the blood on the bat and on her face were an every day occurrence.

Elena grabbed Axel's arm and whispered, "You're not going to let her go out there without you, right?"

"Hell, no."

"Good." She smiled. "I'll stay here. You go." Her breath hitched with a sudden idea and she brought her lips to his ears to say, "You can keep an eye on her power and let me know the stats. Like, how heavy is an item that she lifts with her mind?"

He narrowed his eyes. "I'm not doing that."

She pouted. "Aww, come on. What else do I have to look forward to?"

"My winning personality?"

She snorted. "Right."

"God, I love you." He grabbed her and kissed her beanie.

"I know."

With Daisy already inside, Axel and Elena walked in and then closed the door. He scanned the nicely furnished apartment. *Expensive shit.* Big windows. Slick floors and kitchen appliances. Baby stuff everywhere. An elderly couple played cards at the dining table with a portly fatherly figure and a young woman about Elena's age.

Mary was at the kitchen counter cutting up food. Her husband Flint was at her side picking at the vegetables, and subsequently getting thwacked on the hand for sampling the goods. His frayed baseball hat hid short gray hair and dark eyes. He stood taller than his wife, but she commanded the room. There was something about Mary's aura. Axel had met them briefly when he'd carried Daisy in after pulling her from the storm drain.

Further into the apartment, before the sectional and TV screen, a young man carried the baby. With burgeoning muscles, he looked to be in his late teens. He bounced the bundle in his arms and showed it the patterns on the television. Longish shaggy hair. Hearing aid on each ear.

Mary looked up as Daisy walked toward her. She didn't put down her knife but carried it and deftly twirled it in her fingers as she met Daisy halfway near the foyer entrance. Flint followed behind to meet them all near the door.

"What happened?" Mary checked Daisy over.

Flint asked, "Are you hurt?"

Daisy glanced at Axel and Elena. "Some Faithful attacked us. We're fine."

"Did they want your blood sample?" Flint asked, scratching his peppered beard.

Daisy shrugged. "No. They didn't even know I'd defected. Where's Parker?"

"It's just us," Mary answered grimly. "Everyone is out in the city. Griffin is... not doing so good. He's gone dark—completely blacked out and is now hunting down greedy sinners without remorse."

Axel stopped surprise from showing on his face. They were being so candid in front of him. It was strange. They'd been hush-hush last time they'd all met, even though Axel knew their crime fighting secret. Was it because Daisy had brought them home to meet the parents?

Could he be so stupid to think that was what was happening here?

Daisy's face paled as she spoke to Mary. "What will you do?"

"Parker and Alice are trying to restrain him and bring him home." Her eyes turned downcast. "We'll have to lock him up until he's stable."

"He might never emerge from that state," Daisy pointed out.

"We need Lilo." Mary slipped her hand around Flint's waist. She fit under the taller man's arm. Their ease and affection with each other warmed Axel's chest. Mary leaned against her husband. "We need all the mates. Without them, they're all ticking time bombs."

A silence descended. Thoughts flickered in Daisy's eyes. The set of her jaw hardened. Her shoulders straightened. Through it all, Axel couldn't shake that feeling he was privy to secrets he shouldn't be. They trusted Daisy because she was their family. But Axel? He'd helped them once to save her. It would be foolish to suddenly give him all the house secrets like this. Something was going on and he wanted to know what.

Mary's gaze landed on Elena as though just realizing she was there.

"This is my sister, Elena Alvares," Axel introduced.

"Hi." She gave a shy smile.

"Nice to meet you." Mary softened immediately, her eyes landing on Axel again. "I'm glad Daisy has brought you here, but I'm sorry it's under such trying circumstances. You're welcome any time, Elena. For as long as you need." Mary noticed Elena sliding glances to the young man with the baby and pointed. "That's Alek. He's Misha's brother and Amari's uncle. You look about the same age. If you know anything about soothing babies, you're more than welcome to give him a hand. Be mindful he's deaf."

Elena's cheeks flushed. She looked at Axel and hesitated.

"Go say hi," he said, inwardly hopeful her curiosity would turn into something more to keep her interested in life. Maybe she would meet a friend. A friend meant she was thinking of a future. To Mary, he said, "She used to babysit for the neighbors."

The relief on Mary's face was obvious. Axel felt better knowing Elena was welcome, even though he still couldn't grasp why. Was knowing their Deadly secrets enough to put them in the circle of most trusted? Or maybe they were taking their lead from him. He was trusting them. They were trusting him. Whatever the case, Elena would be looked after, no matter what happened to him out there. He gave his sister's shoulder a squeeze and she dropped her backpack by the kitchen counter before heading into the living room to introduce herself to Alek. Within seconds she'd taken the baby from him. He should probably let Mary know about Elena's condition.

"She has medication in her bag—"

"Mary?"

The panic in Flint's voice brought Axel's attention back to them. Alarmingly, Mary's irises had turned milky white—all the color gone. She stared as though looking into the distance. Her muscles stiffened, the tendons in her neck stood out, and she jerked uncontrollably. The long dark braid flapped against her back. The knife slipped from her fingers and landed with a metallic clank on the floor. Daisy and Flint rushed to catch her.

Daisy dropped her bat and sank to the floor with Mary. She held Mary's head in her lap while Flint took his wife's hand.

"What's happening?" Daisy asked, a tremble in her voice.

"She's having a vision," Flint explained, brows pinched.

"But I thought those stopped years ago."

"They did."

The confused look they shared did little to assuage Axel's nerves. A vision? As in a psychic vision? Axel's parents were superstitious. They used to say all their troubles emerged because they crossed the path of a *bruxa*, a witch, and had displeased her. Axel had always been a believer in the mystical, even before these heroes with superpowers emerged. But seeing it in person was something to get used to, just like seeing that ball freeze in front of Daisy's face.

"Do you need me to do anything?" he asked.

"She'll be fine," Flint said. "It's just like an epileptic fit, she needs to ride it out. She needs to experience the vision."

"How can you be so calm when your wife is like this on the floor?" Daisy gaped.

Flint looked her squarely in the eyes and said, "A minute ago, I wasn't. But now I'm trying. What does your gut tell you about that?"

Daisy studied Flint long and hard before saying, "You have hope."

"That's right," he said with a fond smile as he stroked his wife's hair. "When you love someone, you keep the faith."

Everyone in the room stopped what they were doing and crowded around. The younger woman who'd been playing cards asked, "Do you want me to call the ambulance?"

There was no need. Mary became lucid with a gasp. She clutched Flint's hand, then twisted to see Daisy and clutched her hand still crusty with dried blood. Tears formed in Mary's eyes.

"What did you see?" Daisy asked. "What is it?"

When Mary tried to voice her thoughts, but couldn't get the words out, the hairs on the back of Axel's neck stood on end. Something was very wrong. Nothing physiological. Mary seemed fine. It was the vision. He felt it in his bones.

"Give the lady room," Axel said and shooed everyone back to their places. Victims hated being gawped at. "I'll get you water."

Mary's knuckles were white as she clutched both Daisy's and Flint's hands, their heads bent together as they whispered. He gave them privacy and went to find a glass in the kitchen. He tried not to look back at their hushed conversation. As he filled the glass from the faucet, he lifted his gaze and locked eyes with his sister. Standing in the great room across the expanse and near the tv, she patted the baby's bottom as it slept soundly in her arms. Alek had gone to his family and hand-signed in quiet conversation with them. It took some effort, but Axel schooled his expression into something calm and easy. He shot Elena a comforting smile so she wouldn't worry, and then went back to the group.

"Here." He handed Mary the glass.

She accepted it gratefully but only took a sip.

"Can you stand?" Flint's voice was way too raspy for Axel's liking, as though he was trying to hide his distress.

Mary nodded and leaned heavily on her husband as she raised to her feet.

"Why won't you tell me what you saw?" Daisy gritted out.

"I don't know what I saw, *mija*." Mary shook her head. "I... I don't know."

"You say you trust me, but you're keeping things from me."

Mary grasped Daisy by the loose fabric at her sternum. At first it looked like she was going to attack, and Axel stepped forward to intervene, but then Mary's fingers flattened over Daisy's heart, and she patted. Her face softened and she whispered with such pain in her eyes.

"Daisy, it was always meant to be you." She patted her again. "Gloria made you special, so you have the tools to lead this family. It was never meant to be me or Parker."

"Parker was born to lead," Daisy quipped.

"Maybe with this." Mary tapped Daisy's head. "But you lead with this." She tapped Daisy on the breastbone. "Do you understand?"

"No." Daisy's exasperated tone sounded an inch from snapping. "Because mine is broken."

Mary glanced at Axel. "Not for long."

Daisy's cheeks turned pink, and she started scratching her palms. She shook her head and then stared at Mary for a moment longer before announcing. "I'm going now. Axel, you stay here."

"Oh, no you don't." He stopped her just as she got to the door. He had no idea what had passed between Daisy and Mary, but it felt significant. Somehow, he knew Mary would be on his side about this. He wouldn't be left behind.

"I have to." Daisy's eyes flashed. "This business with Julius has to end, and I have to be the one to do it. I know him better than anyone."

"You don't look happy about it." She looked scared, resigned, but determined.

"I told you why." She scowled and lowered her voice. "I'm not the hero. I will never live up to their expectations. You heard what

Mary said to me. She puts me on a pedestal and I'm not that person."

"So be yourself."

"What?"

"I mean…" Axel surveyed the room. Everywhere he looked he saw goodness. From the matriarch of the family, to the way her doting husband cared for her, to the way the rest of them rallied to care for the baby who could very well end up orphaned, to his own sister mustering her strength to stay positive. He knew exactly what Daisy felt when she didn't see herself fitting in here. But he saw the same thing Mary did. Daisy had something special. She'd survived decades of brainwashing, abuse and torture, and still she wanted to walk out there and make things right. She just needed to find a way to feel like she fit in. "I mean you're perfect the way you are, Daisy. Stop trying to be their hero and just be you. Trust your instincts."

She blinked up at him like he'd told her the most insane thing ever. For a moment, he thought he had.

"Your instincts have gotten you this far, Daze."

A hesitant smile formed on her beautiful lips.

"You mean… just let go?"

"None of us are going anywhere. Just let go."

eight
DAISY LAZARUS

AT FIRST, the thought of letting her instincts loose was liberating for Daisy. She felt like she was soaring as she left Wyatt's apartment. Axel's words were the wings she'd always dreamed of having... *Just let go...* Maybe she could be like a bird, trust her instincts and fly. But then again, maybe she'd fall. Everything came crashing down when she realized they would be going nowhere without a plan.

She stopped at the elevator without going in and leaned on the baseball bat, a little tired. Her muscles ached. The fresh scars from Julius's 'exploratory surgery' while she was imprisoned pinched at her stomach. But she was determined to come up with a plan of action. Her mind had the right idea, but her body leaned harder on the bat. For some reason, she had a hard time leaving it behind. It wasn't the game it represented; it was the feeling of rightness when she looked at it. The bat was her weapon, no one else's. Not a sniper gun. Not a bullwhip. Not a knife or sword. She'd used it to protect.

Let go, but go where?

Two days earlier, Daisy's siblings had raided every Faithful clubhouse she'd known, but they couldn't find the missing partners.

They'd turned up empty. The Faithful also wouldn't have stuck around the old haunts if they knew something big was going down, so searching them had been a long shot, but an important step in taking down the Syndicate.

Now, only half the family continued to look for the missing mates, not that the other half didn't want to—their resources were just being pulled in different directions. If Daisy could find the mates, reunite them with their partners, then the chances of the Seven going dark would be seriously mitigated. With eight of them at full strength, they could take on any weapon Julius released.

And there would be weapons. Julius had many fingers in different pies. Daisy was sure something bad was coming. She'd seen a black site full of mech fighter suits, replicate tanks, rabid sin-sensing animals, and sentient plants. The international Syndicate ring might be disbanded and destroyed, but it would be stupid to think Julius hadn't kept something in isolation for his own dark plans.

She turned her mind back to the mates while Axel waited patiently beside her. Parker and Sloan had installed trackers on most of them but, unlike the nano-trackers in her tattoo, theirs were in watches. And they must have been destroyed because none of the trackers worked.

Daisy had no idea where the mates might be. All this thinking, and she'd come up with nothing.

Axel tried to hide his yawn behind a stretch, but Daisy noticed. It was late for him. He wouldn't be able to keep up with her for the rest of the night. She only needed a few hours sleep to refresh herself.

She knew all this but when he followed her out, she allowed him to stay. She had to admit a part of her enjoyed his eternal optimism. And there was something about touching him. He soothed her loud mind. But as much as she enjoyed his company, he had to go home at some point, and she would have to continue alone. It was safer that way.

When Julius had her captive, holding onto hope helped beat back the abyss of despair. Hope had come in many forms, one of them being the crushed flower she'd stolen from the bonsai plant her family had kept in her honor. She'd focused on it for so long, even after the petals had disintegrated. Axel had also been a tiny part of her defense against complete annihilation, and he hadn't even known it.

All he'd done was sneak food in to her. It seemed like a small thing, but she saw it as someone else going against the grain. He was the splash of color in the gray.

Once Daisy started ruminating about the tall, fit man next to her, she couldn't stop. She found him incorrigible, young, and perhaps a little naive which was surprising considering the daily tragedy he faced as a firefighter. But that same optimism was dangerous. His joining the Faithful was a classic example of that. He had no idea about the real consequences of exchanging his mortal life for his sister, even if it was for unselfish reasons. He'd condemned his sister to be reborn as a powered and controlled clone, existing purely to be a soldier in Julius's unholy war against sin and he didn't even realize it.

All because he couldn't bear the thought of a life without her.

"I've been thinking," Axel said. "They didn't know we weren't on their side anymore."

"The Faithful?"

"Yeah. What if we can use that to our advantage?"

"You mean… go back?"

He rubbed his eyes and yawned again. "Yeah, I mean, the club-houses are obviously disbanded, but there's always some other communication method. I could try some contacts and put some feelers out."

"Are the group chats still active?" Her eyes narrowed. "Has Julius tried to contact you?"

"No, but I took their cell phone from the batting cage. With everything happening, I forgot to show you." He dug into his pocket and showed her. "Maybe we can use it."

She studied him. He was right. The two of them now had an incredible advantage. They could lure out more Faithful and then follow the breadcrumbs until they found where Julius hid. Someone had to know. Just as they were standing there contemplating, a message came through on the cell.

Axel read it. His brows lifted.

"What is it?" she asked.

She tried to take the phone, but he held it back. She went for it again, but he evaded her a second time. Scowling, she met his eyes expecting a cheeky game face, but serious brown eyes were leveled on her.

"I'm with you on this, Daze."

"Fine."

"Say it. I'm coming with you."

"Just show me."

Reluctantly, he handed her the cell. As she read the message, her hope lifted.

Boss-man has job for us. Dusk tomorrow. Crow's nest. You know the drill.

"Whoever sent this is in contact with Julius," she mumbled. "They said boss-man."

"Crow's nest is the shipping container yard. We meet them there tomorrow," Axel said. "And we find a way to get to him."

Daisy pocketed the phone, a fact Axel noted but didn't comment on.

"You should get some rest," she said. "Go back to Elena. I need to pick up supplies."

"She's fine with your family. I'm not leaving you by yourself."

"Axel, I'm fine." She gave him a derisive look. "I can handle myself."

He folded his arms and became an immovable mountain. Daisy suddenly had a vision of what he'd be like in his job—picking up injured people, carrying them like he had with her. His scowl deepened. "You were sliced up not that long ago and almost drowned. When I pulled you from that storm drain, you were barely breathing. I know you have some kind of fast healing, but I also know what it's like when someone is hiding how they really feel. My sister does it all the time. So, I'm not leaving you alone."

"Fine." Why did she like his response? "Come with me."

Satisfied, he dropped his scowl. "Where we headed?"

"To my old apartment in the Syndicate Tower."

First, they needed a mode of transportation. To get to the Lazarus House garage, they had to go through the headquarters in the basement. A strange vibe filled the air as she walked out of the elevator and into an empty hallway. It felt like a ghost town, but she knew the rest of her siblings were out on the streets, either hunting down replicates, stopping rioters and looters, or looking for their mates. None would be sleeping yet.

Axel cleared his throat. She glanced up at him. At least with no one here, she didn't have to tell him about the mating bond. If he knew he had a connection to her, she'd have a hard time convincing him to go back to his sister after this little excursion.

Straightening her shoulders, she strode forward and stopped at the weapons room. The door was ajar, and she could see inside. Lined along the walls were various swords, guns, and devices she could use to help her with her task. She went in.

"Wow," Axel said, following her. "This is some shit."

He touched a few items. On instinct, Daisy put down the baseball bat and went for the military grade sniper rifle in the case. She hauled it over her shoulder but then froze under the weight of a memory.

"Pretend it's a game," Julius urged.

Daisy settled herself stomach first on the hot asphalt of the building's roof. She looked down the scope of her sniper rifle and counted the milling people. They were ants. And ants should be squashed. That's what Julius always said.

"I'll give you fifty bucks for each one you hit."

"I don't want money," she mumbled.

"What do you want?"

"Anything?" she asked, excited and turned back to squint at him.

His tall figure blocked the sun. All she could see was the dark space he filled. "Well that depends on how many you hit."

"I want to go to the zoo."

"Take down twenty and it's a deal."

Daisy shook the memory away and hate filled her. She'd made it to the zoo in the end, but Julius never came with her. Some nameless nanny did. Daisy's life had been full of his empty promises.

She put down the sniper rifle, collected the bat, and headed for the operations room. Axel followed but then stopped somewhere behind her. She caught him staring into the viewing window of the medic room. His jaw flexed.

"This is where they took you," he said. "After we rescued you."

She glanced at the operating table, medical equipment, and recovery gurney. She'd laid on that cold surface for hours while they pumped fluids into her via an intravenous needle, but she'd been in worse situations. The scars on her body proved it.

"They wouldn't let me go in," he said, then met her eyes. "I didn't like it."

"They didn't know then," she said.

"Know what?"

That you're my mate. She shrugged. "Never mind."

He opened his mouth to respond, but voices in the operations room stole their attention. Someone was back. Daisy jogged into the room. The wall screens played out news reports from around the city: fires; the Mayor talking at a press release about delayed assistance from the federal government; grainy cell footage of one of the Deadly Seven in action and his full support of their help to manage crime.

Daisy was wrong. No one was back. It was just the news reports. One drew her closer. The more she saw, the more her heart rabbited.

"Shit," Axel said, a grim tone in his voice. "That's your brother, right?"

On the screen, Griffin—Greed—stood in his battle gear with a hurricane of metal junk whirling around him. His eyes were cold, like no one was home. Mary had said something earlier about Griffin falling under his sin's influence.

"AIMI," Daisy asked the air. "What's the time stamp on the news report on screen five."

"What you're seeing happened twenty minutes ago."

"Do they need help?"

"Parker and Alice are incoming with Griffin. Would you like me to ask them if they need assistance?"

"No, it's—"

The basement door leading to the garage swung open. In came Parker and Wyatt carrying Griffin's limp body between them. Alice raced in after, her blue eyes wild. She wore a similar battle suit to the Deadly Seven and the hood was pushed down to reveal her wild copper hair.

"I'm sorry," Alice blurted. "I'm sorry but I had to do it."

"Stop apologizing," Parker answered gruffly. "You had to knock him out."

"Where do we put him?"

"Fuck, I don't know," Wyatt barked.

"I do." Parker jerked his head toward the corridor leading back toward the elevator and the main apartments. "I refitted the storage room."

"Refitted it to what?" Alice gaped.

"An insulated cell."

Griffin murmured and his head lolled to the other side. "Lilo…"

"He's coming to," Parker said. "Hurry."

They rushed Griffin away. His boots scrambled on the ground, leaving a muddy, wet stain that might have been blood. Daisy followed to see Alice open a glass-windowed concrete door. Parker and Wyatt dumped their brother inside. The room had a plastic-like lining over thick concrete walls.

"Wyatt, out!" The second Wyatt and Parker jogged out, Parker used his immense strength to roll the heavy door closed and shouted, "Lock the cell door AIMI. Now!"

Two seconds after they heard the lock click into place, and the air pressure in the room sealed, Griffin's furious face appeared behind the window, and he slammed his palm against it. Then he stopped. Cold dead eyes stared out at them.

Every metal object in their vicinity rattled. From the weapons attached to bodies, to the exposed pipes in the ceiling, to a rattle filtering back to them from the workshop.

"I thought you said it was insulated," Wyatt said.

"Clearly not enough." Parker tilted his head to the speaker in his hood. "AIMI, sedate Griffin in the insulated cell."

Instantly, gas spurted from the ceiling behind Griffin. He looked back at the mist and then his body flopped. He landed unceremoniously on the hard floor with a muffled thud that reminded Daisy of the time she'd sniper shot all those homeless people. It was the same sound they'd made.

"I'm so sorry. This wasn't supposed to happen," Alice mumbled.

"Babe." Parker's giant hands swallowed Alice's face as he cupped it. "Stop apologizing."

"You know what my job is," she blurted, voice tight. "You know why I'm here. I said I would do it. If I have to kill him to stop him, I will."

"I know." Parker sighed and rested his forehead on Alice's.

"What happened to Griffin?" Daisy asked.

"The gaps between his blackouts are shortening," Parker said. "We can't trust him anymore."

"He deliberately wounded a civilian," Alice said with a wince. "I had no choice but to take him down."

Daisy's brows winged up. "You managed to take Griffin down on your own?"

Alice's eyes turned hard and she lifted her chin. "I have contingency plans to take down each and every one of you." She paused and kept her eyes on Daisy. "Especially you."

"It will never come to that," she promised.

Somehow, Daisy's words bolstered them. It was as though she'd stepped back in time and sang a song to cheer them up. The lifting of their spirits was a tangible shift in her gut—a fizzing flutter—and it invigorated her.

"So, you're just going to leave him in there?" Axel asked.

"There's nothing else we can do. He's unstable without his mate."

Daisy could virtually see the cogs turning in Axel's mind. He'd taken in a lot of information while working as a Faithful. Toward the end of his time there, Julius had brought him in as a close contact.

Daisy had been stewing over the possibility that he knew he was her mate, but he might have already figured it out.

Wyatt faced Daisy. "Do you have any news?"

From the eager look in his tired eyes, and the flutter of hope that tickled her belly, she guessed he meant news about the location of his missing mate. She shook her head and his shoulders slumped. In all her time knowing and researching this angry brother of hers, she'd never seen him admit defeat like this. His despair wrapped steel fingers around her heart and squeezed.

"We might have a lead on Julius, though," she said.

Wyatt looked up. His hope surged so swiftly that Daisy almost swooned.

Axel explained to them about the Faithful attack and how he and Daisy hadn't initially been recognized as defectors. Still reeling from Wyatt's hope, she watched Axel talk to her family. They listened with wary respect. She wasn't ready for him to know what his role was in her life. She wanted to keep that separate for a little longer. But the more she thought about it, the more she realized it was a stupid resistance. The sooner Axel learned he was her mate, the better for the fate of the world.

What Daisy wanted had never mattered. She should know that by now.

"We're going to intercept a meeting tomorrow," Axel explained. "Then we're hoping to trace them back to Julius. We'll find out where your family is."

Wyatt nodded. His downcast eyes shifted to the elevator leading up to the apartments and he started walking. Two steps in, he looked over his shoulder and said, "I'm going to check on my daughter. Keep me posted."

Parker and Alice were the only ones left.

"That blood from the Faithful?" Parker asked, looking at her stained face.

She touched her skin and then glanced down at the baseball bat in her hand. She'd forgotten about the spatter.

"She whaled on them," Axel said. "She saved my sister's life."

Parker heard it all with a steady expression. Then he nodded toward the door. "You heading out?"

"If we're going to fit in with the Faithful again," she said. "There are a few things I need to pick up from my old apartment."

"At Syndicate Tower," he confirmed.

She nodded. Alice stepped forward. "The Sinners are there keeping an eye on the site where the replicates were digging. I'll tell them to let you in."

"Thank you."

With a renewed sense of purpose, she went to the glass cabinet housing her Deadly Seven uniform. She was the eighth member. It didn't make sense that Parker gave her a suit. There could be only seven. But she took the white face scarf off the dummy and pocketed it. Then she gestured for Axel to follow her.

"Let's go."

nine

DAISY LAZARUS

DAISY STRODE into the Lazarus House garage and surveyed the performance vehicles. From Parker's Bugatti to Wyatt's Ducati, every vacant spot in the garage was filled. Most were black armored vehicles except Liza's and Joe's sedans. And then there were just the flashy, useless cars. Axel whistled through his teeth at the extravagance.

"Jeeze, Louise," he said, scratching his head. "Talk about a billion-aire's wet dream. Shall we take the Lambo?" He pointed at the sleek, low car.

She shook her head and pointed at the black motorcycle. "That one."

Axel straddled the bike and put a helmet on.

"Hold my bat," she said, then swung her leg over before him, essentially pushing him backward.

Axel didn't complain as she fitted herself between his legs, put her hand on the throttle and fired her up. Ninety decibels of horsepower roared to life, shaking the walls. There was only one helmet. She gave it to Axel. He protested but she wouldn't accept his misplaced chivalry. Daisy walked the bike backward until they were at a position where she could angle out of the driveway.

The sound of the motorcycle was the only sound on the drive back across town. The curfew had begun and, surprisingly, the citizens stayed in. But the worst of them would lurk in the shadows, and any corner they rounded could bring trouble. The journey took less than ten minutes, but in that time, Axel's grip on her waist slipped in his exhaustion.

The Tower was at the southern end of the Quadrant, right up against the city highway. Julius enjoyed looking out over Mid-Town and further down to the Southside slums. He liked to see the wealth of a city on one side, and the shit on the other.

He used to say it reminded him of his mission, but she always thought it made him feel like a king when he wasn't. He was just a desperate madman who missed his family.

Daisy wasn't sure what she'd find when they arrived. Days ago, Parker and Alice had chased Julius into the basement here where they thought Daisy was being kept prisoner. But it hadn't been the basement. She had been in the sewers beyond.

She took the bike to the underground lot and forced her way inside through a half-lifted metal door. The building used to be filled with offices for dummy corporations they'd used as a cover. They'd run most of their high-level Syndicate strategy from there—well, Daisy and Julius had. It had also been where Daisy laid her head to rest. Most nights, Julius also slept in his office on a couch. He hadn't returned to his family home for years.

Too many painful memories, he'd said.

Somehow, she didn't think he was talking about how he locked her in the attic to "protect" her. She now knew it was to stop her from roaming about and touching his dead family's belongings. And she supposed, there would have been an element of not wanting Daisy to discover the truth about the world—how not all of them were falling under the influence of sin, how her family was still alive, how there was hope.

They parked the bike and walked into the basement lobby entrance. Glass sliding doors were locked. Crime scene tape covered it from side to side. She pulled it down and then pried the glass door open with her fingers.

"Slot the bat in when I open it," she said to Axel.

"Won't the alarm go off?"

"The Sinners will have it disabled."

After they opened the doors, two women in black skin-tight clothing, hoods and red scarf-masks emerged. They dropped their scarfs and hoods to reveal their identities. One was an Asian brunette, and the other was a Caucasian blond. They took in every inch of Daisy's and Axel's body, checked behind them to see if anyone else followed, then waved them in.

"I'm Tawny," said the blond. "Alice said you were coming. Leila and I have been guarding the gate."

"The gate?" Axel's brows lifted.

"The gate to Hell," Leila replied, matter of fact.

"It's not Hell," Daisy said to Axel, placating him. "Julius is a madman. Don't listen to them."

Both Sinners pivoted and glared at her.

Leila said, "Hell, the Afterlife, another dimension. Whatever you want to call it, sin-sensing replicates want to go there because it's where they sense the largest concentration of sin. If Julius succeeds, there's no telling what will come through. Raven foresaw demonic forces in her psychic visions. She said the gate has evil mystical energy. If it opens, the replicates and the state of this city will be the least of our problems."

Axel visibly paled. Daisy rolled her eyes. "It's not true."

"How do you know?"

"I know because he spent his life working on replicates so he could bring his wife and daughter back to *life*. This other nonsense isn't what he does. His original plan failed, and rather than accept defeat, his pragmatic mind took a sidestep to come up with this cockamamy plan to bring his wife and daughter back."

Tawny folded her arms. "We saw the replicates target that spot ourselves. We saw their ripped to the stumps as they tried to dig through. Julius killed his lead geneticist right there."

Leila added, "All of our occult research mentions sacrifices. Well, one was already made."

Daisy stared at the two women. Parker had said they truly believed there was something else at play here. He didn't think it was heaven or hell. But he did say other dimensions were a possibility. There were still things of this earth none of them understood—how Daisy had been able to stop a baseball moments before it hit her face was one of them. She wasn't even sure Parker understood Daisy's part of their mother's research. He was vague about it any time Daisy asked.

They all stared down through the darkness of the damaged lab to the hole in the wall and beyond. The sound of sewage water trickled back to them, along with an unpleasant smell.

Tawny shuddered and hugged herself as she eyed the hole. "It feels wrong. Like someone walks over my grave every time I look at it."

Daisy concentrated on the hole, on the small gust of air coming out and the hollow sounds within. The hairs on her arms lifted. Her stomach twinged with the sense of despair or maybe it was something else, like Tawny said. The darkness felt wrong. Daisy's eyes traveled over the broken wall that made up the hole into the sewer, trying to locate something—anything—logical that could explain the feeling. Like Parker, she would much rather face something flesh and blood.

"There?" Axel asked, pointing to the hole. "The gate to Hell is in the Cardinal City sewer, and I walked through it a few days ago?"

This time, Daisy couldn't raise the energy to deny. She scratched her face. Dried blood came off under her nails and she winced. She needed to shower. Axel needed to sleep. She would continue this tomorrow.

"Whatever it is, just keep Julius out. Or at the very least, raise the alarm when he gets here," Daisy said, ignored their *duh* look, then gestured for Axel to follow her back through the makeshift lab and into the elevator.

As the doors closed around them, and they stared out over the destruction of the lab, she realized it had all been fake. Nothing in this building was tied to the Syndicate's real purpose. Just like her, it had been a means to an end for Julius. Tomorrow, she would find the truth.

"HOW LONG HAS the Syndicate owned this building?" Axel asked as Daisy opened the door to her apartment.

"A few years," she replied.

Her place was the only apartment on the floor. In fact, it was the only *habitable* room. When Julius took over the empty building, he'd given Daisy an entire floor while he kept the one beneath and used it as his office. She'd hated having so much space, so had it furnished into an apartment. Outside the walls, the rest of the floor was just a dark concrete shell. She had her room set up with a view of the Quadrant Park. Far beyond that, farther than the eye could see clearly, was Lazarus House.

Up here, with the pretty view, she felt like a bird.

She turned on the dim lights and saw it for what it was, a cage of her own making. An illusion. Inside the small apartment, a bed sat by the window, a closet by another wall, a kitchenette and bathroom against the third, and a couch with books and wilted potted plants on shelves. That was it.

At some point during her stay, she'd placed her plants in self watering pots. Now it smelled like dying nature. Overwatered roots and rotting soil.

She was surprised her room was untouched. She wouldn't have put it past Julius for him to destroy everything in retaliation for her betrayal.

Axel went straight for her bed.

"Come here," he said as he sat down on the plush comforter and toed his boots off.

"Why?"

"Because I want to hold you while I sleep," he grumbled and fluffed up the pillows.

Her heart rate spiked, and she tensed, unsure what to do with his sudden confession. He took her confusion as an excuse to elaborate, and when he spoke, his tired husky voice plucked strings Daisy didn't know she had. "I want to put my arms around you and know that you're safe. After the night we've had, and the day I've had, I want to feel the heat of a woman I adore against my body."

Cocky, self-assured, and hard to resist. This was the other side of youthful optimism.

He smiled wryly with a slow look up and down her body and then gave a composed stare. "Come on, Daze. You know we share a special bond. There's no point denying it."

Special bond. So, he knew? "How do you know about that?"

He reclined on the bed and rested his hands behind his head. His lashes drooped with lethargy as he mumbled, "You lean into my touch when you pull away from others. Come here. Don't make me wait. I'm tired."

There was nothing in his tone or body language that revealed he expected denial which marveled Daisy. How could someone who'd seen her dark history firsthand talk to her like that? Like... he already had her. Like she had been sleeping in his arms for centuries.

He popped one eye open with a warning grumble. "I swear I won't let myself sleep unless you're here."

"Emotional terrorism?" Her eyebrow arched.

He shrugged. "I'll use whatever tool I have to get you to lie down with me."

"I have to shower," she blurted and headed for the bathroom.

He jolted upright, his eyes blinking open. "I'll wait."

She stopped with her hand on the doorframe. "Go to sleep."

"No." He shook his head stubbornly. "Have your shower. I'll keep an eye on the door and make sure no one goes in."

Humor rippled through her body. He was clearly half asleep and had no idea what he'd said. Who else would go in the bathroom but one of them? This entire building was deserted except for the Sinners in the basement.

Shaking her head, she went into the bathroom and quickly showered the blood off her face and hair. When she emerged in a towel, he sat on the edge of the bed resting his head in his hands, eyes closed. As quietly as she could, she went to her closet, but as soon as she opened the door, the white leather Falcon battle suit assaulted her eyes. She'd had multiple suits made. So many were ruined after blood stains, but she'd liked the symbolism.

Now, like her entire life, it was all a lie. She pushed aside the hangers and considered putting on day clothes, but she was a little tired too. Maybe her family was right, and she was still healing from her ordeal. Sleep would be welcome for a few hours until dawn. She chose a soft camisole and panties, plaited her long damp hair, and then padded quietly back to the bed.

Axel still leaned on his hands. He'd removed his shirt and jeans, but remained in his boxer shorts. Leaning forward like that, his muscles pulled taut, his long lashes fanning his cheeks, his breath even. Asleep. A rush of affection surged as she brushed a lock of brown hair from his face. His brows lifted as though he tried to open his eyes but couldn't. He mumbled something in Portuguese. Daisy was sure it was a demand from the tone. In that moment, seeing him bathed in the soft blue light of the moon, hearing the smooth timbre of his voice, and smelling his raw earthy scent, she couldn't think of anything she wanted more than to be in his arms.

She pushed him down and helped him under the covers, then climbed across him so she could face the window. This was the only way she liked sleeping, watching the world below, waiting for dawn to wake her up. It reminded her of the mornings she and Parker would wake before the sun, lie on the roof and cover themselves with food so the pigeons would find them. Then they'd scream and shout so the flurry of wings fluttered all around them, tickling them. It was the closest they could get to flying.

To freedom.

The instant she rested her head on a pillow, Axel tugged her against his body. He burrowed his face into her neck and sighed heavily as he rested his arm over her body, caging her in.

"Why do you smell so good?"

"Probably the pheromones," she murmured. She'd never had someone hug her like this. Not since her childhood. Not since her siblings and Mary. It had been so long. It took her a long minute until she relaxed.

"Probably."

Daisy tried not to tear up as she fell asleep, but Julius's voice was in her ear taunting her.

"Suck it up, my darling. No time for tears when the world is burning."

As if he sensed her distress, Axel murmured something soothing and then kissed her nape. As his breathing evened out, she decided to listen to the other voice in her head—Mary's.

"... you have the tools to lead this family."

"Parker was born to lead."

"Maybe with this." Mary tapped Daisy's head. *"But you lead with this."* She tapped Daisy on the breastbone. *"Do you understand?"*

"No. Because mine is broken."

Mary glanced at Axel. "Not for long."

Daisy covered Axel's hand on her breastbone and closed her eyes.

This, she thought. This right here was another thing she knew for sure.

ten

AXEL ALVARES

AXEL HAD the best night's sleep. A sexy woman in his arms, a comfortable bed, and... well, that was all he needed.

He lay behind her, watching the silhouette of her body as they faced the window. Soft purple hues painted her feminine curves as she laid on her side. From the dip of her waist to the swell of her hips. He didn't care for the wondrous sight of dawn lighting the city outside. He only had eyes for her as she drew sleeping breaths. The only way this would be better was if she faced him instead of the window.

Last night when he'd asked her to sleep with him, he thought she would refuse. He also thought she might leave after her shower, and he'd wake to find her missing. But she'd allowed him to envelope her, and she'd cuddled back. He'd been prepared for a lot of resistance and had worked out scenarios in his mind on how he would chip away at her icy cold walls, but she'd melted into him like hugging was her natural state. Natural, but forgotten. Until now with him.

An aching need to always have her close, filled him to the point of pain. It had stayed with him throughout the night. He couldn't understand why his feelings were so intense. His parents had always said their relationship was love at first sight, and he believed it. Right up until their death, they were hopelessly in love. His father would massage his mother's feet nightly in front of the television, and she would dote on him and spoil him, especially at the dinner table.

When they were sick, they still managed to find time to care for each other—even when one had come straight from vomiting in the toilet. This kind of dedication was his guidance. Seeing them all but crawl to each other, to give their last breath to each other, it was the kind of love Axel wanted in his life.

To not be alone at the end.

He smiled. Daisy had stayed. She'd let them embrace, which meant somewhere inside she wanted him as much as he wanted her. It had to be that. At the very least, she was willing to give him a chance. And in chaotic times like these, having someone to hold made it all more manageable.

He glanced down the line of her body and closed his eyes. He inhaled deeply. There was something about her scent that triggered every primal urge in his body and pulled his muscles tight. He exhaled and opened his eyes, then trailed a finger from her shoulder down her arm. Goosebumps erupted on her skin as he slid his hand over her waist, hips, and then around to her flat stomach. He tugged her against him.

He must have fallen asleep, because it felt like seconds later that the sun shone high, and Daisy twitched under his touch. It was late in the day.

"Daze?"

He pushed up on an elbow for a better view of her face. Sweat dappled her upper lip and plastered her camisole to her body. Her brows pinched together. Even the escaped strands around her face were stuck down and wet.

"Hey, *minha margarida*," he shook her gently, but she hunched forward into a fetal position, exposing the purple scars along her spine. She trembled.

His vision turned red at the bruising. This was Julius's fault. The scars, the ones he could see and the ones he couldn't. Fuck that bastard. That Axel had ever made a deal with him made him sick to his stomach. In sleep, Daisy was a delicate flower. His *margarida*—his daisy. She didn't deserve this. It broke his heart.

"Daze." He tried shaking her again.

She stilled under his touch. So hot. So quiet that he thought her breathing had stopped.

"No," she mumbled, her eyes still closed. "No. Get off. No!"

A pillow beside her head started to float. Then the blanket corners lifted, then every little knick-knack and potted plant levitated. Books in shelves rattled and slid out. It was like they'd entered a zero-gravity zone. Daisy was telekinetic. First the ball, and now this.

"I said get off!" she shouted.

He snatched his hand from her shoulder. Tears glistened at the corners of her lashes. The items in the air twirled and rotated around them like they were in the center of a household tornado. Wind whipped past Axel's face. A pot crashed into the window, spilling dirt. He ducked as another stormed past his head.

This nightmare had to end.

"Daisy it's me. Axel." He rolled her to face him. She lashed against him like he was hurting her. God, she was so strong. He flattened himself on her, hoping to contain her panic like a weighted blanket. "Daisy, you're fine. You're dreaming. Wake up."

Luminous violet eyes popped open. She gasped. She gulped in air, hyperventilating.

He tightened his embrace and stroked her head.

"Shh," he said into her hair. "You're okay. It's me. You're okay."

Every floating item fell in disarray. Whimpering, she pushed him off and then slapped her stomach. She fumbled to lift her camisole and checked her skin. A long, angry purple scar stretched from her belly button to between her breasts. It was fresh, rough, and bruised. She sighed and tugged her camisole down. She dropped her head to the pillow and squeezed her eyes shut.

"A dream," she whispered, her bottom lip trembling.

Axel's gaze was glued to that purple, jagged scar and it turned him cold. Without thinking, he shoved up her camisole again to reveal the old wound. So long. So... violent.

"Who hurt you?" he growled. He had a fair idea, but he needed her to confirm it. To say it out loud. Make the devil real. Make him a target.

"Julius." She propped up on her elbow and glared down her body. "I swallowed strands of his wife's and daughter's hair. He thought he could cut me open and find them."

Air left Axel's lungs. He lurched off the bed and stumbled to his feet.

Can't see.

Can't think.

That bastard had cut her open and fished around *inside* her stomach for two single strands of hair. This was beyond what he'd ever imagined. She acted like her nightmares were no big deal. Was she so used to this sort of treatment that she'd become numb to it? Was it only in her dreams that her true fears came out? He breathed heavily, raging at the opposite wall so she wouldn't see the fury in his face. Axel wasn't a naturally violent man. He'd stomached the things he'd done as a Faithful for Elena's sake, but now all he could think of was violence. It clawed at his insides like a ravenous beast.

"I'm going to kill him," he snarled.

He pivoted, saw her surprise and complete utter devastation, as if she was shocked at his reaction for her. He would kill the asshole to prove to her someone cared. He would find a knife, gut Julius, and then rifle around in *his* stomach like he had with this precious woman. He climbed over Daisy and took her still-shocked face in his hands.

"No one will ever hurt you again," he promised.

She blinked up at him.

"I won't let them. Do you hear me? Do you believe me?"

He tried to show her with his steady touch and gaze. He meant what he said. Never again would she tremble and quake from fear while in his arms.

Daisy wrapped her fingers around his wrists. Their eyes locked. Then she lurched forward and kissed him. Her tongue swept out and brushed his lips. She nipped and licked with breathless abandon. She tasted him like he was a drug. And then her mouthwatering scent bloomed, and he was a goner. Done. Dead.

"You smell so good," he mumbled between kisses. "I want..."

His body swelled with need for her. He scorched with want. She gripped his hair, tearing strands in her passion. They clashed. They demanded. Then she pushed him, rolled him to his back so she could straddle him.

A goddess stared down at him. White hair. Violet eyes. Luminous skin. He saw not the scars on her body, but the warrior she'd become. No one could be this perfect for him... right?

Her chest heaved as she breathed. Each lift pressed hard nipples against her camisole. Desire ignited down his spine. He arched forward to kiss her again, but she shoved him down with a frown.

"You're my mate, Axel," she said, concern etching her features. "You need to know that's why I smell so good to you. That's why you want me so badly."

He jerked back with a scowl. "Fuck that. That's not why."

Surprise plastered her face. "What? You know?"

"Daisy, I want you because you're hot. I want you because you inspire me. I …" His words stopped as he registered what she'd said. *Mate.* All the Deadly Seven had mates. They were the partners so important that when removed from the hero, the hero turned dark with mindless rage. Like Griffin had at the loss of Lilo. And Axel was this person to Daisy—her balance. Her other half. "Daisy, are you telling me I get to be with you forever?"

Something shuttered in her features. "I'm sorry. I know it's fast. We hardly know each other."

His mind whirled. He was her *mate.* Him. *Fuck me.* "I get to keep you. Wait." He squinted at her. "I get to keep you, right?"

"I guess if that's what you want."

A broad grin broke out on his lips. Of course, it's what he wanted. It meant all these feelings he'd been having for her over the past year could continue. He kissed her again. This one was deep, slow and passionate and it sent all the blood in his body rushing to his cock. He groaned and flexed his hips upward.

She moaned, "Do that again."

He did. She gasped. He did it again and watched the color rise in her cheeks as she drew pleasure from his touch.

"Daze," he whispered against her lips. He had nothing else to say, just her name as he gripped her braid and clenched tight, holding their lips together. He'd fantasized about this moment in his dreams. He'd jerked off to it in the shower. *Mate.*

A piercing alarm went off.

Daisy bolted upright. Her hand covered his lips as if to shush him.

"What is it?" he mumbled through her fingers.

She cocked her head, then looked at her shrieking cell phone on the bed side dresser.

"We have to go," she sighed and climbed off him with a rueful glance at his very hard, very painful erection pushing against his boxer shorts. "I'm sorry about—you know."

"Hey." A wry smile curved his lips and he grabbed her as she pulled away. "Hold that thought. We'll come back to this."

Humor danced in her eyes and she tickled his cheek. "You're cute when you're demanding."

"Cute, huh? When I'm demanding." Oh, he saw what was happening here. She didn't think he could be alpha enough for her. With a mischievous urge, he placed her hand over his dick and shot her a challenging look before lowering his voice with intent. "Like this?"

She rubbed him and he groaned, instantly regretting his tease. Then she pulled away and switched off the alarm on her cell phone.

He rolled to his side and enjoyed watching her pert, panty covered ass wiggle as she walked to her closet. One side of the cotton was caught in her buttocks. He wanted to pull it out with his teeth. He sighed and flopped onto his back to stare at the ceiling like a swooning teenager wondering how he got to be so lucky.

Mate...

He didn't give a shit if they were about to hunt down the bastard who hurt her. He didn't care if they might die, and the world could be ending. He'd slept next to Daisy. He'd hugged her. He'd kissed her like a lovesick *amante* and she'd just told him he would get to do it again. For every damned night of his life. He kept grinning at the ceiling until he felt grainy bits of dirt on the sheets and craned his neck with a frown.

He sat up.

"Daisy," he blurted. "You made everything float."

"What?" She slotted her feet into jeans and shimmied them up her hips.

He swung his legs over the bed and found his pants on the floor through the mess.

"You made everything float," he repeated. "Did you not see? Look."

She surveyed the room, taking in the pillows, plants, books, and other items crashed about. The room had been semi-tidy when they'd gone to sleep. She buttoned her jeans and then put a fallen plant back on the coffee table.

"I did this?" She frowned. "I guess I wasn't paying attention."

"You're telekinetic." He shoved his shirt over his head and tugged it down, wincing at the uncomfortable hard-on still straining his pants. *Later*, he promised it. The next time he had Daisy alone, he was finishing what they started. He checked the time on his watch. "We have about a few hours before we need to be there. Why did you set the alarm so early?"

She cocked her head, confused. "We have to scope out the place first."

Of course. "Do we have time to eat?"

"We can find something on the way."

While he put his shoes on, she went to her closet and stared. He came up behind her and slipped his hands around her stomach and rested his chin on her shoulder. She stared at her Falcon white leather suit.

"I don't want to put it on." She shuddered.

He hugged her tighter. "So don't."

"But we have to infiltrate the Faithful."

He reached past her and picked up the coiled white braided bull-whip and the Falcon half-face bird mask. "Just these will do."

She nodded with relief and then shamelessly slipped off her camisole right in front of him. She found a sports bra, put it on, and then added a shirt and leather jacket. He'd stood dumbfounded the entire time. Before she made it to the door, he closed the gap between them and pushed her against the wall.

"When we get back…" His voice was a low purr as he cupped her nape. "We're finishing what we started."

"Axel," she said, but he swallowed her protest with a searing hot kiss she had no choice but to take. When he broke away, her hand landed on his chest, and she frowned.

"Is this real?" she whispered. "Us?"

He covered her hand and squeezed. "What do you think?"

"I think…" She gave a self-disparaging shake of her head. "I don't know what to think."

"Then don't think. Feel." He held her palm against his beating heart so she could feel the heat. He slid her hand down to where he ached most, so she could feel his attraction. Then he kissed her knuckles with a smirk so she could see his determination. "That real enough for you?"

She blushed and couldn't meet his eyes.

"For you, Daze. I ache for you."

Her lashes lifted and she smoldered. Gone was the bashful woman. In was the vixen. That raging spitfire he'd glimpsed fighting to protect Elena and him at the batting cage. Relentless. Determined. Loyal. She flicked her wrist, and the white bullwhip length flew up. She caught the end and used the length across the back of his neck, forcing his head down until their lips met. But didn't kiss. She was a lioness playing with her food.

"Baby, you're teasing me." His lips fluttered against hers as he spoke.

She laughed and pushed off. "Let's go."

He watched her as she sauntered to the door. Before he followed, his eyes tracked to where she'd left the baseball bat. He jogged to pick it up.

"You've got the something old," he said and indicated to her Falcon mask, sword and bullwhip. "Here's something new."

Her eyes widened gratefully as she accepted the bat and clutched it a little like a security blanket.

"Something borrowed." She grabbed his shirt, yanked him close and gave him that elusive kiss. Then cupped his balls. "Something blue."

He chuckled. When she wasn't doubting herself, she had a wicked sense of humor, and he loved it. Her smile was brighter than the dawn and when she walked outside, it tugged him after her. With each passing minute they'd spent together, she became more confident, happier, and stronger. The idea that the shadow of a single man had taken her sunshine away brought his violence back.

Fuck Julius. He was going down.

eleven

DAISY LAZARUS

THE CLOUDS DAISY walked on evaporated when they arrived via motorcycle at the shipping container yard being used as a Faithful meeting point. They'd stopped at a burrito place brave enough to remain open and grabbed a quick bite, then headed straight here. Now it was twilight.

She'd hoped to be early to scope out the place and find the best vantage point to spy, but they'd spent longer than planned eating… and at her place. Their lateness gave her a trickle of unease.

She didn't like being unprepared.

But as it turned out, they were right on time. They pulled into a parking lot and noticed Faithful in white robes converging—disappearing through the gap between two towers of containers. Some wore the Halloween mask, some wore casual clothing with their faces exposed.

No one policed entry. There was no yard security—probably paid to look the other way, or even perhaps part of the curfew. No workers operated the cranes. As far as the eye could see, it was a ghost city made of primary-colored containers stacked on top of each other like children's building blocks. Flashes of white, the ghosts.

Daisy shook her head. Once she would have been happy with this turnout. Now the food she'd recently eaten made her feel sick. She did her best to avoid the incoming crowd and drove the motorcycle behind a container at the back of the yard. As she checked her weapons—katana strapped, bullwhip at her belt, bat in her hand—her inner alarm bells triggered. What if Julius had now warned everyone about her defection?

They could be walking into a trap.

Best to spy on proceedings from a safe spot. She wished she'd brought her sniper rifle. But if she had brought it, it would have been too easy to pull the trigger. She clutched the baseball bat tighter.

No one even cared that they walked into the yard. Were they fools? Or just overconfident?

Regardless of no one glancing their way in the parking lot, Daisy and Axel went in the opposite direction to where they saw the Faithful headed, took a long route around and backtracked to the meeting spot between a collection of containers.

Daisy used the bat like a walking stick and crouched as she heard voices. They were getting closer. There were no lookouts here. She glanced at Axel, also crouching and wary.

"I'll give you a boost," she whispered and pointed up the uneven container stack they stood by. There was an edge between the containers. It would make a climb easier here than other more evenly stacked containers near where the voices were coming from.

He gestured at her. "Shouldn't I boost you first?"

"I'm stronger."

He stared blankly for a moment but then must have realized the logic of her words. She held the bat like a step. He planted a boot on the wood. She heaved him up.

Axel wasn't a small man. Slabs of hard muscle covered his body. Being a fireman meant he needed a strong core and the ability to lift bodies out of buildings. Sometimes that extra bulk made a man less limber, but Axel swung his long legs up and over the first container with little effort. Instantly, he rolled onto his stomach and reached over the edge for her.

She didn't take his hand. She tossed him the bat and smiled.

There were two ways she could get up. Simply jump or use her bullwhip to lever herself up. At this height, option one was the easiest. She took a running leap and launched herself into the air, easily making the distance to the container roof, parkouring up, and latching on with her hands. Within seconds she was on top, then leaned down to lever him up to her level.

Axel made a low whistle in his teeth. "You're incredible."

Daisy was grateful for the cover of darkness, because her cheeks heated in what she was sure was a blush. Which was ridiculous. She'd never cared what anyone thought about her modified abilities. Would she ever get used to having someone praise her the way Axel did? Genuine and not for selfish reasons?

On the ride over, she'd stewed over her reaction to him after waking. Her nightmare had rocked her foundations, yet he'd soothed her. More than that, he'd looked at the evidence of her pain and vowed to keep her safe.

No one will ever hurt you again.

Someone else had said that to her once and it had been a lie. There were things in this world he had no control over. No one did.

Axel pointed at another container stack next to them. "That way," he whispered.

They stayed low and hurried along until they climbed two more containers. Approaching the area where the main group congregated,

Daisy crouched as they arrived at the lip of the container closest to the meeting.

Two barrels of fire burned brightly. A spark combusted in one of them, letting off a loud crack. The flickering flames sucked Daisy into a vortex of memory.

Smoke singed her nostrils. It rasped in her throat. It burned her eyes. But she didn't need to see. She could feel her way there.

Follow the sadness. Make it stop.

There. Toward the end of the room, tossing computers off desks. It was the woman behind the mirrored window. Daisy knew because she'd always felt her despair, just like she'd felt her joy every time another of Daisy's siblings was born.

That joy, that radiant spark of effervescence in Daisy's gut, would herald their arrival. Like sweet molasses warming her insides. Those were the purest days in Daisy's life. At the door waiting, feeling, hoping, praying, and then the cry of a baby as a nun brought the new addition through the door.

Then the door would close.

And the lady behind the mirror would despair once more, just like she was now. Daisy ran full pelt into her, rocking her backward from her vicious embrace. All Daisy could think was that cuddles always worked with her brothers and sisters. They worked.

Not this time.

The sad woman with the long black hair stroked Daisy's hair, and her despair thickened to mud.

"You shouldn't be here, sweet one." The woman's voice trembled and broke. "What have you done? Run. Run back to your family now while you can."

Flames licked higher around them. Glass broke. Something made a loud bang and Daisy screamed. She hugged tighter. Fear trembled her bones but she wouldn't let the woman go.

Cuddles worked. They WORKED.

"You have to come," Daisy cried, choking on the smoke.

"I must see this through. I must make sure it's all destroyed so no one will hurt you again."

The woman pushed Daisy back. She looked down at her like a fierce warrior, a halo of dark smoke about her head. Determination set her jaw and she screwed up her face. Tears glimmered in her eyes.

"The fire, the fire!" Daisy cried. "It burns."

She dragged Daisy. She hurt Daisy. She pulled her crying and kicking and screaming through the smoke and flames until they hit a wall with a heavy metal door. All the while she croaked words to Daisy.

"Nothing burns forever, my child. You are the only one who will truly understand that."

Fire burst. The woman cried in pain as flames scorched her back. She opened a metal door. Arctic air blasted out. She tossed Daisy in.

Daisy rounded on her, wanting to scream, but there was no air. No time. Flames were everywhere. So hot. So hot.

"No one will hurt you again," the woman said.

Fire exploded, engulfing her. It caught Daisy on one side of the body. She was thrown back into the cooler and landed on glass vials and jars. The roaring fire muffled. The smoke lessened.

The door had closed.

"Daisy?" Axel whispered low. "What's the matter?"

She shook the memory away and gulped in air. She eased back from the edge so she could gather her thoughts. She'd stifled them all, locked them all in a deep dark place where nothing flew but only sank. But since meeting Axel, so many memories were surfacing. It was as if they'd been waiting for a safety net.

"You look like you did when you woke," Axel said, inching closer.

Daisy wiped the back of her lip. Sweat came away. She wanted to pull her jacket off. It suffocated her.

"Fire," she blurted and shook her head.

He glanced down at the barrels. "It's contained. It won't hurt you."

"I know that," she hissed back, then flinched at her tone. It wasn't his fault. She exhaled, long and slow then met his eyes. "I'm sorry. It's just that I've been having flashbacks to the day I was burned."

He reached for her, but she flinched away. He scowled and dragged her down to the container roof and forced a hug on her. Unless she wanted to alert the enemy to their position, she had to take it. She wanted to laugh at the ironic absurdity of being hugged right now. But Axel tightened his embrace until she relaxed.

She squeezed her eyes shut and submitted.

She hugged him back.

They laid under the night sky, the wind caressing their faces, the lullaby of nearby voices in conversation, the distant sea, and they hugged.

Eventually, Daisy's heart rate settled, and she could breathe again. She stopped sweating. She stopped fearing.

"You good?" he murmured.

Sounds below drew their attention back to the gathering. They crawled to the edge of their container until they could see below. Daisy almost vomited when she saw what some Faithful wheeled in— a cage full of plants.

The sentient, sin-eating kind. Monsters.

twelve

AXEL ALVARES

"WHAT KIND OF *CARALHO* IS THIS?" Axel murmured to Daisy, hardly believing his eyes.

Below them, plants writhed through the gaps in the chicken wire cage. The undulating mass of shadows hinted at something behind the leaves. Axel did a double take. Did that vine unfurl and try to hold onto the arm of the Faithful pushing the cart?

His experience as a Faithful had been running terrorist type attacks, and toward the end, he'd learned a little about the Lazarus family, but plants that moved? What other pies did the Syndicate have their fingers in?

"I didn't know he had any left," Daisy murmured, aghast.

"Any left of what?" Axel asked. "Plants?"

"One of the Syndicate scientists bred biologically enhanced vege- tation that hunt sin. I let one escape." She was silent for a good while before continuing. "At the time I didn't care about the damage it might have caused. I felt its despair and wanted to help it. As it turned out, the plant fed on innocents. It evolved and took on their traits. It became a monster. In the end, its despair worsened. If it wasn't for Tony's fire, it would still be alive hunting and feeding on anything that moved."

"Shit." Axel scrubbed his face. "I never heard about these."

"You wouldn't. Julius kept them at the black site along with sin-sensing animals, mech suits and other weapons. After the plant I released created too much public havoc, Julius decided they didn't have the funds to fine tune the process and said he destroyed the rest of them. They were too hard to control... but I guess, lack of control is an asset now when—"

"When chaos is what they want."

With a growing sense of doom, Axel and Daisy quietened themselves to hear the proceedings. A platform dais made of packing crates had been set up between the fire barrels. A hush fell over the waiting Faithful. One stepped onto the platform. He removed his mask. Firelight flickered on a saggy face. Axel narrowed his eyes at the aging man.

"I know that guy," he whispered. "Sam, or something, I think. He always argued with me when I had to give orders. Said he had better ways of doing it."

"He might be the one in contact with Julius now," Daisy suggested.

"Maybe." But he wasn't convinced. Axel himself had gone from a nobody in the Faithful ranks to a potential right-hand man of the boss simply by being in the right place at the right time.

Axel had never agreed with Sam. There was nothing appealing about his personality. Sam was a smoker who had something wrong with his lungs. Maybe emphysema, maybe cancer, Axel wasn't sure. He only knew that the man blamed everyone and everything except himself for the state of his health. Axel hated him. Elena and his parents had done everything right for their health, yet they copped a mystery disease no one had a cure for. And then here was Sam running headfirst into sickness, expecting a handout for his second life. He still smoked like a chimney any chance he could get.

He used to call Axel a boy scout.

Another cage wheeled in. A second Faithful stepped up to the podium. His mask remained on.

"The time for enlightenment has finally come!" came the muffled voice from behind the mask.

Cheers rang out.

"Your patience and loyalty will soon be rewarded," Sam said, taking over. "You can see with your own eyes the future the Syndicate predicted is coming to pass. Sinners are being wiped from this earth. The bridges have been destroyed and no one is coming to save the citizens of Cardinal City. Only one question remains. Do you want to stick around to see it?"

Murmurs rumbled through. People shifted uncomfortably. Seeing them from up here, Axel saw the truth. They were just like him. People who'd been conned into believing it was every man for themselves. Unease pulled his stomach into knots. Some of the Faithful behind those masks were just women and men with sad lives. People who should be pitied. Helped.

That woman in the dress with socked feet and slippers. She had three grandchildren. Axel had seen her knitting at one of the clubhouses. He was never a regular visitor like the other lost Faithful, but he'd gone a few times to check them out. He'd never asked this grandmother why she'd joined the Faithful—it was taboo to do so—but he knew she was loved by her family. She wore colorful friendship wristbands. Someone's child must have loved her enough to make them for her.

Next to her was a vet who'd lost his leg in action and lived on the street. Another Faithful Axel recognized had a drug habit he'd struggled with his entire life. He was a family man and believed his wife wouldn't be able to tell the difference if he came back as a clone. Another woman wanted her life insurance to go to her daughter who couldn't afford to go to college.

They all had sob stories. Some of them worse than others, and some of them nastier and greedier than others. Not all of them criminals.

Axel turned to Daisy. Her head canted as she took in the crowd, and then the plants.

"They're going to feed the people to the plant," she murmured.

"Like a sacrifice?"

She nodded.

"Why?"

"It's how the plants evolve into something that hunts."

"We can't let that happen," he said. "These people have been conned."

Her scowl hit him in the center of his chest. "They know what they signed up for."

"As did I."

Her jaw clicked shut and she speared her gaze down at the group, hopefully considering his words.

"I don't like this, Daisy," he said, to drive his point home.

"Me neither."

"Who will take the honor of being the first?" shouted Sam.

Butterflies soared in Axel's stomach. He could feel something insidious coming. Something else Daisy could have nightmares about. Among the crowd of thirty or so Faithful, no one answered. His nerves relaxed a little, and then Sam clicked his fingers and the masked Faithful next to him stepped forward and yanked a random follower from the crowd.

"This is what you've been waiting for!" Sam bellowed at them. "This is your moment of freedom. Don't be afraid."

The victim was the grandmother. Axel could see in her eyes she tried to be brave, to convince herself that Sam's words were true, but even in this low light, the fear flickered there. Tendrils from the cage snapped and flicked.

"We have to stop this," he whispered harshly.

"But…" Daisy responded, eyes locking on Sam, then darting back to the grandmother as she clearly grappled with the situation.

Axel thought maybe he knew why. Sam could be the link back to Julius. Daisy wanted to focus on that in case it lead back to her siblings kidnapped mates, but now they had a moral conundrum to solve. One she'd likely never had to face before. Save these bad people, and potentially lose the one chance they have of finding Julius or let them die. She only knew how to be bad. He couldn't fault her for the decades of brainwashing she'd received at the hands of an evil megalomaniac.

"Daisy," Axel urged quietly. "We have to stop this. Letting them die is bad."

"But we'll lose our advantage."

"I used to turn a blind eye to all this damage, but I was wrong. That was also bad."

She blinked at him. "You want me to save the plant like I did before?"

"I want to save the people who were conned into doing the Syndicate's dirty work."

Understanding dawned in her eyes. She pulled her katana from her shoulder harness and replaced it with the baseball bat, squashing the narrow end hard into the sheath until it fit and held.

Axel put his Faithful mask on. "So I'll go down and say there's a change of plans—word from the boss."

"No." Daisy slipped on her Falcon mask. "I'll do it. You stay here."

"We both go."

"You don't trust me?"

"With my life," he promised. "I just don't want you going in alone. I'm in this with you now, Daisy. For better or worse."

She stared for a moment at him, contemplating, then grinned. "For better or worse."

But they were too late. The plant didn't wait for the cage to be opened. Vines shot through the cracks and headed for the grandmother. Tendrils wrapped around her like a mummy's bandages. She lost control of her bowels and whimpered, crying that she'd changed her mind.

The horrific sight caused upheaval in the crowd and confusion set in. Some of the more rotten souls cheered, some backed away. Daisy stood. Wind whipped her silver hair, pulling strands from her ponytail. Vivid violet eyes latched onto him and then she leaped off the container, two stories high. Her bullwhip flew toward the plant— cracked as she whipped and sliced tendrils in half, releasing the grandmother before Daisy landed on the floor.

She's a fucking goddess. The way she moved. He was in awe. *An avenging Valkyrie.*

The crowd scattered from Daisy.

She unfurled herself from a crouched position and readjusted her mask. White feathers on the top ruffled along with her silver hair. Axel watched her cant her head from side to side, and almost believed she would sprout wings and fly like the angel of death she emulated.

Sam barked orders, pointing and waving. Surround the newcomer. Axel darted the aim of his gun about, not sure where to focus. Who would attack Daisy first. Would any?

Would a bullet stop a plant?

thirteen

DAISY LAZARUS

FROM THE MOMENT Daisy's boots connected with the cool concrete, she sensed something wrong. Like a buzz in the air, a tangible tingle, it sparked an inner alarm. But why? Slowly she surveyed the space, waiting for the first person to attack—if any.

But none came.

She almost slumped in disappointment. She was ready for a fight. Wanted it. Having Axel by her side had made her feel more confident about setting things right. She wasn't quite sure who was her enemy —Sam, for sure. But the plant? She sensed its despair the way she'd sensed the first plant abomination. It had absorbed a man and together they'd become something new. Something unwanted and miserable.

She sensed the grandmother's sadness… she felt it in *all* the Faithful like nails down the chalkboard of her stomach. They were all so miserable, they were almost prepared to sacrifice themselves to this burgeoning creature. She didn't understand why Axel said she should save them.

They were so sad.

Then she remembered the memories. The cuddles she gave her brothers and sisters when she was young. Gloria's final words to her. *Nothing burns forever. You're the only one who will truly understand that.* Gloria didn't mean actual fire. She meant the pain of despair, the heat and the violence, the destructive consuming power of it. Daisy used to make people laugh to douse that scorching feeling.

In the end, none of these people had volunteered to sacrifice themselves.

There was hope.

This grandmother weeping on her knees. That robed man cowering in the corner. That plant desperately trying to fulfill its urge to feed. Her own endless despair. All these things could end. They could be reversed. She was already living proof of that possibility.

Nothing burned forever and, sometimes, precious things grew out of the ashes.

"No more sacrifices," she announced, facing the crowd. "Enough."

Sam narrowed his eyes. "Falcon. I didn't expect you here."

He didn't know. Good. Maybe she could use her old position to influence them.

"I am." She rolled her whip back into its coiled position and clipped it to her belt. "You can all leave. Go home."

"But the boss gave us orders."

"The boss is insane."

No one moved. They looked at her with confused, shell-shocked eyes.

This isn't working. They expected Falcon to be bad. She had to show them what could grow from the ashes. She took a deep breath, a chance, and tossed her mask on the ground.

"I am no longer following him. He's a liar, a sick man, and I should never have believed in him."

"I was also wrong." Axel emerged from the shadows around the side of a container. He tossed his Faithful mask into a barrel. Flames sputtered with the melting plastic. The acrid scent filled the air.

"None of what is happening is worth it," Axel said. "Even if Julius was honorable with his promise to clone you all—which he's not, I can assure you—it's not worth it. Some of you are here because you're protecting loved ones. And you have to see that people are dying. If we let that creature loose, innocent women and children will die. They could be the very people you're trying to keep safe. I didn't sign up for that, and I know many of you didn't either."

He came to stand next to Daisy and a strange feeling washed over her. She felt lighter, as though she really did have wings.

"No," blurted Sam. He looked at the Faithful. "Don't listen to them. They're trying to confuse you. She's not worthy anymore. Her faith has been rocked and now she's trying to take us down with her. This is a test of our faith."

Axel opened his mouth, but before words came out, Sam ripped open the cage door. Thick jungle-like leaves shuddered. For a moment, the plant's despair abated. Then it sprung from its prison with a speed Daisy had forgotten it capable of. Sam pushed Faithful into Daisy's path, into the plant's path. That's when she saw it wasn't just one plant, but many. They'd all been huddled like livestock. Some had bipedal viney feet, others rolled and flowed like bubbling water. They weren't as advanced as the one she'd fought in the sewer, but dangerous all the same. If these plants fed, they would evolve.

Fear for Axel prickled her skin. She glanced at him. One tendril would paralyze him. But he was tugging Faithful by the robes, shoving them the other way, ripping their masks off, shouting for them to go home. It was over. No more Faithful. Spread the word. Daisy returned to the creatures with a scream, unleashing the fury of her katana and slicing through anything green in her way.

She had to close the cage before it fed and evolved. Doing her best to avoid lashing leaves and green things, she slammed her shoulder against the cage door and heaved it closed. The gods must have been smiling on her because the plant inside wasn't mature enough to fight back. Just like the ones she'd met in the cages in the Syndicate black site, it operated on base functioning. She closed the door and slotted her katana in the latch.

"You fucking bitch!" Sam shouted from down the darkened corridor. "You're ruining everything."

Sam turned and ran. Daisy's heart leaped. If anyone had contact with Julius, it was him. She couldn't let him escape. Uncertain, she glanced at Axel, her conscience.

He must have known what she was thinking. He glanced at her.

"Go!" he shouted, and pointed after Sam. "I've got this covered."

She started jogging, then turned back and pointed at the caged plant. "Burn it."

He nodded grimly and she took off.

DAISY TOOK to the container tops to track Sam. He wasn't hard to follow. His white robe billowed like the sails of a skew-whiff ship. Unlike the other Faithful, she sensed no despair in this one. With each step, the hunt bloomed in her gut, and her need to unleash swelled beneath the surface of her skin. She followed him, but her past followed her.

She wasn't in the maze of a container yard, but in the maze of a dilapidated house. She was fifteen. The stench of wood filled her nose. Mold. Mildew. Blood.

Drip drip drip.

Daisy flattened her back against a wall. Her heart bucked like a rabid horse. Wide eyes took in every dingy corner of the room. Perked ears strained for her adversaries' breath.

Men.

Women.

She had no idea where Julius found these people, but they smelled funny. They smelled like the old roadkill she'd been forced to scrape off the road as punishment once for failing to do as she was told.

"This is what happens when we lose sight of our goals," Julius had said. "Decay."

Something held Daisy back from attacking Sam. And it wasn't the old, warped instincts to hunt him like an animal, like she'd had with the homeless people. She'd slaughtered them, one by one, hoping to gain an iota of praise from the only man who'd ever given her attention.

Daisy had the sudden urge to go back to Axel, to touch him and look into his eyes.

She swallowed.

How could she trust her instincts if they'd led her to kill so much? Her palms itched. She glanced down, half expecting to see dark stains on them in the shadows, but there was nothing. Her yin-yang tattoo was a little on the dark side, but still manageable.

The sound of a can being kicked sharpened her focus. She followed Sam across the stacks to the rail yard where a train was being loaded.

"Go, go!" Sam shouted, waving to another Faithful lifting heavy crates into the car.

The masked Faithful stopped and stared at Sam. He registered the danger and quickly closed the sliding door on the car.

Hurry.

Daisy reached for her katana only to have her fingers close around the baseball bat. She'd left the katana with Axel. She only had the bat or the whip.

And the other skill.

The telekinesis.

If she could learn to harness it, she wouldn't need a katana. But for now, she didn't have time. Sam was getting away. The train started creaking and rolling. She leaped off her container and landed hard on the dirt. Pushing effort into her legs, she pumped them hard and fast. Her arms following suit and driving her onward, chasing after the fleeing Faithful as he caught up to the train.

The air in her lungs labored. She was unfit. Still recovering. All the more reason to end this quickly.

Only twenty feet away, the Faithful inside the train car reached down and boosted Sam up. They tumbled into the carriage. With her eyes locked firmly on the gap, Daisy didn't notice another Faithful appear behind Sam with a gun in his hands. He pointed at Daisy.

He fired. She flinched and jolted to the side, hoping to swerve and miss the bullet. Nothing hit so she kept going. Another gun shot. Another swerve to avoid getting shot but it slowed her down. The train was leaving, faster and faster, and their only link to Julius was on board. The last car passed, and her thighs were on fire, but she wasn't giving up.

She had to do this.

Had to prove to everyone that she had what it took. That she could be a part of this crime fighting family, to forgive them for leaving her, and to fix her mistakes. That she *wanted* to. There was no Axel being her conscience. There was no Parker telling her what was necessary. No Mary with her expectations. This was all Daisy. A turning point, she could feel it. A way to balance the dissonance in her life.

Faster, faster, she urged herself forward on the track. Within five feet of the caboose, she released her whip from her belt and snapped it out. The tip curled around a bar on the end like a tendril. She gripped tight and used the whip to pull herself up. With a last painful yank that felt like her arms would pull out of their sockets, she landed on the platform at the back of the boxcar.

Heaving lungfuls of air, her body wanted her to rest. But she wouldn't allow it. It also smelled funny—musty and stale. She rose on shaky legs and tried to open the back door. It wouldn't budge. So she secured the whip to her belt before going up and over. With the train not at full speed, she jogged across the roof with relative ease.

Urgency nipped her tail.

She had the sense that if she didn't end this fast, then it would be too late. She didn't have the stamina she once had.

The third car from the rear was the one Sam hid out in. She'd seen him leap into it. Lying flat on her stomach, she put her ear to the roof. Too noisy. Nothing but the clickety-clack of train tracks. She wrapped her whip around her waist and then secured one end to an exposed U-bolt on the car roof. Then she eased her head over the side. The whip pulled tight, stopping her from slipping and meeting the tracks. She needed to lower herself enough to look inside.

Head over the side, her long silver hair streamed down from her ponytail. She gripped the sliding door handle and peeked through the two-inch gap. Dark inside. Musty. But light cracks through the wooden car revealed three Faithful in dirty white robes, masks off, talking. Sam was one. She also recognized the second. But the third was more familiar. He looked like one of the mercenaries Julius hired but he was dressed in the acolyte robe. Since when did he convert to a Faithful?

Didn't matter.

What mattered was that she got her hands on the cell phone Sam used to contact Julius. Then Sloan could trace the calls made and find out where he was hiding. If Sam wasn't the one who'd contacted Julius, then one of these other two must be.

Daisy tested the tension of her whip against the U-bolt and then flipped her entire body over the edge of the train. She twisted midair and dangled near the door. Her arms strained against her weight. Her feet kicked as the tracks whizzed below. On her exhale, she kicked open the sliding door and swung in.

Her bat was swinging for the head of the second Faithful before they registered she was there. She knocked him out and went for Sam.

"Give me your cell phone," she demanded.

His eyes widened and he scrambled further into the dark cabin. Daisy launched after him, but the third Faithful grabbed her hair and yanked. Pain sparked in her scalp as she jerked backward. She cried out. A sliver of doubt hit her, of fear, and then vengeance filled her with red hot fury. Her face screwed up and she shut off her bodily sensations. There was no pain. It was the space of emptiness she'd survived in her entire life. The cold place that had kept her safe. She used the bat to sweep his feet out from beneath him. The Faithful hit the floor with a jarring thud.

She turned her back on the fallen Faithful and stalked into the dark recess.

"Give. Me. The. Cell," she gritted out.

Sam reached for a second door in the back and hauled it open. Blinding wind rushed in and Daisy winced. It was only a second. But it was enough for Sam to toss the cell out.

"No!" Daisy reached for it, instinctively trying to catch it with her new gift, but she didn't know how.

Horrified, she watched as the tiny handheld object wobbled in the air then continued sailing down to the tracks where it shattered into a million pieces.

"Fuck you, Falcon," Sam spat. "You can't stop what's coming. No one can."

The fury in her system compounded tenfold. It bubbled and sizzled and burned like the fire in the barrels back at the yard. That cell was her retribution. That cell was her forgiveness. Their clean slate. And he'd dashed it away.

Her fist tightened around the bat. Pain in her palm. She stared at the landscape whizzing past for long hard moments while heaving air into her abused lungs. And then the dam broke on her restraint. The fire in her body rose up her neck to coat her vision red. She rounded on Sam and punched him in the face. His head snapped back and hit the wooden cabin wall. Dazed, he slid down to land on his ass.

But she didn't stop there. She kept hitting him. With her fist. With her bat. With her boots. She unleashed her pent-up rage at the world on him. The unfairness of it all. All the effort she put into being good. Useless. She took it out on Sam until his blood was as much on her face as his.

Then she rounded on the other two. One was still unconscious, but the third was awake and wide-eyed as he backed up against the wall.

"Where's Julius?" she blurted.

He shook his head.

"Where are the kidnapped partners of the Lazarus family?"

He kept shaking his head.

She fisted his robe at the collar and shoved him. *"Where!"*

Daisy let go. He slumped. She raised her bat, ready. The Faithful whimpered and she pitied him. To end like this—

"He called from a landline!" The Faithful shielded his face. "That's all we know."

"What good is that to me?" she snarled, feeling that ire raise again.

"I don't know. But that's all we know."

"You're cowards," she said. "You follow like sheep and can't think for yourself."

Something in her words settled on him. His fear dissipated and he glared at her. "And I suppose you can?"

Her bat was in his face before she realized her arm had moved. Despair sliced into her gut, stealing her breath.

Tears stung her eyes as she lowered herself and hissed, "I'm nothing like you."

He flinched again and tried to get away from her. But his eyes were settled. In his head he truly believed her to be like them. Her palms itched. *The blood.*

Daisy dropped the bat with a gasp. She'd done this of her own accord, and that was the most horrifying realization of them all. Her despair surged again, and she had to check the status of her tattoo. The yin-yang symbol edged into the dark. She had to get back.

Had to get to Axel.

To... absolution.

Gasping in stuttered breaths, she glanced around the cabin. What was the cargo on this train?

The Faithful saw her looking.

"It's too late," he said. "As soon as the animals are unleashed on the city, everyone will be decimated."

The smell. She crinkled her nose. That's what it was. This cargo train was filled with animals that had been modified to hunt sin and end it. She scrubbed her face and looked outside. They'd left the yard near the docks and were headed toward the city. But they hadn't left the cargo track yet. If she could keep this train headed in the right direction, this track would lead across the Vermillion Bridge... the same bridge that had been destroyed in Julius's attack on the city.

She shot the Faithful a dark look and then booted him in the face.

He went out like a light. She wiped her face with her shirt and refitted the bat in her back holster. With a last rueful look at the three she'd taken down, she considered tossing the Faithful over the edge and giving them a second chance at life. Wasn't that what Axel had said? Even the Faithful needed a second chance.

But she couldn't do it.

She couldn't bring herself to save them. Braving the gushing wind at the door, she wrapped the still dangling bullwhip around her forearm, and then swung back outside the train, hoisted herself on top, and untied the whip before jogging across the freight vehicles. Gravity tried to pull her back but she kept her footing.

There had to be someone driving. Someone who could change the track directions.

The further along she went, the more she heard and smelled the animals. Screeches. Barks. Growls. All kinds of furry creatures had been twisted into monsters for Julius's sick gain.

She slotted herself into the gap between the engine car and the first boxcar. The cabin door was unlocked. She pushed herself through, prepared to fight.

Empty.

No. Despair coming from behind her.

Pain exploded over her head. She staggered forward into the controls. Her vision blurred but she wasn't down yet. The person behind her rushed at her again. She rolled, flipped her whip out and wrapped it around his neck. She looped the length on a stick controller and used it as an anchor. She pulled. His head slammed down, trapped on the instrument board. His eyes rolled and he slumped, falling to land in an unconscious heap on the tiny floor space.

The clickety-clack and animal sounds seemed to grow in volume.

Daisy bent and slapped the man on the face until he roused.

"Where is this train headed?" she asked.

He groaned and tried to roll away from her but she held him firmly beneath her grip.

"Don't make me force it out of you."

His eyes latched onto her face. The white's showed. She didn't know what he saw in her eyes. Or maybe it was the blood on her face. Or the pain of her sticky fingers clamping his jaw... but he blurted, "Quadrant. Monorail."

Daisy checked ahead. They were on the original seaside track, but up ahead was the junction. "Who's changing the tracks?"

He pointed at a remote wedged into the instrument panel. She picked it up and inspected it. Two lights. One for each line. The light for the line heading into the city was on. She pressed the button beneath the other. It lit up. Daisy held her breath as the train plowed onward. It wasn't until they passed safely over the junction that she exhaled. And with her breath went all her resolve.

"You've doomed us," he croaked. "We'll head straight into the sea."

"Maybe that's a good thing," she murmured, looking at her red stained hands.

"What happened to you?" he whispered.

"Julius," she whispered back. "He made me like this. He lied to us all."

Daisy locked eyes with the stranger and, like electricity crossing wires, understanding passed between them. In his eyes, she saw her own suffering. Confusion. Despair. Maybe that's what he'd seen in hers when he'd blurted the truth.

The corner of a white card poked out from the inside of his white robe collar. She went for it. He tried to stop her but she was too fast. What she saw stopped her heart.

A family photograph. Him, with a healthy-looking complexion, not sallow and sour like it was now. A woman. Two children hugging his legs. Daisy's eyes burned.

"We don't have to let him win," she croaked. "There's still time to be better."

Family first. That's the mantra Mary peddled. Daisy wanted to believe it. She wanted to *feel* it.

The Faithful peered into the darkness ahead. He glanced back at the train cars. Then he straightened himself, lifted his chin, and shoved her out the cabin door.

AXEL ALVARES

AXEL HADN'T BEEN FAR behind Daisy after she'd run after Sam. He sent the Faithful on their way and then tipped the barrels of fire onto the plants and made sure they caught. There had to be nothing left. He was prepared to wait and add fuel, but as it turned out, the barrels had oil inside. It poured like a flaming river onto the creatures and shriveled them up.

Knowing he'd never catch Daisy on foot, he returned to the motorcycle and followed. He weaved in and out of the container stacks, hunting her down corridors until eventually he hit the rail yard and saw her leap onto the train. He followed as the train sped up but had no idea what to do next.

Should he do as she did and find a way to get on board?

He was no superhero.

He settled for staying behind to be there if she needed him. A few minutes down the bumpy track, she emerged bloody from a boxcar and climbed to the top of the train. He'd shouted to her, but his voice was lost in the wind. Something was wrong. He could sense it in the air.

It was more than the fresh blood spray on her face. Her expression was pained. Was she hurt?

She disappeared again—this time, only for a few minutes before she was ejected from the engine door, landed hard on the limestone rubble and rolled into the brush. With his heart in his throat, Axel veered off the track and skidded, his wheels turning and kicking up dust as he slowed. He climbed off the bike before it stopped.

"Daisy," he bellowed, stumbling after her.

He pushed aside tall foxglove weeds until he found a fallen angel lying still beneath the moonlight, silver hair splayed like she was asleep. Time stood still as he hovered his ear over her mouth and checked for breath.

She gasped and opened her eyes. Vivid violet eyes locked onto him, registered he was no threat, then bolted upright and chased after the train now quickly receding into the distance.

"Daisy, what—"

She ran, slick and fast and with silver hair streaming behind her. He jogged after her. They only made it a few hundred feet and then a fiery explosion in the distance slowed them. Axel grabbed Daisy and yanked her back. They stumbled but he caught her against him.

Anguish contorted her face as she glanced at him and then the wreckage. He squinted to see better. The train...

"I think..." He swallowed. "I think it's gone straight over the damaged bridge and into the sea. Shit, Daisy. That could have been you."

The pained look on her face worsened. She looked at him as though the sea would rise up and pull her down. She stepped back.

"Daisy," he whispered, and reached for her. He wanted to comfort her. To tell her it was okay, but she slapped him away and let out a strangled cry as she attempted to breathe and not cry.

"He pushed me out," she eventually said. "Why would he do that?"

Axel squinted down the line at the fireball being swallowed by black rolling water. "There were other people in there?"

She shook her head. "I don't think so... just the Faithful and some modified animals. I was going to do it. I was going to run the train into the sea but he—" She held her hands before her face and her breath hitched. She shook her head and wiped her palms on her pants. "This isn't working."

"What?" God, he was confused. "Daisy, what?"

But she strode back to the motorcycle, shaking her head the entire time. Axel jogged after her and took her shoulder.

"What isn't working, Daze?"

"Me!" She rounded on him. "I'm not working."

Tears leaked from her eyes. She wrenched her gaze away and tried to pick up the Ducati but her fingers slipped. She stubbornly tried to right the fallen vehicle but kept stumbling.

"Hey," he murmured.

He took her hand and pulled her to him, be damned with her resistance. He wrapped his arms around her and held her close. Tight. Like a vice.

"Daze, it's okay. I've got you."

She stayed stiff in his arms, and then suddenly softened. She melted into him and shuddered as her tears leaked out.

"You're not hurt, are you?" he ventured.

She shook her head against his chest. He cupped the back of her head and stroked, uncaring of the tacky resistance from the blood. To him, it only made her more human. Vulnerable. She was a warrior, but a warrior with cracks in her armor.

"Then what? Did they do something to you... say something to you?" She refused to talk. "Daisy, tell me so I can fix it."

She pushed away and the look on her face stabbed him in the heart.

"It's *me* who's broken. You can't fix me." She sniffed and wiped her nose, then picked up the motorcycle and turned it on. "Let's go."

Clenching his jaw, he stared at her long and hard.

"No." He covered her hand on the throttle. "I want to know what happened."

Eyes full of animosity slid to him. Hate like he'd never felt before speared him, yet somehow, he knew it wasn't directed at him. But at herself.

"I happened," she spat and waved down her bloody front. "I beat them within an inch of their life and then kept going." Anger poured off her in waves. "I wanted him to die. I wanted them all to hurt the way I've been hurt. I want them *all* to lose. And I... I can't stop myself. Whether you're there or not, I can't stop." Her jaw clicked shut. Her expression deadpanned. She became the uncaring Falcon again. "I'm a murderer. A villain. This is me, your mate."

"Daisy. What you're feeling is happening to all your siblings, not just you."

"No. They don't do it on purpose. I do."

"Daze—"

"Get on or walk," she barked.

Scowling, he climbed on and wrapped his hands around her small waist. He was at a loss for words as she drove them out of the yard. She was hurting and he wanted to make it right. He wanted to fix it for her, but he was starting to see there might be nothing he could do.

Maybe it wasn't his job to fix her.

Maybe she couldn't be fixed.

All he knew was that he could promise her one thing. He would be there if she broke apart. Every damned time.

THEY ARRIVED at Lazarus House in the early hours before dawn. During the ride she had stayed quiet and tense. He tried to talk again when they stopped in the garage, but she walked away and didn't look back.

Axel wasn't sure how long he stood there, his fingers twitching at his sides, but when Mary pushed her petite body through the door leading to the basement headquarters, he jolted.

"Daisy's back?" she asked quietly.

He nodded but couldn't bring himself to talk. He'd failed. Wasn't he supposed to be her balance? Wasn't he supposed to be the one who she would go to and feel better? Maybe it wasn't her that was broken, but him. Maybe he was blinded by his hope.

"Your sister is asleep in our apartment," Mary said. "Come in. There's a spot for you on the couch."

He slumped and followed her inside, his feet dragging although he wasn't tired. The cold, empty hallway stared at him with dark eyes, waiting and judging.

"I'm sorry, Mary," he said as they walked through the darkened basement rooms.

"It's not your fault. It's mine." The elevator doors opened to allow them entry. Once inside, she punched the button for her floor. "I made her this way. The blame rests on me."

"But I thought Julius trained her to be like this."

Sad eyes slid his way. "He only had control of her because I left her behind."

"I'm sure you couldn't help it, just as I'm sure there is more than one person to blame."

She shrugged.

They went up the levels in silence. When they arrived at what he assumed was her floor, the doors opened and stayed open. She didn't walk out. She took a breath and faced him.

"Is she going to be okay?"

"I don't know," he confessed. "She has moments when she jokes." Axel smiled to himself at the memory of them sleeping. "In those moments, I see a whole new person who is so magnificent that I feel like I'm bathing in sunshine. And then…" He frowned, looking at his fingers both soot-covered and bloody. Must have been from Daisy's face. "Then the darkness takes over, there is hate in her eyes, and everything is cold. But the worst… the worst I see is when there's nothing."

Mary made a strangled laugh and covered her mouth.

He glowered. What was so funny?

"I'm sorry." She smiled with unbound joy laced with tears. "You said she joked with you. She *smiled*." Mary exhaled slowly, forcing herself to gather her tumultuous emotions. She nodded. "She's coming back to us."

"Mary," he warned. "I just told you she's empty half the time."

She gripped his arm and looked him in the eyes. "My dear boy. She used to be empty *all* the time. There is hope yet. And you're giving it to her. We must have faith that she will find the rest of her way home."

With a huff of satisfaction, Mary straightened her shoulders and beckoned him into the hallway. When they arrived at a door, she stopped him with a palm to his chest.

"You can go in and see your sister, but then I want you to return to Daisy."

He raised his brow.

"And before you complain that I'm telling you what to do, get used to it. You're part of the family now, Axel. Trust me when I give you direction."

131

He stared at her palm on him and sensed that if he tried to remove it, he would lose his hand. This deadly woman had Daisy's best interests at heart. But did she have his... or Elena's?

"Mary," he cautioned, slow and steady so she picked up his vibe. "As much as I'm falling for Daisy, there is no one in this world I care for more than my sister. No one."

Mary assessed him from top to toe. She stepped back, her hand dragging off his pec. Her chin lifted in respect.

"Elena is ours too, now. Anything she needs, we will supply it. Including our love."

A lump formed in Axel's throat, and he coughed to cover it. "Okay."

"Okay?"

"Yes. I'll see my sister and then I'll check on Daisy."

Mary entered the apartment on silent feet. Axel tried his best to emulate her, but she was a goddamned ninja as she moved. If she wanted him dead, he wouldn't hear her coming. But as he followed her through the dark apartment, he realized he was behind her. This assassin of epic proportions was giving him her back, as she had done since he'd arrived that morning.

She meant what she promised.

She trusted him. And if she trusted him, then he should trust her.

"In here." Mary opened a door a few inches.

Inside, the only light came from the predawn hues coming through the window. On a bed, wrapped in cozy blankets and surrounded with pillows, Elena slept soundly. She looked good. Peaceful. He frowned down at Mary.

"Did she talk to you about her illness?"

"Only that its terminal. The doctors don't have a cure." She paused. "And that the same illness took your parents."

"Was she okay?" No sickness. Nothing to worry about?

"She took her medication on time. She ate a full meal."

Axel exhaled. "Good. Thank you."

Mary closed the door and looked at him expectantly.

He nodded. "Take me to Daisy."

MARY TOOK Axel to Daisy's apartment. Before he went in, she handed Axel a pile of folded clothing.

"Some clean clothes," Mary said with a pointed look at his dirty shirt.

"Thank you."

"No, Axel. It's us who needs to thank you. I know this isn't what you signed up for."

"To be fair, I signed up for cloning my sister. So... um, yeah..."

Mary's eyes twinkled. "I like you."

That felt like the stamp of approval from a tiger. "Thanks?"

Mary's mood sobered. "You need to know something."

His forehead crinkled.

"No one else could go from perfect to pieces and then back again. But she did. She is the leader this family needs, and you'll help her realize that."

"You sound so sure. Why can't you go in there and tell her that? It seems like this declaration needs to come from you."

"I tried. But she doesn't want to hear it from me. I burned my bridges."

Her words stayed with Axel long after he'd entered Daisy's apartment and closed the door. From perfect to pieces and back again. He rubbed his chest. But he followed the sound of the shower running into a bedroom. The door was ajar.

"Daisy?" he ventured, poking his head in.

No answer.

Inside the bedroom, steam billowed from the adjoining half-open ensuite door. Axel put the clothes on the double bed. Potted plants flourished on shelves. The scent of jasmine came from somewhere.

"Daisy?"

Still nothing.

"I'm coming in."

fifteen

DAISY LAZARUS

HOT WATER SPRAYED DOWN on Daisy as she laid fully clothed on the shower floor. She watched the water dribble down her outstretched arm. Watched as dried blood softened and turned the water a mix of brown, orange and pink. Watched it twirl with her silver hair before it circled the drain. Some left, some returned to her body.

She fixated on that cycle.

Water falling.

Water cleaning.

Blood leaving.

Blood returning.

It always returned.

The moment they'd returned to Lazarus House, her mind had shut down. *Shower*. All she could think about was to get to the shower. *Clean the blood. Wash*. But she didn't have the energy to stand. She laid down and that's when things had fallen apart. Blood circled back to her. It wouldn't leave.

And she couldn't get up.

The death of enemies that weren't her enemies was a stain she would never remove. Not just Sam. Not just the driver. But all of them. From the first homeless person Julius made her kill, to the replicates she'd put down, to the Faithful who needed to be pulled into line or silenced. She had been Julius's sword.

And now she was the same for the Deadly Seven.

The sad part was, she didn't know who she was without the blood running down that blade.

Special One, Gloria had called her.

The true leader of this family, Mary had said.

Mate.

Savior.

Villain.

They all said.

The driver's eyes before he'd pushed her out the engine door haunted her. The family picture was still in her hands as she'd landed. Her eyes skated across the bathroom and saw the frayed and bloody edge of the photograph on the counter, about to tip off the edge.

She'd intended to only have a shower, but the picture had fallen out of her pocket. She'd picked it up, tossed it there, and then collapsed on the shower floor.

Why did the driver save Daisy? He had a family. The memory wrenched her soul tighter with each passing second, suffocating her from within. He'd seen something in Daisy. That look they'd shared felt like he was drowning, and she was the life raft. But instead of holding onto her, he pushed her. He saved her from drowning too.

She didn't even know him.

She was a monster.

Why were people helping her when, if they looked inside and stripped open her chest, they'd find a cavern where her heart used to live. She squeezed her eyes shut. The burn. It spread from the back of her throat. It heated her skin. It hit her eyes. She squeezed tighter. Held her breath. Fire leaked from the corners of her lashes. *Stop. Don't—*

"Daisy?"

Axel. Don't cry.

"I'm coming in."

No.

The burn. It leaked. She choked on a breath. Held it. Screwed up her face.

"Oh, Daze," he breathed, and it was the pity in his voice that opened the floodgates of her hell. Sobs wracked out of her chest. Her vision blurred. She clawed the tiles. When will this anguish end?

"Daze. Let me turn this off," he muttered.

"No. Let it wash me." *Clean me.*

"You're still in your clothes."

"I know."

He paused. He sighed.

She was a burden. Even to him. She would always be a burden. Couldn't do anything right.

"Why are you here?" she blurted, trying one last time to push him away.

When silence answered her, she thought he was gone. The tears she'd held back burst forth again but this time, there was no sound. There was hardly enough air.

And then…

He reached over her, gathered her, and laid down behind her. In the wet. In the shower rain. Holding her close.

"I could tell you that Mary sent me," he said, voice low and rough. "I could tell you that I've been in a daze since I met you. I could also say that there's something pulling me to you in the way the shore calls to the sea. But the truth is, my truth is… I don't know why I'm here." She tried to hunch away from him. "Stop it," he scolded. "No more. Let me take care of you. Let me cuddle you."

Those last words. They broke her.

Unable to stomach the sight of blood circling, she rolled into him, buried her face in the comfort of his chest and cried. She cried for all that she lost. The years. The lives. Her soul.

She cried out the pain in her soul until the emptiness didn't feel so raw.

At some point, Axel slipped his hands under her arms and thighs in a way she imagined him using frequently in his job. He hoisted her effortlessly, shut off the faucet, and stepped out of the shower. He wrapped a towel around her like a cocoon, and then carried her to bed where he laid her down gently and patted her dry.

Her eyes remained closed, hiding. She couldn't face him. The shame.

The mattress depressed as he climbed on before her. The pillow tilted as he laid his damp head next to hers. He caressed her hips. His breath tickled her face.

She should be cold. But warmth emanated from him like a cozy fire.

"I don't know why I'm here," he finished softly. "But that's okay. What matters is that I'm not going anywhere."

Her eyes opened and were caught immediately in the snare of his. She gasped. His were hot, dark and glistening as though he was on the brim of breaking too. But there was no despair. Never would this man's sadness hurt her. Somehow, she was unsettled about that. He shouldn't suffer alone. She touched his cheek and he pushed into her, chasing her touch.

"Why?" she whispered. "I don't understand."

"Is that so bad? Do we have to figure out everything right now?"

"I suppose not."

"Good." He exhaled and tugged her closer before closing his eyes.

She watched his gorgeous face for a moment, marveling at it so close. A tiny freckle on the bronzed skin beneath his left eye. A tiny scar on his upper lip. Stubble peppering his jaw. Thick, thick lashes swept down like the wings of a dark angel.

She spent some time being aware of her body's sensations. She felt as tumultuous as a sea in a storm. Up. Down. Up again. Axel brought them up. His very presence made her feel good. Not just the mating thing where touching him reset her internal sin equilibrium, but his demeanor. What she'd thought was pity, wasn't. Someone who pitied her wouldn't have hugged like he had. They wouldn't have taken care of her. They wouldn't be here right now.

She knew exactly what tolerance was. Julius had displayed it daily for her. He'd never truly wanted her around. He'd placated her and left her as fast as he could. He'd never once cuddled her. He'd never stayed when she'd been sad.

But Axel did. Not only did he stay, but his body language—all at peace and languid—said he seemed to like it. Axel truly liked her company. The sudden thought had her heart pitter pattering in her chest. She became hyperaware of her wet clothes, of the damp towel beneath them.

"Axel?"

"Mm-hm."

"Are you tired?"

"No."

"Are you pretending to sleep?"

"*Meu pai* always said when your wife is ready for bed, you're ready for bed. That way you'll always be—" His eyes popped open with a guilty look. "Never mind."

"Were you going to say ready for *it*?"

"No," he scoffed, as though it was the most ridiculous thing.

"Your dad said that to you?" she pressed.

A pink hue touched his cheeks and ears, and she couldn't help but reach out.

"No." He scrubbed his face. "I mean, yes. But he didn't know I understood what he meant. He thought he was being cryptic. Shit. I didn't mean to assume. Especially not now."

Her lips curved on one side and a flush chased away the emptiness her tears had wrought. "I like that you assume."

"You do?" He opened one eye.

"I like that you told me to stop pushing you away. I like that you walked in here like you belong. You keep pulling me from the brink." She sucked in a breath then let the truth out. "I like that you're here."

"Me too." He twirled his finger through her hair.

"I like that too." Her eyes followed his action.

"Then I'll do it forever."

She snort-laughed again. "You're very romantic."

"I practice in the mirror."

"No you don't."

"No. I don't." His gaze softened. "I like that I make you laugh."

"Me too," she whispered.

"Then I'll do it forever."

They stared deeply into each other's eyes, and she felt something shift within her soul. Another broken piece found a home. She wanted to kiss him. To see if more broken pieces fit somewhere, but his eyes turned serious as he found another strand of her hair to twine.

"Are you going to tell me what hurt you back at the yard?"

She deadpanned. "I don't want to talk about it."

He stopped her from turning away. "That's the only way you can set it free."

"How would you know? You're only twenty-five."

He shrugged. "I'm wise beyond my years. Spent most of the past decade rescuing people from burning buildings and parenting a sick sister. Much of the time before that caring for sick parents. Age has nothing to do with it."

"I'll bet they were wonderful parents. I'll bet they loved you very much."

"You're deflecting, but yes. They did." He brought the strand he twirled over her front, then collected another to make a crisscross pattern on her wet sweater. "Elena and I loved them."

"How did they die?" She paused. "If you don't mind me asking."

"Same illness that's taking Ellie."

"I'm sorry."

"Not your fault. But thank you."

She touched the sadness on his face and wished she could rub the wrinkles away. His gaze sharpened on her as she tried.

"See this is another thing I like about you, Daisy," he murmured, his voice oh, so intimate that it sent chills chattering through her blood. "You've been beaten and hurt but you still try to soothe others."

"You've only just met me." She lowered her hand with a self-deprecating shake of her head.

"Stop saying that." He brought her hand back to his face. "I met you a year ago. I saw you plenty. I noticed you, Daisy, even though you didn't notice me. You used to bring potted plants to the club-houses when you didn't think anyone was watching. You were the first to organize luxuries for the Faithful like a billiards table or a gaming center. Even though half of them didn't deserve it, you gave them things. It wasn't Julius. It was you. You hated their sadness. You wanted to bring them a glimmer of joy, of normalcy, of hope in a dark time."

"But then I hurt them if I needed to. Their deaths stain my soul."

"He made you."

"Maybe I wanted to." And there it was. The cold hard truth of the pain she kept locked in the cage of her heart. "That's why I was in a state at the yard. I *wanted* to hurt. Sometimes that's a faster way to eliminate the despair. It feels good."

"Does it?" His brow raised. "Does it really? In here." He patted her chest. "Or do you feel like you have a purpose when you're doing it. Maybe taking orders from Julius meant you didn't have to worry about making mistakes."

Her lashes lowered.

He lifted her chin, so she met his eyes again. "But, Daze. Mistakes are how we learn. We need them."

"They don't feel good."

"Not when you make them alone."

His words hung suspended in the air between them for a moment before he stroked her hair and whispered, "Go to sleep. You're tired."

"But you're not tired." She stifled a yawn. "I should be able to stay awake longer."

"You were also tortured not long ago."

"I'm fine." She leaned in to kiss him, to prove she was okay.

It felt right. Needed. He opened his lips and kissed her slowly back. As soon as she tasted him, everything clenched tight in her lower stomach region and she shuffled closer, hardening their contact.

"Daze…" Axel gave a pained groan and pulled away. "You have no idea what you do to me."

"Show me." She tried to kiss him again, but he stopped her with a shake of his head.

"I'm going to regret this, but you need to rest." He exhaled and started stroking her hair again. "I'll be here when you wake."

"Hug me?" she mumbled, as sleep stole over her vision.

"Always."

As Axel's arms surrounded her, she knew he was right. They didn't have to know all the answers now. This was another thing she knew for sure. And being in his arms, surrounded by his heat was everything.

Daisy woke to the sound of the shower running. Maybe she hadn't turned it off. She sat up and noticed something else not right. Axel wasn't beside her.

He said he would stay.

Feeling her sanity tumble into the darkness again, she tossed the still damp blanket away and went for the bathroom door. It was open a crack.

She gasped.

Axel was in the shower. Naked. One hand on the tiled wall, his biceps bulging and rock hard. His other hand on his swollen erection, squeezing and stroking. His eyes were closed, his head dipped, and he frowned as he worked himself. As if it hurt.

From the safety of her dark room, she watched through the crack, unable to tear her gaze away from the mesmerizing water sluicing over his muscular body. How the rivulets carved patterns down the toned hills and valleys. How his pecs and abdominals flexed with each stroke, beating in a visual symphony.

Should she leave him be?

Or...

Axel looked up. He locked eyes with her.

sixteen

DAISY LAZARUS

DAISY FROZE.

Her skin tightened. Was he going to kick her out? Tell her to leave? Ignore her?

No. Axel's hand tightened around his cock until the tip went dark. His cheeks flushed, his brown eyes brightened, his chest heaved with ragged breath. All the while, the hot spray of water showered around him like a storm. And then his gaze scorched a path from her head to her toes and he stroked again. Slowly.

A challenge?

Defiance ran through her. She slapped her palm on the door, opened it, and stalked in.

"Your pheromones leaked while you slept," he said, voice dark and husky.

Pheromones?

He'd been aroused, and rather than waking her, he'd come here to see to himself. Daisy wasn't sure if she was impressed that he cared for her, or angry that he'd not picked her to help relieve his need. Her gaze darted down to where he rubbed himself. Water dripped off the swollen tip and for some reason, the erotic sight made every sense in her body ache to touch him. To have him touch her. She needed it.

But did he want her here?

She nodded at his erection, barely able to speak through her dry throat. "So… that is for me?"

Heat flared in his dark gaze and his upper lip curled.

"Of course it's for you," he growled. "It's *always* for you."

"Then stop."

"Stop?" He blinked. For a moment, it looked like he would let go, but then his eyes narrowed. "No."

"But I want it."

"Then come and take it."

Daisy smiled. So this *was* a challenge. They studied each other, sizing each other up, waiting to see who would break first. She peeled off her sweater and dropped it on the floor. Next was her T-shirt. Then her bra. The instant her breasts were exposed, her nipples hardened. Axel watched her every movement like she was a movie. And it made her hotter. Aroused. Through it all, his breath grew faster, more ragged, and he increased his pace. *Cheeky bastard.* She wanted to be the one to touch him. He knew it. She shucked her jeans and then stood there, naked, while he boldly looked his fill, not even once catching on her scars.

Come and take it.

Fine.

She opened the glass shower door, and fitted herself under the stream, pretending to ignore his need. Hot liquid sensations trailed down her body like a caress. His breath stuttered at her closeness. Only then did she face him, expecting him to have faltered, but he backed up until he hit the wall, a self-satisfied smirk on his face.

"Give it to me," she demanded, suddenly irrational.

His eyes flashed with amusement, but he didn't let go. She

reached for him. He stepped to the side. A tiny snarl escaped her lips. She pushed his shoulder against the tiles. He slammed hard with a *puh* of breath falling from his lips. She wrapped her hand over his and held his gaze.

They both stopped stroking.

They breathed.

"You said it's for me," she accused, and tightened her grip over his hand.

He threw his head back, exposing the thick column of his neck and Adam's apple rolling in a slow swallow. Every line of his body was tense. Every muscle stretched taut. This was a battle of wills he wanted to win, or he was testing her—making sure she wanted this, was ready for it.

Maybe he also knew she needed an edge to her lovemaking.

"I'm not a sunshine and roses girl," she said. "I'm dirty and dark."

She squeezed tighter. His lips parted. His breath turned ragged.

"Look at me," she demanded. He rolled his head back to her and opened drowsy eyes. The fever was back. She could virtually see her pheromones take hold of him. "Let me."

"Fuck, you're hot, *minha margarida*." Lust-drenched eyes traveled over her. "You're everything I need."

He gave over control. She almost dropped to her knees but wanted to see the change come over him. She wanted to know what effect she had. Wanted to see him come undone in her hand. Wanted to know she could have a feel-good effect on someone. With one hand on his shoulder, pinning his bulk to the wall, and the other hand fisted around his velvety hard length, she pumped him hard.

His eyes rolled. Fluttered. And she loved it.

"Too fast," he gasped.

She shook her head, spraying water. She kept going. He was so hot beneath her touch. So indomitably masculine. This powerful body carried people out of burning buildings. He'd carried her out of the storm drain. For her, he melted. He gasped. Panted. Struggled to breathe.

"Daze—" His breath hitched, panicking as he approached climax.

His lower stomach clenched. He swore, bit his lip, and then he spurted white, ropy jets over her fist and stomach. When he was done, his gaze darkened, and he smeared his release over her stomach with possessive pride. She squeezed him, as if to say, *That was because of me. Take note.*

His jaw hardened when he met her gaze. Uh-oh. He didn't look happy. He'd wanted to savor this, but she went fast. She grinned, touched her tongue to her upper teeth, teasing him.

"Your turn," he ground out, voice gravelly. "I'm going to make you come so fucking hard you'll see stars."

He picked her up, twisted their positions and flattened her against the wall. The rush thrilled her to the bone. An element of danger buzzed off his skin and she was here for it.

"I like this," she breathed, eyes drinking him in. She'd never had weak lovers. They had to keep up with her. Axel was exactly what she didn't know she wanted. Some distant part of her had to wonder if this was fate.

If fate was real.

It was one thing to pair her with someone biologically, but in carnal need? In passion? How could Gloria have known this person was her match in every way?

He was strong, domineering, relentless. He held her face in his hands and crushed her lips with a brutal kiss, forcing her mouth to open, plundering with his tongue. He roughly squeezed her breast, plucked her nipple until she cried out, and then dropped to his knees.

"Axel," she gasped. She clawed his head.

He growled against her mound, then lifted her leg over his

shoulder and spread her with his fingers. His mouth hovered an inch away from where she needed it, and he looked up. Pure, masculine entitlement scalded her. Hard, irreproachable, and unwavering eyes pinned her.

"This is for me." He tossed her own words back at her. Except, where hers was a question, his was a declaration. An understanding. He inserted his fingers and thrust into her. "Only me."

She nodded. Tugged his hair. A wild grin split his face and then he licked between her legs. His tongue flicked her clit relentlessly, harshly, just as cruelly as she'd worked him. She cried out at the sensations throttling her, choking her, blinding her. *God, yes.*

She felt alive.

She felt... wanted. Needed so badly that he couldn't control himself.

"Axel," she sputtered through water spray as her climax started to build. *Not yet.*

"Too wet," he said, drawing back. "I want to taste you, not water."

He shoved her an inch to the side, out of the stream, and then reinserted his fingers into her, using his thumb to work her as his tongue had. His long-lashed gaze lifted to study her with smug satisfaction as she squirmed on his hand, just as she had watched him.

Something about this connection clicked another broken piece into place. He was the same as her... somewhere deep inside. This man meeting her pound-for-pound was hers to keep.

Sensation built, rising like a tidal wave. Her eyes rolled. The back of her head hit the tiles.

"Eyes to me, Daze," Axel growled. "Look at the person making you come."

Feverish, and hot all over, Daisy locked eyes with him. She moaned loudly as her orgasm crested. Felt her body shift outward.

The floor tilted. Water exploded, splashing the entire bathroom. For a moment, she wasn't sure what had happened. Her vision blurred. Her mind drifted. And then Axel stood, running his strong grip along her thighs to hold her up with a proud smirk gracing his lips.

"What happened?" she gasped.

"You happened. Or should I say, I happened to you." He caressed her hips, over her still quivering stomach, and then gave a proprietary squeeze of her breasts. She bit back a moan at her sensitive nipples and her reaction only deepened the masculine entitlement she saw in his eyes. "Your gift, Daze. You released it when you... unloaded."

"I did?"

He kissed her, tasted her lips, and then smiled against them. "I like it."

She drew his lip between her teeth and pressed down. His chuckle came out a breathy grunt through his nose. Finally coming down from her high, she saw the mess she'd made. Water from the shower now dribbled down every inch of the bathroom. It was as if she'd turned the shower head and sprayed it like a fire hose. God damn, she needed to work on the telekinesis. It was definitely there. No turning back.

"We should get out," she murmured and made to move.

"Oh, no." He tugged her back. "We're not done yet."

seventeen

AXEL ALVARES

AXEL TUGGED Daisy back into the shower with him thinking back to when she'd fallen asleep. She'd emitted that sexy, sweet smell of hers and he'd gone hard and stayed hard. He'd tried to ignore his need—for hours—and then he couldn't take it anymore. He'd decided to sort himself out.

Never had he dreamed Daisy would wake and demand to be the one to finish him.

Never had he imagined she'd like it hard and fast.

Never had he thought he'd like it too.

But now... now, as he enveloped Daisy in his arms, now it was time to go slow. To relish her while he could because she still held a distance in her eyes, and he wanted it gone. He wanted nothing between them. He wanted up close and in-your-face personal.

So he gently put her under the shower spray and watched her silver hair plaster down her pale body. He took the shampoo from the caddy and squirted some in his hands.

"What are you doing?" Her delicate brows puckered.

Fucking adorable. How she could go from vixen-on-fire to sweet-and-innocent blew his mind.

"What do you think?" He chuckled.

"Oh."

Like this, when he surprised her with his attentiveness, she was so innocent despite her age. A broken birdy. All he wanted to do was take care of her. He tried to make a mental note, that if she acted all tough, to remember these moments. To remember she was still someone fragile inside before he caved to her whims like he'd done when she refused to tell him what bothered her.

He cleared his throat. "Turn around and face the wall."

She did. He lathered her hair slowly, taking his time to massage her scalp and then down the length of her hair. When he was younger, and his mother was sick, he'd had to wash her hair while she laid in bed. He'd used a pan and a jug. Then she lost her hair, just like Elena was losing hers. Maybe, one day, the illness would come for him. To dispel the memories, Axel massaged down Daisy's scalp to her neck, digging in all the soft spots he knew would feel good.

Her groan of appreciation traveled down his spine and stirred his cock. Ready again. Fuck. He didn't think this was ever going to change. He'd always react like this around Daisy.

"Feel good?" he murmured.

"Mm-hm." She rested back against his pec.

The position gave him the perfect view down her sudsy front, including the firm breasts and erect nipples. He swept her skin. Slipped his fingers through the suds, traced around her feminine shape, washing where he'd released, enjoying her melt for him.

"Thank you for letting Elena and me stay in your home." He moved them under the stream, so the shampoo washed from her hair. "I feel better knowing she's safe."

Daisy turned and looked up at him. She blinked through the

water. "It's not really my home. Not yet. Not like it was with…" She suddenly frowned and finished her sentence softly. "Not like where I used to live with Julius, I suppose. But then again, that wasn't really my home either—"

She cut off suddenly and started.

"What is it?" He tensed and brushed his thumb over her cheek.

"I… there was something one of the Faithful said on the train. He said Julius called him from a landline phone connection. At the time I thought it was useless information but…" Violet eyes met his. "What if it's from my old childhood home?"

"It could be any landline, though. Right?"

"Yes, but Julius had always kept his old home. No one else knew it existed, but me. I lived there when I was younger, but he hated me touching his wife's and daughter's things." She scowled. "I hated that too. They were dead. Long and buried, yet he kept his daughter's room exactly as it was the day she'd died. He once caught me sneaking in there and playing with her dolls. Wasn't long after that he started locking me in an attic fitted out with a toilet. That would be the perfect place to keep a group of people."

A prickling sensation came over Axel. "Where is the house?"

"Just outside city limits."

"But the bridges…"

"If we head down to the slums, the gap between the mainland is small. We can take a boat across the river. Or we might be able to find a helicopter." She turned the faucet off. "We'll go now."

WITHIN THE HOUR, they were dressed and driving on Daisy's motorcycle down to the south end of Cardinal City. Before they'd left, Axel had quickly checked in on Elena, only to find her having the time of her life gaming with the boy she'd met on the first night, Alek. Elena actually looked at Axel like he was cramping her style, so he quickly left. He tried not to think about the dark circles that had been under her eyes and hoped she wasn't just putting on a brave face.

Despite being mid-afternoon, the further they drove down to the tail end of the city, the worse the conditions were. Looting in broad daylight. Muggings in the street. Bodies laid on the side of the road in the gutter. Axel's stomach clenched when he saw one of the CCFD trucks trying to get through to an accident, but an angry mob was pulling the hose down. He should be out there with them, but he was needed just as much here.

Helping Daisy could end all this chaos.

He forced himself to keep his head down and focused on the road ahead as Daisy weaved the motorcycle through debris and garbage and people wandering the streets. The smell of shit and piss grew stronger the closer they got to the riverside banks. Unlike the center of the city, where the debris from broken bridges was being cleared, here it was left to fester like a pustule on a dying man.

Daisy stopped the bike when she couldn't get any further beyond the chunks of pitchmen and asphalt. She parked and they got off.

"I wish you'd stayed with your sister." She glowered at him as she checked her weapons. A pistol at her hip and a katana buckled across her body and sitting over her shoulder. She'd left the baseball bat at home. But she wasn't wearing a battle suit, like her siblings. She wore a sweater and jeans. Her long silver hair was tied back in a ponytail.

He had his own gun in the waistband of his jeans. He knew how to use it. He would be fine.

"Daze," he said, an eyebrow arching. "The rest of your family might be okay with you going off on your own, but there's no way in hell I'm letting you scout a potential hideaway of a mad man without back up."

"They're not exactly okay with it," she mumbled. "But they have no choice. We're stretched thin."

Most of them had been out searching the city, but Wyatt had been in the basement with his baby and Mary and Flint. They'd said to report back immediately on what Daisy found. Griffin still wasn't doing so good. They were worried and didn't want to leave him, but they would come running if Daisy's hunch proved correct. They would take down Julius together.

"I would have preferred not to tell them at all," she admitted.

"But I'm sure you're glad you did."

"I didn't want to get their hopes up." Her teeth ground. Her nostrils flared. "I suppose it's too late to complain now."

"Damn straight." His lips curved on one side. "Remember what I said about making mistakes together? I'm here with you, whatever happens."

For a moment, her eyes softened, then she hardened them and jerked her chin toward the crumbled bridge. He followed her gaze to where seagulls jumped over the rocky rubble. Cable wires and metal poles stuck out at odd angles.

"Flint arranged for a boat to be hidden somewhere behind there," she said.

"Careful. There could be live wires."

"There it is." She pointed to where a speed boat sat moored on the riverside dock.

They jogged over with a wary eye along the coast. A boat would be precious cargo right now. That or a helicopter was the only way out of the crime-riddled city but those with access to an inflight vehicle had made a mass exodus once the bridges were blown.

Axel felt the unnatural weight of eyes on them as they approached the empty boat.

"Was the skipper meant to meet us?" he asked.

"Yeah. Flint said to meet him here and pay him."

"With what?"

"Safe passage."

Axel's brows went up, but he shrugged. He supposed if the skipper wanted off the island city, and Daisy could provide an escort, then at least it wasn't costing them cash. Then again... what would the man need an escort for? The hairs on the back of his neck prickled and he surveyed the shore. No one was in sight. Seagulls squawked under the overcast mid-afternoon sky. After a few moments of eerie silence, he turned to Daisy.

"Maybe we should just go," Daisy suggested, scrutinizing the boat. "I'm sure I'll figure out how to hot-wire it in no time."

"Maybe you should practice."

"What?"

"Your gift." He pointed at the water. "You moved the shower water. Maybe try something with that."

She gave him a dubious look. "A few droplets of water is different to a river."

"What does it feel like?" he asked, trying something new. He was determined to get her feeling good about her gift and if Flint made a deal with a skipper for safe passage, then they should probably stick to it. "When you connect with something and move it."

Her gaze turned inward as she thought about it. "I never really paid it attention. It seems to come out when I'm not thinking about it."

Axel strode to the river and dipped his hand in the water. He scooped some out and tossed it at her. She dodged with a scowl.

"What gives?"

"I thought maybe if I surprised you, then you'd find a way to stop it."

Her scowl deepened and she wiped her face. "It didn't work."

He shrugged. "I'm no expert at this, Daze. But I think you need to get a grip on what you can do because, if we find Julius, and he has replicates around him, then we'll need every weapon in your arsenal."

"I know." She pouted.

"How can we train you?"

"Pigeon. He'll know."

"Parker?"

She nodded, then brooded at the water. Axel followed her gaze. The mainland shore was visible on the other side through the murky air. Somewhere over there, Julius could be based. And if he was… then Daisy would have only him until backup arrived.

"Hey!"

They both turned to see a man running toward them full pelt down the sodden shore. The messenger bag strapped over his shoulder bounced. Behind him, three men chased.

"Shit," Axel muttered and sloshed into the water to get to the boat. "Get in."

Daisy splashed after him, but didn't get in. She rounded and sighted her gun at the three men chasing.

Axel looked for keys, just in case they had been left under the visor or seat. Nothing. He turned back. The men were close enough Daisy and Axel could see they were trouble. One had a crowbar. Another had a gun.

Daisy's gun fired. *Pop! Pop! Pop!*

All three pursuers fell to the ground in quick succession. The man Axel assumed was the skipper ducked, worried he'd get shot, but quickly realized he was fine.

Axel stared at Daisy.

She deadpanned. "What?"

"I think maybe next time, aim to maim. Not kill."

She tucked her gun into her pants and then climbed into the boat.

The skipper tossed Axel the keys as he approached. "Start it. There are more coming."

"Just exactly who are the men I was forced to shoot?" Daisy ground out, a guilty glance thrown Axel's way.

Feeling frustrated, he forced himself to focus and put the keys in the ignition. The engine purred to life.

Now on board, the skipper took control. He pushed the throttle and the boat zoomed forward. Within seconds, the wind blew in their hair and the Cardinal City shore receded.

Still frustrated, Axel realized why. The body count was growing. He had no idea who those chasing the skipper were, or why.

"Who are you?" Axel asked. "Why did my girlfriend just kill three men for you?"

He hated that Daisy now had more stains on her heart. He hated it more that she was more concerned with his reaction to it than the actual task. The skipper slid his gaze to Axel and considered his answer. He didn't answer fast enough, so Axel stepped in with his own pistol aimed at the man's throat.

"I won't ask you again," he gritted out.

"I'm no one," he replied. "Just a man escaping the city."

"Why were they chasing you?"

"I owed money. That's all."

"So, my girl killed three innocent men trying to claim their debt back?"

The skipper laughed, and Axel caught missing teeth. But not the kind you lost from old age. The man was maybe forty, no more. He looked in good health. Decent clothes. No bum or hobo.

"They aren't innocent, believe me." The skipper gestured to his mouth. "They pulled my teeth out. I borrowed money to fix my boat. Times got tough. I took too long to pay them back."

"Sure," Axel said wryly but put the gun away. He wasn't sold by any means. But he could see the answer wouldn't be clean.

He was just pissed others were taking advantage of Daisy. Had Flint known this would happen? Still scowling, he sat down next to his girl.

She looked at him strangely.

"What?" he grumbled.

"You said girlfriend."

"Sorry. Mate, I guess. But no one else will understand that."

The smile that crossed her lips barreled into his heart. She looked at him with such emotion that he had to smile back.

"You like it when I get all macho?" he murmured to her with a brow waggle.

She blushed and her gaze skated away. "Maybe."

He grabbed her waist and pulled her onto his lap, then burrowed his lips in her hair right behind her ear and inhaled deeply as they glided over the smooth water.

"I'll always want the best for you, Daze. I'm not afraid to fight for it." She squirmed into him, and for a moment, he felt like they were Bonnie and Clyde. The strange thought stuck in his head, and he knew, that if he let it, if he didn't have Elena in his life to ground him, things could get very messy and dark for him.

He was the kind of man who went all in. And Daisy had the power to get him to do anything. He would kill for her... if it kept her clean. To avoid her crying like she did in the shower. Axel held his face in the crook of Daisy's neck the entire journey to the mainland. Her sweet feminine scent pushed out the brine in the air and drugged him.

It reminded him of their shower.

It made him dream of more.

A life together. A life with a sister who wasn't dying. A life where the world wasn't falling apart. A life where he could take Daisy to a real baseball game and eat hotdogs that spilled mustard over her shirt. And then he would take her home and clean her up. In the shower. More than once.

He sighed and she patted him.

It was still possible. He hoped for that.

eighteen
DAISY LAZARUS

AS THE BOAT approached the shore of the mainland, Daisy had trouble detaching herself from Axel. His body was warm. He felt safe. Not only had he cuddled her the entire journey, but he muttered all the things he wanted to do with her when this was all over.

Baseball games. Dinners with the family. More showers with her.

So caught up in the lullaby of his voice, she wasn't watching the skipper. She didn't notice him deliberately steer the boat to a sand bank until it was too late, and they were tumbling hard onto the floor. A gunshot cracked through the bay, stopping her heart and her lungs.

Axel?

In a panic, she checked her mate beneath her. Had she shot him? Had one of their weapons misfired? Was he hurt? Panic scorched her veins.

But his hard gaze was locked solidly behind her. His arm was up and aimed, the barrel of his gun smoking. She twisted in time to catch the skipper flopping to the ground. Her own gun in his hand tumbling to the ground.

Daisy scrambled off Axel. "What happened?"

He slid his gaze back to her and got to his feet. "He tried to kill you."

"What? Why?" she breathed. "We were his protection."

Axel's face paled as he, no doubt, registered he'd just killed someone. Daisy bent and searched the skipper. Inside his bag was a pouch filled with uncut diamonds. She shook her head in disbelief.

"So, he was a thief. He lied to us."

When Axel didn't respond, she looked at him. His tanned skin usually full of color now had a greenish hue.

"Hey," she said, squeezing his arm. "You saved my life."

"I know." He nodded, as if trying to convince himself.

It killed Daisy to know he had blood on his hands because of her. His gaze snapped to hers, as if he could read her mind.

"I would do it again," he promised. "I'm not sorry."

"You should leave the dirty work to me."

"Fuck that shit, Daze." He yanked her flush to his chest. "What did I tell you?"

"Together."

"Damn straight. Now let's get out of here before someone sees."

AXEL REMAINED quiet behind Daisy on the drive to Julius's house. They'd hot-wired a motorcycle they found in the dock's parking lot, but she didn't think that was why he didn't speak. She feared the kill was getting to him. Daisy still dreamed about the face of the first man she'd killed. Her palms still itched from the blood.

This would haunt him, regardless of the logic behind it.

She wasn't sure what she expected when they arrived at Julius's old family home—her old home. Maybe she thought it would be like they'd left it. Frozen in time. But the yard was in disarray. Overgrown weeds, grass and plants covered the suburban two-story home. The rest of the street was perfectly manicured, especially the house across the street. Daisy remembered an old couple living there and wondered if they were still alive. The old man used to always wave at them if he was in the yard.

Julius never waved back and soon, Daisy had stopped too.

She cut the engine, climbed off the Yamaha, and strode up the front path with a growing sense of dread. Axel jogged to catch up and caught her hand in his. He gave her a small smile when she glanced at him, surprised. The look he returned said he understood this would be difficult for her.

So many memories. Rarely any of them good.

She squeezed his hand and surveyed the yard. A broken swing on a magnolia tree. Julius hadn't liked her playing on that. She would lie beneath it and watch it sway under the shadows cast by the leaves, and she'd dream about when she and Parker would invite the pigeons.

"I thought it would be looked after," she said, unable to hide the strain in her voice. "I thought maybe if it was, then he could still be using the place."

"He could still be inside," Axel pointed out.

"Maybe." But she wasn't convinced. The place looked deserted.

Hand in hand, they walked to the front porch and kicked the door in. The smell of gas was instant. It watered her eyes.

"Nope." Axel tried to drag her out, but she tugged him back in.

"We have to check."

There was something urging her in, and she couldn't explain it. A gut feeling. An instinct.

"Fuck." Axel gritted out and propped the door open to let air gust in. "I'll see where the leak is coming from."

He moved, but her fingers tightened around his hand. For some reason, she couldn't move. The sight of the house assaulted her. Inside, her childhood remained.

Nothing was out of place.

Unlike the yard, in here it was frozen in time. From the foyer entrance with its fake flower arrangement, to the living room beyond and the leather couches facing each other, a scratch down one almost invisible in the dust of time. Vases and knickknacks on the buffet were also dust ridden. Cobwebs laced between flower stems.

Those couches facing each other.

She vividly remembered the day she arrived. She'd come from a second lab where Julius had put her after the fire. He brought her here to give her a home, he'd said. But she'd sat across from him, looking up at him from the far side of the coffee table separating them, and all she could think was that he was over there, and she was on this side.

Little did she know she would never succeed in crossing that divide. Daisy cleared her throat.

"I'm okay."

Axel glanced down at their joined hands. "Come with me to the kitchen. If the gas is on, I need to turn it off."

She nodded and stayed with him, squeezing his hand. He made short work of checking the stove top, found all gas knobs had been turned on, and promptly switched them off.

"Deliberately switched on," he mumbled. "From the concentration of the smell, it's been on for a while." He shot her a concerned look. "Like someone was waiting for you. We need to be careful. I need to open windows and flush the gas out."

He leaned across and opened the window over the sink, then tried to leave her—she assumed to open more windows. Another nod from her but she felt helpless. Her training went out the window. She didn't want to let go of him.

"We'll go wait outside until it's safe," he suggested, eyes stark. "Together."

She could sense he was concerned.

"I'm okay," she told herself as they walked back to the entrance, intending to leave as he'd suggested, but she stared through to the living room once more and frowned at a clean spot on the buffet. A dark ring in the dust stood out. Odd. "Something's missing."

With her eyes locked on the buffet, she stepped forward and wished she hadn't.

Trip wire.

An explosion ripped through the house, shaking its foundations. Her gift surged outward, protecting them. Two kinetic powers clashed—one natural, one her—causing a second blast of force. They jerked backward and fell. Their hands broke apart. The sense of *despair* suddenly strangled her. She gasped and clutched herself, curling into a ball.

"Daisy." Axel held her up. "We have to get out. The kitchen is on fire. It's spreading. It's a miracle we haven't been fried, but I think you saved us somehow. I saw the explosion come and then hit an invisible wall."

"Ungh." She shook her head, unable to focus on the fire or what she'd inadvertently done. "Something else is wrong. I feel... I feel..."

She tried to focus on the despair. On the bone chilling darkness spreading from her gut. So many... she glanced up, moved around a few steps, and homed in with pins and needles prickling the back of her neck.

"There are people here," she blurted.

Her eyes stung as the fire heated up the house. Flames licked up the walls, propelled by the gas leak. With supernatural speed, it spread throughout the house and try as she might, she had no idea how to repeat what she'd just done to protect them from the blast.

Axel glanced up. "Fuck. I can hear them."

Daisy couldn't move. Her lungs wouldn't work. Her brain stopped. It was stuck in a loop. Fire that had almost killed her as a child. It was happening again. Trapped.

Axel went into business mode. He yanked Daisy's hand hard. The despair winked out with his contact, and she snapped out of her daze.

"But we have to save them," she blurted as she stumbled after him out the front door.

"I'll get them. Wait here. Call your family."

He deposited her on the grass and turned back to the house, searching up and down until they both saw it at once. The tiny attic window. A face peering out of the gloom.

"Max," Daisy breathed, shocked. "They're here. The mates. I can sense multiple types of despair. It must be all of them."

"I need a ladder," Axel said and started jogging around the house.

"Garage," she suggested. "There used to be gardening tools in the garage."

The fire was still contained at the house, so when they arrived at the garage, and broke in, it was safe to enter.

"How can I help?" Daisy followed him. "What if I break the attic window while you get the ladder?"

"No. The fire is spreading fast. I need to vent it first." He searched the dim room covered in disused garden supplies and boxes. "Go call your family."

"But…" She had to do something.

Her family wouldn't get here on time. She wanted to run in and help them… but she couldn't move. Her feet were glued to the floor.

"Daisy," Axel barked. "Get safe and let me do my job."

She blinked. "You're a firefighter."

"I got this." He clapped her on the shoulder and then jogged out

165

of the garage with a ladder under one arm and a crowbar in the other, tossing over his shoulder, "Get me the garden hose."

She jolted into action, went straight to where she remembered the outside faucet to be, but discovered no hose. Damn it. She turned the faucet on, anyway and willed herself to move the water with her mind. All she could manage was spluttering and spraying.

Stupid idea, anyway. God, she was stupid. *Useless.*

She ran back to the front yard and, with her blood slowly freezing in her veins, she watched her mate set up the ladder and climb onto the roof. He shouted through the window not to break the glass until he'd vented the room to avoid a backdraft.

The flames were growing, getting thicker and hotter and louder. Daisy's vision started closing in as she pulled out her cell phone and struggled to breathe. With shaky hands and blinking to see straight, she dialed Parker.

He answered in two rings.

"Daisy." His deep voice was a welcome baritone warming the ice in her veins.

"Pigeon…" she choked.

"What is it?" His tone sharpened. "Where are you? Are you hurt?"

"I'm… I'm okay. It's the house… They're here. They're here."

A pause. "The mates?"

"Yes," she gasped, pacing. "The house is on fire. Axel is trying to get to them in the attic, but… I don't know. The flames are spreading. There was a gas leak… I don't know!"

"Sit tight. We're on our way."

He cut the call and she collapsed into a crouch, steadying her woozy self with fingers on the crisp grass. A loud crash drew her attention back to the house, now billowing with black smoke.

Axel was sliding from the roof top, angling his feet for the ladder. Did it work? Did he find a way to vent?

He must have. He hit the glass window with the crowbar, but it wouldn't break. He tried again and again, then seemed to communicate with whoever was through the window. A desperate look came over him and he glanced down at her, his brows lifting in the middle.

She jogged to the base of the ladder and looked up.

"It's made of something tough," he shouted down, shaking his head.

Memories crashed into Daisy, memories she'd tried to suppress. Hours, days, weeks locked in the attic. It was her prison cell for when she'd failed to complete her training required. It was the place he sent her as punishment. But she'd forgotten about the window. She could always see the sky through it. She wasn't even sure if she had tried to break it and escape. She had nowhere else to go. But he'd always told her she'd never get out.

"Try your gift," Axel suggested.

"I can't even move the water from the tap to the house," she exclaimed, exasperated.

"You can do this," he said down to her. "I'm sure of it."

She shook her head and stepped back.

"Daisy. Look at me." His gaze was hard and steady. Sure. "When we pulled you through the drain with Parker, do you remember that grate? It had been welded shut. I always thought it was a miracle we broke it. I thought maybe it was all Parker and his brute strength, but there was a part of me that wasn't satisfied with that answer. Now I know why. Our bond had triggered then, didn't it?"

She paled but nodded. When her fingers had brushed his through the grate, that's when she'd felt all sense of despair dissipate from her gut.

"Are you saying I helped move that grate with my gift?"

"Yes." He turned back to the window to address them inside. "Step back. The glass is going to break."

Then he slid down the ladder like a pro, his boots hitting the ground with a thud.

"Now, Daze." He faced her toward the window. "Focus on the window. Break it. Same thing you did for the grate. Deep breath. *Go.*"

There was something about Axel's confidence. Something about the way he believed in her. It clicked another broken piece into place. She sharpened her stare on the window, glared, and then pushed her awareness outward. Like a fumbling child first learning to walk, she felt her mind grasp at the solid surface. An invisible hand in her control... but harder, more lethal. She tested the window, felt herself slide into the minuscule cracks, and then pushed everything she had into those tiny spaces with a scream of effort.

Every cell in her body swelled. But she kept pushing with that gift, kept swelling until the dam broke. The glass shattered and blew off the frame.

Axel used his body to shelter her from shards falling on them like acid rain. The instant the glass settled, he was back up the ladder, his body moving before her mind had caught up.

Something warm trickled down from Daisy's nostril. When she wiped it, her hand came back smeared with blood. Dizziness swarmed her mind and her vision blurred but she took a few deep breaths and reined herself in.

A cloth was thrown over the broken windowsill. A hand emerged, then a head of dirty brown, wavy hair.

Lilo.

IT TOOK mere minutes for Axel to extricate everyone locked in the attic and help them down to the yard across the street. Daisy, who'd been pale and stilted throughout the fire had woken up the moment Lilo climbed out the window.

She'd helped the pregnant woman down with care, murmuring softly into her ear, no doubt telling her about the family being on the way.

Except Lilo's husband, Axel realized. Griffin was locked away in a cell, blacked out and beholden to the whims of his sin.

Joe, Liza's mate, was the last through the window with Max climbing out just before him. By the time they all got down and safe, Daisy had enlisted a neighbor to help supply cups of water and blankets to the distraught victims. The elderly couple who owned the house directly opposite were more than happy to help.

The mates were dehydrated, hungry, tired, and all shell shocked. But as far as Axel could see, they were in one piece and uninjured.

Axel kept away other neighbors wanting to help put out the fire. "Leave it to the professionals," he said.

This was the biggest mistake he saw in his job. Civilians thought they could put out fires with garden hoses or buckets. They forgot about the gas lines running through the walls. There had already been one explosion. All it took was for another to turn them all to cinders.

There were things he could do, but he knew that the moment he turned his back, someone would try to jump in and help him. It wasn't worth it to save a house. Especially one Daisy had such bad memories in.

He stood behind the white picket fence in the elderly neighbors' yard, watching the fire glow and crackle from a safe distance. Others watched from their property lines and gossiped amongst themselves, but for the most of it, they'd heeded his warning not to get close.

They'd been so lucky. If he'd not opened the kitchen window and left the front door open… if Daisy hadn't been able to shield them with her gift…

Daisy came to stand with him, but then Misha, the blond woman with curly hair launched into her, wrapping her in a tight embrace.

"Thank you," Misha, cried. "I knew you would find us. I *knew* it."

Max, the tall, tanned Australian owner of Nightingale Securities walked over to Axel. Joe, the only other male there was FBI. Axel hadn't officially met any of them so he introduced himself.

"I'm Axel," he said, holding out his hand. "Daisy's mate."

Joe's thick Italian brows lifted. He shared a look with Max who immediately narrowed his eyes at Axel. They both shook Axel's hand when a brown-skinned woman with fiery eyes stuck out her hand to him, too.

"I'm Bailey," she said. "Tony's mate. Is he… are they all okay?"

"They're okay except…" His voice trailed off and he couldn't help looking to where Daisy tossed a blanket over Lilo's shoulder and handed her a cup. Dr. Grace Go, Evan's mate directed the water to those who needed it most. She had dark circles and sallow skin herself but must have been keeping tabs on the health status of her fellow prisoners. She must be a good doctor if she continued to put the needs of others before herself.

Bailey gasped, "Griff? He's not…"

Axel's gaze snapped back to her and the men. "He's alive and uninjured. He's just not himself." He lowered his voice, not wanting to alarm Lilo. "He's been locked up because they can't control him. He's gone dark."

"Liza?" Joe clipped.

"Sloan?" Max added.

"They're both fine. They should be on their way here."

Fine wasn't exactly the right word, but again, he didn't want to worry any of them. He also didn't think it was his place to announce the inner workings of the Deadly Seven. He made his excuse and went to Daisy.

"Do you need anything from me?" he asked. "Has someone called the fire department?"

Grateful violet eyes washed over him. It was enough for him to see she felt adrift. She glanced at an elderly couple keeping their distance on the front porch.

"I told them to call," she muttered, "but they seem a bit skittish."

He touched her shoulder and said with a calm tone, "I'll sort it out. You keep updating these guys on what's been happening. They want news and I don't want to alarm them." He paused. "I told Joe, Max, and Bailey about Griff."

She sighed. "Okay. I'll break it to Lilo."

Axel walked up the porch steps to the elderly couple.

"Hi, folks," he said. "My name is Axel. I'm with the CCFD. I'm off duty, though. We need to call the local department about the fire."

"It's done," said the man, scratching his long beard. "Are they okay? What happened?"

The old lady's eyes narrowed. "I always knew there was something off about that man over the road. He didn't treat that girl right. No sir."

"And the state of that yard?" The man shook his head.

"Thank you for your help and hospitality," Axel said. "We'll be out of your hair as soon as we can." Sirens in the distance carried. "Looks like the locals are here. They'll put the fire out, but until then, it's best you stay safe here on the porch."

They nodded to him.

"You need anything else? Food?" the woman asked.

A cell phone rang from somewhere. Axel frowned and scanned the yard to see Daisy pull hers out and answer. He turned back to the couple and answered their question. "I'll let you know. Thank you again."

"Suppose we're lucky we ain't so bad as the city folk right now."

"Mm," his wife agreed.

They continued talking quietly amongst themselves as Axel jogged down the steps to Daisy's side, tensing as he passed Lilo with her face buried in her hands sobbing and Grace and Misha trying to console her. Daisy must have told her about the state of her husband.

"They're all alive and fairly well," Daisy said into the handset. "I'll put her on."

Daisy held the cell out to Misha. "It's Wyatt."

Misha shot a guilty look at Lilo, but then the moment she put the handset to her ear she burst into tears. Daisy spoke up so everyone could hear.

"They couldn't track down a helicopter, but their boat has landed on the mainland. They should be here in fifteen."

"Do you think that's wise?" Joe said, folding his arms. "I mean, all of us in one place at the same time. It can't be a coincidence the house set on fire the moment you arrived."

"How did you know we were here?" Bailey asked.

"Daisy had a feeling," Axel answered.

"A feeling." Max's brow went up.

Axel could see the suspicion in his eyes and shut it down immediately. "She used to live here. Her suspicion had nothing to do with you all. It was sheer luck that we happened across you. Your family has been searching night and day for you, and with the city bridges blown—"

"All of them?" gasped Bailey.

He nodded. "Every access into the city has been destroyed. Replicates have been deployed. Faithful still loyal to the Syndicate are wreaking havoc."

"And you," Joe said, turning the full force of his gaze on Axel. The intimidation in his stance would set criminals weak at the knees. "Who exactly are you?" He glanced between Daisy and Axel. "It seems like you two are comfortable with each other. More than I would expect after meeting only days ago... I'm assuming."

Axel fidgeted under the scrutiny.

"You assume right. I was one of the Faithful—"

"*Was* being the operative word," Daisy interrupted and glared as she came to stand by his side.

No matter who they were, what they meant to her siblings, she was with Axel. He put his arm around her shoulder. And he was with her.

The fire department and police arrived at the same time as the Lazarus family. Cars, trucks and motorcycles filled the small street, giving the neighbors something else to gossip about. Before a black SUV rolled to a stop, the door opened and out ran Sloan. She quickly gathered her footing and went straight for her husband, almost bowling him over with the force of her hug.

Axel and Daisy stood aside as the rest of the family arrived, all coming from various vehicles. They'd taken the journey across the river. He searched for Elena, just in case, but was glad to see her missing. As were Flint, Mary, and possibly Alice. With any luck, they were back at Lazarus House, keeping an eye on the extended family staying there.

Tony, looking gaunt and tired, found Bailey and studiously checked her for injury before slamming his lips on hers. Evan was by Grace's side in an instant, pulling her into his tattooed arms. Joe and Liza embraced. Tears burned the back of Axel's eyes at the emotional scene, and he cleared his throat.

He bent to kiss Daisy on the head and mumbled, "You did this, Daze. You brought them home safe."

He didn't say it to give Daisy public recognition, but Parker heard from where he'd stood next to Lilo. He murmured some words to her before locating Daisy. In quick strides he was with them, towering high with his face stern.

"He's right, Daisy," Parker said. "You did what none of us could do."

Despite the sound of the fire department deploying their men and equipment, his booming voice carried over the yard. Enough to make every person pause and face Daisy as the weight of Parker's words settled.

"It was luck," she blurted.

Aw, hell no. She wasn't going to palm this off as luck. "Maybe us getting here," Axel said. "But not us getting them out." He met Parker's eyes. "We couldn't open the attic window. It was some kind of bulletproof material—"

"Ballistic glass," Parker said. "For an attic?"

"Your father used to lock Daisy up there when she was younger."

"Oh, Daisy…" Liza's hand flew to her mouth.

Daisy's gaze turned downcast, so Axel tightened his hold around her shoulders.

"The point is," Axel continued, "that when we failed to get in, when the building was burning down around them, she used her gift to get them out. Even though it made her nose bleed."

Daisy coughed and refused to meet anyone's eyes.

"Yeah, I noticed the bloody nose," he said to her, voice low. "You endangered your health for these people."

"For family," Parker corrected, his voice tight. He stared at Daisy long and hard, and then he wrapped his big arms around her smaller form and squeezed her tight.

Axel stepped back as Liza rushed in, then Tony, then Wyatt, Evan, and Sloan. Lilo tossed her blanket off and joined them. With her acceptance, every single other member of the Lazarus brood joined the group hug. Axel lost sight of Daisy's white hair as she was swallowed whole by love, and her childhood prison burned behind them.

DAISY HAD a surreal out of body experience. From the big family group hug to the way she was included in conversation on the journey back into Cardinal City, to the responsibility she was given as bodyguard to Lilo on the boat ride and consequent car ride home.

This love, this acceptance, it felt too good to be true.

She was still floating on this cloud when she returned with Axel to Mary and Flint's apartment to check on Elena. He was covered in soot and sweat like her, but he insisted on touching base with his sister first.

The moment they entered the apartment, they knew something was wrong. Mary's face remained hard, even when Misha ran in to reunite with her baby. The joyous occasion, seeing Amari squeal and kick her baby legs, should have brought a smile to anyone's eyes.

But not Mary.

And when her gaze landed on Axel, Daisy knew why. Something was wrong with Elena. In what felt like slow motion, Axel's hand slipped from hers as he came to the same conclusion. His face paled. His expression dropped.

"She didn't wake up," Mary explained quietly.

"She's dead?" he blurted.

"Coma."

Axel's breath started coming in hard and fast. His broad chest heaved. He swallowed. "Where is she?"

Without a second glance at Daisy, he rushed down the hall to the bedroom Elena occupied and disappeared into a room.

"What happened?" Daisy breathed to Mary.

"I don't know, *mija*," she replied. This time, the term of endearment didn't feel wrong. Mary's eyes were bleak and full of pain. "Elena said she was tired and went to have a nap, but when she didn't come out for a meal, Alek went in to see if she was okay. He couldn't rouse her."

"How long ago?"

"Maybe three hours."

"A doctor?"

"We can't get one in."

Shit. "Grace?"

Mary nodded. "Flint is asking Evan to pass on the message. I think Grace is down to check on Griffin with Lilo, and then she said she would be up."

Daisy shook her head. "Grace needs to rest at some point too."

Mary's sharp eyes studied Daisy. "And you. I see the blood in your nostril. What happened?"

Daisy wiped her nose again, but no more blood came out. She considered changing the subject but instead blurted everything out. Mary had a way about her that, at the start, Daisy had seen as overpowering, but now associated it as coming from a true place of concern. When she was done with her story, Mary's gaze softened and she trailed her fingers down Daisy's ponytail, brushing the strands as she made them settle over Daisy's shoulder.

"You did it, *mija*. Just like I knew you would. You're becoming the leader this family needs."

"I don't understand."

"You followed your instincts. You didn't leave the house, even when Axel wanted you to."

"It wasn't like he knew at the time. And as soon as he found out, he was the one who took the lead rescuing them. Without him, I'd have failed."

"Your mates are very important," she said, nodding. "They're imperative to your survival, both mental and physical."

Daisy's chest constricted and she glanced down the hallway Axel had gone. She took a step and then stopped.

"Should I—" Daisy met Mary's eyes, not knowing what to do.

Mary lifted her chin stoically. "Tell him Grace is on her way."

"And then what?"

"Then be there for him. Do what you do best." At Daisy's questioning brow, Mary tapped Daisy on the sternum. "Listen to this and you'll never steer wrong."

DAISY ENTERED Elena's room on quiet feet. In the dark, Axel hunched in a chair, his head in his hands. Elena was lying face up, her lips parted, her breath coming with long gaps between. It smelled like death. Sour. Stale. Old.

"I'm sorry," Daisy whispered and touched Axel's shoulder.

He shrugged her off with a frown and refused to meet her gaze. Daisy's stomach dropped. She went cold. This was her fault. He didn't say it, but he thought it. Why else would he flinch away from her?

Her throat thickened and burned at the back.

She didn't know what to do.

Axel had quit his job so he could spend time with Elena. He'd joined the Faithful hoping to give her a second chance at life. The brave face he'd put on, the eternal hope and optimism he'd had at the time their bond triggered was nothing but water under the bridge. Gone.

Before she could say anything else, Grace, followed by Evan, rushed into the room. She looked like she hadn't had a moment's peace since they'd rescued her. But she didn't complain. She was a star. Evan watched his mate caring for Elena with pride in his eyes.

If Axel didn't want Daisy's compassion, then she shouldn't be there. This was a private moment for him and she was intruding. Feeling a numbness take over, she stumbled out of the room and into the empty kitchen and living room. Where it had previously been full of people, it was now empty. Misha's family must be with her in Wyatt's apartment. Mary and Flint were probably reuniting with the other siblings or checking on Griffin.

Daisy glanced back at the hallway, hesitating, wondering if maybe she should go in anyway, but then chickened out. He didn't want her there, and if Elena died, he would blame Daisy.

It's what Daisy would do.

It's what she *had* done.

She'd blamed Mary for something out of her control. Mary had been in Axel's shoes. Of course she'd wanted to save Daisy, but she also had grave responsibilities. Mary had to save the world, not just the other Lazarus siblings. No one intentionally left Daisy there. It wasn't personal.

Just like Elena's situation. It was dumb, bad luck.

How they responded now was what mattered.

Daisy walked toward the exit but promised herself she wouldn't be long. Axel needed her. She would be back.

twenty-one

DAISY LAZARUS

DAISY FOUND MOST of the family in the basement at the door to Griffin's cell. Lilo, straight from her captivity and still wearing dirty clothes, had her palm on the door. She spoke into a microphone connected to the cell while everyone else looked on from various positions around the nearby rooms.

Lilo rested one hand on her swollen belly, the other stroked the door, as if she could soothe Griffin though the thick concrete and whatever else Parker had built the room from.

Daisy knew what Griffin would look like. His veins would be popping in his forehead. His gaze would be dark. He'd be the bull about to charge.

"There's too many of you," Daisy said quickly, making sure she kept her distance. "I'm assuming you want Lilo's presence to calm him. She can't touch him, so it's unlikely she can block out the sin he's feeling. The further we all stand back, the better Lilo's proximity will work to bring him back."

The spectators nodded, seeing the truth in Daisy's words. And she would know. She was part of the experiments on how to turn them all dark.

"Griff, honey, I'm back. I'm safe. The baby is safe. You can stop worrying now." Lilo's voice tightened. "Come back to us."

She continued to speak to her husband as they all gathered further down the hallway and spilled into the operations room. It might not be far enough, but it was better than standing right next to the cell.

Just like upstairs in Mary's apartment, Daisy felt like an intruder. A voyeur. On the outside looking in. She wanted to feel more connected to the man inside the cell, but the truth was she barely remembered him. Just like Sloan and Evan, Griffin was one of the younger ones. But she wanted the chance to get to know him. She wanted to get to know them all.

"He's going to be okay," Parker said, coming up to her side. "It might take some time, but he'll get there."

"What if he doesn't switch back?" she whispered, not wanting her voice to carry and alarm Lilo.

"He will."

"How can you be so sure?"

His brow arched, and she couldn't hold in her amusement at his classic reaction. Her brother. Pigeon. The most arrogant man on the planet, but also the smartest she'd ever known.

"What about you," Parker said. "Are you good?"

She snorted. "Good is a gray area."

"Yes, it is. But I was talking about your gift."

"I should probably train," she mumbled reluctantly.

"Any time you're ready."

"Now?" she asked hopefully.

He glanced at his fiancée standing closest to Lilo at the edge of the operations room—looking down the hallway. The burden on Alice was to eliminate Daisy and her siblings if they went dark… and couldn't be saved. But for some reason, they allowed her here.

Hope battled despair in the room. Daisy felt it in her gut. From her siblings standing by in the operations room, to Mary and Flint in the hallway closer to the cell. The grimy fingers of her sin weighed down the tingling butterflies of hope. She'd never felt such a unified collection of belief other than in this moment, and she didn't want to be the one to burst their bubble.

Griffin may never come back from the brink.

Like Parker, Alice was full of confidence, but where he outwardly professed his, she remained humble. Alice flicked her gaze Parker's way and gave him a small smile. That was all Parker needed to decide.

"Let's do this now," he said to her.

"Actually," Daisy said. "Can you give me ten? I just want to check in on Axel and Elena."

"Proud of you, Daisy." He flashed her a toothy grin. "You've come a long way."

Her cheeks heated at the praise, and she scowled, to which his grin widened.

"Be prepared for a walloping," he teased.

She scoffed. "By a pigeon?"

Her nickname riled him, just like she knew it would. His smile dropped and he said, "Ten minutes."

Daisy was still smiling as she entered her apartment and collected as many potted plants as she could carry before returning to Mary's and Flint's. Axel was in the same spot as she'd left him, hunched over with his head in his hands.

Grace and Evan were gone, but had left fluids on an IV drip feeding into Elena's arm.

Daisy placed the plants about the room and then gathered Axel something to eat from the kitchen. She put the food plate on the bedside furniture, and then borrowed some of Flint's clothes and put them next to the food.

"I'm going to be in the training room," she said quietly. "If you need me, just ask AIMI and I'll be right up." She hesitated when he lifted his pained gaze to her. "Try to have something to eat. If you need a shower, my place is yours. I left some clothes."

When he didn't respond, she returned to the basement. It was fine. He needed some time. This would be hard for anyone.

Parker waited for Daisy on the exercise mat. He'd taken off his shirt and wore simple basketball shorts. His bionic arm glimmered under the halogen lights as he grazed metal fingers across the array of weapons on a rack behind the mat. But he didn't pick any.

He turned her way and gave her outfit a disapproving onceover. "Jeans?"

She shrugged and removed her jacket. "Doesn't matter what I wear. The Falcon will eat the Pigeon."

Parker scoffed. "You sound like an old martial arts movie."

"I watched a lot of them at Julius's house." She went to a side wall where a low, long bench stretched, and placed her jacket down. She toed off her boots and peeled off her socks, and then retied her long ponytail. The weight of Parker's attention followed her every action, and she knew he wanted to ask questions, but held them back. Now wasn't the time to worry about hurt feelings.

"What do you want to know?" she asked without facing him.

Instead, she padded over to a wall plastered with charcoal sketches. They must be Evan's prophetic art. Parker sidled up to her, his brow puckered as he also scanned the pieces. He gave a breathy grunt as he folded his arms.

"He's drawn so much over the years," he said. "After we learned he'd dreamed about my retirement party and didn't realize it, we thought all his art should be public so we can all study it. If you see anything familiar, let me know."

"Like this?" She pointed at the note she'd pinned to Max's chest when she left him in the municipal district with a bomb strapped to his chest.

"That's actually the note you wrote," he pointed out.

"Oh. It is?" She couldn't remember much of the past few years. It all felt like a blur of despair, angst, and confusion. It made her sick in the stomach to think about. She refocused on the note and recognized her handwriting. *The answer is in your blood.* That's right. Julius had not only tasked Daisy to strap the bomb to Max, but he injected Max with poison despite Daisy's protests. She didn't like that and rebelled by writing this note. It might have been her first rebellion against Julius.

Through her scrawled clue, her siblings had deciphered the cure for his blood poisoning. As a mate, Max could accept Sloan's blood via transfusion. Her advanced regeneration capabilities temporarily transferred to Max, helping counter the poison's effect.

This healing process only worked between mates, and of course, one way.

Apparently, their maker had built this failsafe into their DNA, so they weren't used in the future as some kind of regeneration cash cow to end world disease.

Didn't stop Julius trying though. Daisy had lost count of the number of times she'd had her blood extracted.

Parker caught her distasteful expression and directed her attention elsewhere. "When you get time, check these other sketches. Let us know if you recognize any faces or places."

"I'll take a look."

"Good. Let's get moving."

Daisy joined her brother on the exercise mat and shook out her hands. Just outside the room, she glimpsed some of the family gathered around Griffin's cell. They'd inched back closer.

She returned her focus to Parker. To say the experience was weird was an understatement. Somehow, even after eight years of living in a lab, being told they were going to be warriors against sin, she'd never believed it. She'd spent her days wistfully imagining flying away, playing pretend, and singing songs. She'd been living a dream, even in the cold, small four corners of that room.

Decades had passed.

Her old stubborn brother who was too serious then was now a hulking brute—still too serious. She smirked at him. A twinkle entered his golden eyes, so much like a lion's that she sometimes forgot he wasn't one.

"What?" He squinted.

"Nothing. It's just... you and me. We've come so far yet, some would say, we haven't changed at all."

"Oh, we've changed." He flexed his metal hand and Daisy immediately thought of the tight scars down one side of her face.

"I thought so too," she mumbled. "But... seeing you all, getting to know you again, it feels like..."

She shrugged, unable to come up with the right words.

"Feels right," he offered.

Their eyes locked and she gave a short nod. "Feels right, but still distant."

"Master Yoshi always said, fall seven times, stand up eight." He strode to the weapon's rack and removed a short shuriken throwing star. He tossed it and caught it. "Keep getting up, Daisy. Eventually you won't fall."

"But what if you're pushed?"

"It matters not how you hit the floor, but what you do after. Who knows, maybe you'll even fly." He winked.

"Were you always this obnoxious?"

"You would know." He held out his palm. "Now, take this from my hand without moving an inch."

She gestured at his torso. "And you needed no shirt for this activity."

"I thought we would spar. I changed my mind."

"Sure." Daisy glanced outside the door to where Alice stood in the hallway leading to the cell. "The fact your fiancée is watching has nothing to do with it."

Her brother's cheeks turned a brighter shade of pink. His mouth opened, closed, opened again. Then he huffed and put his shirt back on and shot her an *Are you satisfied* look.

"You were right," she pointed out dryly. "I would know. Nothing's changed in decades. You're still the same grandstanding show pony you always were."

The lion peeked out of Parker's eyes and Daisy thought she might have taken it too far, and then he scowled knowingly.

"And you're still trying to use your wit as a distraction." He waggled his finger at her. "I've got your number. Always did. You hated doing the chores and would pick a fight. Being the biggest, I was blamed. For every cuddle you gave, you also had a devious sneak attack."

She tried to hide her smile but failed miserably.

"Okay. Enough horsing around. Do the hard work, Daisy. Move the shuriken."

"I don't know how." She tossed up her hands and rolled her eyes. There. He had the ugly truth out of her. "I learned by trial and error. I learned by watching martial arts movies. Occasionally I learned with a teacher. But for the most part, Julius tossed me in the deep and told me to not die."

"Well," he said stoically. "Now you have us."

His words settled on her like a warm blanket. He motioned for her to sit cross legged facing him on the mat. He placed the metal throwing star between them and said, "Let's start with basic meditation techniques."

"Seriously?"

"As a heart attack."

And he was. For the next fifteen minutes, Parker guided Daisy through various exercises designed to give her an acute awareness of her body. From her breath to her heart rate to the level of activity in her mind. It was a crash course, but she got the hang of it fast. Her busy mind calmed.

"Now," he said, voice low and slow. A rumble close to a purr. "Keeping your eyes closed, I want you to remember back to a time you accessed your gift."

She exhaled and conjured the time she'd stopped the baseball mere inches from her face.

"Think about how you felt intrinsically at that moment," Parker continued. "Think about the sensations in your arms, legs, heart."

Her brow puckered. All she remembered was Axel's smile. She shook her head and thought to another time she'd accessed her gift. The shower—*nope*. Not that one. All she could think of was his body. His slippery—*nope*. Start again. The attic window. She exhaled. Now all she could think of was Axel's calming voice, encouraging her.

"I can't." She opened her eyes, frowning. "All I can think of is Axel. I'm worried about him."

And maybe a little in love with him. That she could feel love at all was a miracle, and probably wholly due to her family's unyielding love for her.

"Is his sister okay?"

Daisy shrugged. "She's sick. Probably dying. And instead of spending her last hours together, he was with me."

Parker stared at her, long and hard. "He was with you through his own choice. And he was doing good things. There are a lot of people relying on us right now. Not just one."

She gave another half lift of her shoulder.

"He won't fault you for that."

He already has, she wanted to say but didn't want Parker's pity.

"All right. Back to work," Parker clipped, adjusting himself in his sitting position. "Tell me in detail about the times you accessed your gift."

She bit her lip. Definitely wasn't going to share the shower scene, but she spilled about the others. She told him how Axel suspected her of helping push the grate out. How she fit her awareness into the gaps between the attic window and then added more. How it felt like she was going to explode herself from the effort. By the time she was done, he scrutinized her with such curiosity that she felt on display in a museum.

"What are you thinking?" she asked.

He rubbed his bearded chin. "I'm thinking you have some kind of connection to the molecular space between atoms." He rattled off some other scientific explanation about quarks and neurons and photons that she couldn't quite grasp until he said, "… and of course, the way matter moves is through exacting a force on it so if you wanted to expand the space between atoms, you'd be doing exactly that."

Aaand… he lost her again.

"I don't understand how that's supposed to help me control my gift," she said.

He gave an indignant raise of his brows. "Unless you've studied quantum physics, it won't."

"Right. Well, you'll have to excuse me. I didn't have the opportunity."

Parker had the grace to look ashamed. "I guess I was just thinking aloud. From what I gather, with your gift, if you want something to come to you, contract the space between atoms. You want to exert force, you expand it." His eyes lit up as his thoughts turned inward again. "The possibilities are remarkable, really. Anything from explosions to implosions to theorized access to alternate dimensions."

"What kind of animal is my gift from?" she asked agape, because Gloria had taken DNA from creatures all over the world to give her siblings gifts.

"That's the thing," Parker answered, his eyes narrowed. "There was nothing in Gloria's research. To be honest, I half disbelieved you would gain any gift until you did. Like I said, Gloria started with perfect. Something so perfect she refused to replicate it in any of us."

And Daisy couldn't bring herself to reveal the fact she could sense hope and joy. "I'm far from perfect, Pigeon."

"Aren't we all?" He gave a wry smile, then tapped the shuriken. "Try thinking on that differently. Remember how you expanded the space between the atoms at the window, so for this, don't think of the object but the space between you and it."

Daisy returned her focus to the throwing star. Okay... not the star. The space between. She let her focus glaze over a little and shifted it to the side. To the front. And back. Immediately a feeling of connection grew within her body. It thrummed along her skin like electricity... only it didn't spark. It wended and rolled. It pulsed. She drew some of it in instead of pushing it out, and lo and behold, the shuriken wobbled. As did the fabric on Parker's clothes. And his hair.

"Um..." His lips pursed. "Try and focus more tightly. Like a tunnel."

Daisy huffed. She'd always hated exercises Julius would make her complete. But she knew she couldn't skip this part. So she tried time and time again until her head started to hurt and the shuriken slid an inch toward her on the mat.

"Good work, Daisy," Parker praised. Then he gestured at her nose with a frown. "You've got a little—"

She wiped her nose. Blood came away. Again. "It's nothing."

"You're tired," he conceded. "Using your mind like this is taxing, and you're still recovering. It will get easier the more you practice."

"Great." Sarcasm dripped off her tone. She was a little miffed people kept telling her to rest when she just wanted to be useful.

Raised voices drew their attention to Griffin's cell. Daisy and Parker walked closer to the workout room's door so they could get a better view. The cell door was opening. *Shit.* Parker opened his mouth as though about to stop them. He hadn't given permission. But the cell door swung wide and slammed back against the wall. Lilo jumped back. But only for a step, and then she rushed forward... into Griffin's arms.

Daisy wasn't the only one teary as they watched the lovers embrace like someone would pull them apart. They couldn't get close enough. Tight enough. He clawed at her and buried his face deep in her neck.

Alice's hand covered her mouth. Her eyes glistened. Mary and Flint hugged. Elation inflated the atmosphere and all around, even from her older stoic brother, tears flowed. Parker grabbed Daisy roughly and dragged her into his arms, suffocating her with his big frame as he pulled her into an all-consuming bear hug.

The smile on her lips stuttered. This felt too good to be true. They both looked over at the reunited couple. Griffin pulled away from

Lilo as she said something. He placed his palm on her swollen belly. They faced Daisy. Griffin's expression dropped. They locked eyes. And then he charged toward Daisy.

She tensed.

Oh, fuck.

He came at her like a bull, and she prepared for the horns, but he took her shoulders and slammed her to his front. Griffin, the baby brother she hardly knew, hugged her like she was a lifeline.

"Thank you," he choked out through sobs. "Thank you for bringing them back to me."

Them. Meaning mother and unborn child.

Daisy blinked rapidly. She caught Parker's gaze from their side. Nothing but relief shone back at her. It came from all of them and especially Lilo. Astounded eyes watched on as the man who hated to touch choked back tears and heaved breaths while he squeezed Daisy in his arms.

The fire of acceptance started slow. From the base of her feet to the center of her warming heart until the kindling of familial love erupted. Like an explosion, Daisy's arms wrapped around him. She hugged back.

Eventually Griffin pulled back. Red rimmed eyes crinkled at her. He grabbed her at the base of her skull and held his forehead to hers. Just a small moment. A touch. A thank you and a goodbye.

A reminder that she was on the outside looking in no more.

She was one of them.

Connected.

But as they walked away, as Daisy and Parker followed them all out of the basement, she couldn't help thinking all this happiness was from a stroke of luck. Luck that she'd gone to her childhood home on instinct. Luck that Julius wasn't there. Luck that she'd been able to access her gift and control it enough to make a difference.

One thing worried her the more she thought about it. If Julius had left them at the house, set a trap for them, then where was he?

They might have escaped this trap, but there would be more. And the next one, they might not have luck on their side. So, she'd better start making some of her own.

twenty-two

AXEL ALVARES

"AXEL?" Someone shook his shoulders. "Axel you should get some rest in a proper bed."

He peeled his eyes open to the dark room where Elena slept. Realizing he'd dozed off in the chair, he straightened to check on her, but she was as before. Asleep. Still barely alive.

"Grace has gone to the hospital for supplies," Mary said softly behind him. He craned his neck to meet her eyes as she continued. "She suggested you get some proper rest."

"I am resting here. Thank you." He stubbornly turned back to his vigil over his sister, silently wishing there was something he could do other than pray.

It wasn't like any god would listen to him, anyway. Certainly not the big guy upstairs with Axel's track record.

Evidence of Daisy's compassion surrounded him: potted plants; fresh clothes; food. He'd scowled at her like it was her fault. He'd pushed her away, and she'd still done these acts of kindness. He was a coward for taking his anger out on her.

"I can't go anywhere," he rasped, his feet frozen to the floor. "Elena needs me."

Mary's steady hand rested on his shoulder. He squeezed his eyes shut against the familiarity of it. His mother used to do the same thing as she watched over him while he studied.

His stomach knotted.

When Elena died, he'd have nothing of his family but memories growing cold and distant.

"Grace said Elena could be like this for days," Mary explained. "Weeks, even. There's also the slight possibility she might wake up. You don't want her to see you like this."

Axel tried to hide his snort of derision as he glanced down at the state of his dirty clothes. They both knew no one slipped into a coma unless they were near the end. He watched Elena breathe for a while. It had seemed to even out.

Elena stirred and mumbled something.

"I'm here, baby sister," he said, heart skipping a beat.

Her eyes fluttered open.

"Hey..." She seemed to gather her bearings, and almost went back to sleep but frowned and reached for him. "We were wrong. The end of the world can't wait. It's okay. Go be the hero without me... tying you down."

Her last words were almost inaudible. But he'd caught them. And hated them. He refused to acknowledge them and held her hand for a long moment. Her breathing had become labored from the effort of talking, but now smoothed out. Despite her words, he hoped the doc had been right. Why else would Elena have awoken? If this truly was the end for her, she'd have stayed asleep. Right?

Still... he stayed for another few minutes in case she had another burst of energy.

Maybe she was a little better, he supposed. A doctor would know more than him.

He could do with a shower. He checked the sky through the window. It was completely dark now. He glanced at the stoic older woman still behind him. Did she ever sleep?

Probably not. She had a family of powered vigilantes to worry about.

Daisy had left him clothes and a plate of food. His brows lifted. He could have sworn that meal was different before.

"Daisy returned while you were sleeping," Mary explained. "She replaced the cold meal with sandwiches and put cello wrap over the top."

Axel scrubbed his hand down his face, noting his stubble was long and rough. "I was rude to her."

"She doesn't think so."

He frowned. "She doesn't?"

Mary's voice softened. "She knows you're hurt."

"Still… there's no excuse for taking it out on the ones you love."

"So go and tell her that. She's in the basement practicing her gift. Been there for hours. You should tell her to get some rest. She's pushing herself too far, but she won't listen to me."

"She listens more than you know." He sighed and stood. "I'll grab a shower first, if that's okay."

"Be my guest. Bathroom is down the hall and on the left."

At her words, Axel softened. "You've been so welcoming to us. I can't thank you enough."

Something flickered in Mary's eyes, something that looked a lot like sadness, and she said, "Knowing you will be in Daisy's life is enough. Now, I've charged your cell phone. I'll call you if there's any change with Elena."

BY THE TIME Axel showered and found his way down to the basement, he'd riled himself up into a tizzy. He hated not being able to do anything for Elena. His whole life he was a go-getter. Proactive. That was how he'd ended up as a Faithful. It was a path through the blockade of Elena's illness. It was why he'd joined the CCFD. He'd hated being told he had to stand on the sidelines and watch a house burn.

He couldn't give up now. Daisy certainly wasn't.

The moment Axel entered the basement, he smelled her, and the longing in his chest tugged him on an invisible line to the training room. She sat cross-legged at the center of the exercise mat, silver hair spilling down her back.

During the shower, he made all these plans on how he would apologize. How he would grovel at her feet and beg for forgiveness. But the mere sight of her triggered a need so strong it burst out of his skin.

Axel went straight for her. Didn't say hello. Didn't say anything. He just got on his knees and pushed her to the floor. He covered her body with his.

God, hugging her felt so good.

Her embrace forgave all. His throat thickened and he nuzzled the space where her jaw ended and her ear began.

Inhale.

Sigh.

That's all they did—laid together on the rubber mat and hugged. Her legs entwined with his. Their arms wrapped around each other. She'd showered too. Her sweet feminine shampoo curled over him like petals of an exotic flower blooming.

"I'm sorry," he mumbled.

"It's okay," she replied. "I get it."

He pulled back, needing to look into her violet eyes and feel peace. But when he saw her face, alarm prickled through him. He wiped a trickle of blood from beneath her nose.

"Daisy…" He could hardly breathe. She was bleeding again. The horror of it brought him back to the times Elena or his parents had nosebleeds from their illness.

Shame washed over her. She quickly went to the bench against the wall where she'd left a towel.

"It's nothing," she said, wiping her nose.

He rested his elbow on his knee, praying to keep himself from overreacting. "It's not nothing. That happened at the house after you used your gift."

She lifted a bottle of water to her lips and drank deeply before answering. "I've been practicing. Parker said it would get better over time."

"Yes, over time, Daze," he chided and went to her. He looked deep into her eyes so she could see the concern in his. "You're still recovering from all the loss of spinal fluid, falling off a damned train, and… the other things Julius did to you."

He didn't even want to think about those purple scars on her stomach—what she had nightmares about. The extraordinary will of his mate hit him squarely in the chest. She was a survivor. Not just that, a flourisher. When she was with the Syndicate, she was a woman who moved like a robot, just going through the motions. Now that she'd found her tribe, her family, she made herself bleed because she wanted to help.

"That's the thing. We don't have time, Axel." She shook her head and raised her eyes to the ceiling. "Apparently the Mayor is announcing a State of Emergency. He's asked for the National Guard, but no one is coming. Cardinal City is being ignored by the big brass.

That means things are about to get shitty here if Julius unleashes more replicates... and—" she shot him wary eyes. "He had a hellova lot of them made."

"You've done everything you can," he insisted. "You don't know where they are. You don't know where Julius is. All we can do is wait and deal with the fallout when it comes."

"I hate waiting."

His tone quietened. "Me too."

"How is Elena?" she asked.

"She's breathing a little better. She woke to scold me and then fell back asleep." He frowned. Swallowed. "I hate not being able to help her. If it's something I can see and touch, I can fix it. But this illness? It's taken my entire family from me... and I can't..." He locked onto where the smudge of blood had been beneath her nose and shook his head.

"Hey," she said. "I'm fine. I'm tough... and so is Elena. She's not dead yet."

"I know."

She took his face between her hands. "It's going to be fine."

"Shouldn't I be the one saying that?"

"When you can't, I will."

Gazing into her eyes, he felt like he was swimming in warm waters and the sun shone on his head. He careened forward on a whim until his lips met hers. Her taste hit and he went under, drowning, becoming lost in her.

What started as a chaste kiss built in crescendo until he couldn't get enough. Every inch of his body hardened. His breath became ragged and hot against her mouth. It didn't take long for her to be the same and he fucking loved it. This woman, this tough woman who, through some stroke of luck, seemed to care for him, felt the same as he did about her.

"Daisy…" he murmured.

"Mm?"

"I…" He didn't know. He needed to be inside her. To feel connected. It was the only way he'd lose this jittery fear buzzing through him. His gaze darted over her flushed face, her kiss-swollen lips and he confessed, "I want to have you right here."

He glanced desperately over his shoulder, as if he had any business checking to see if they were alone. As far as he knew, they were. The other basement rooms were dark. Griffin no longer occupied the cell. If any of them were worth their salt, they'd be spending time with their reunited loved ones, thanking their lucky stars they still had each other. Once sure they were alone, he slid his gaze back to Daisy with a low growl, pleased to see a glimmer of excitement echo back at him.

"I want my cock buried so deep in you that you feel it for days."

He slid a finger beneath the spaghetti strap of her singlet and moved it over her shoulder. She shivered as she watched him. He smoothed down her goosebumps. Next, he did the other side. She said nothing, just watched and quaked beneath his touch. And when he dragged the bulk of her singlet down to pool around her waist, his eyes locked onto her sports bra before meeting her gaze for permission because, once he started, he didn't give a shit if they were interrupted.

He'd keep going.

And when she gave a nod of encouragement, he almost lost control. This night wasn't going to end until he was as far inside her as he could get.

twenty-three

DAISY LAZARUS

THE NEED TO be with Axel took precedence over anything else. Daisy forgot where they were. Forgot the practice exercises she should be doing. Forgot her plan to get stronger so she could hunt down Julius. There was only Axel and the wild need in his eyes.

When he'd come in and walked toward her, she'd seen his loneliness and felt an echo of it in her heart. No, it was more than an echo. It was a twin, the other half of his, and she'd instantly known how he felt. How he needed her. Because she'd felt the same way.

He was losing everything he loved. She was gaining those she'd lost. But somehow, they needed each other to bridge the divide, to be okay with the unknown.

She suspected, no matter how old they got, that look between them would always exist. Like the night sky reflecting on the surface of a lake, they glittered for each other.

He gave a masculine grunt of appreciation as he lifted her sports bra to expose her breasts. A dark lock of hair, still damp, fell forward over his bronzed forehead. He dragged his bottom lip through his teeth.

He muttered Portuguese curses as an agonized need ghosted over his face. "You're so fucking perfect. It physically hurts to hold myself back."

"So don't."

Her body reacted. Pheromones leaked from her pores. Axel's pupils dilated as her scent hit him and he gave a ravenous growl of need. He bowed and drew her nipple into his mouth. He licked and flicked the tight bud, shooting sensations into her body, setting her alight. She moaned and dragged her nails over his head, arching into him, already feeling her euphoric arousal wash through her, drowning out any sense.

"Are you sure?" he asked, words muffled around her breast. "Here?"

As in on this mat? "Wherever. I just need you."

He pulled back, determination turning his face hard, and he yanked her yoga pants down her hips, also taking her panties. She removed her singlet and bra and then laid down and opened her knees for him. He stared at her, eyes heating as he reached around his neck to grab his T-shirt. Biceps bulged. Abs clenched. He slid his shirt over his head and off. Seconds later he'd removed his shorts and crawled naked between her legs.

The first long, lick of his tongue down her needy center had her keening, eyes rolling to the ceiling, palms slamming the rubber mat. He was good. Experienced. Demanding.

He groaned against her flesh. "I fucking love the taste of you."

His tongue speared into her, as if to prove his point. He thrust as far as he could, then replaced his tongue with a finger and worked her sensitive nub with his mouth. His finger and tongue moved in tandem to rock her in a motion that coiled everything tight. He paused every so often to whisper sweet nothings in Portuguese—with his lips still between her legs.

Where they'd been relentless and demanding in the shower, he was attentive and leisurely now.

Her orgasm built... crested like the tide. She saw white. To stop herself from screaming she bit her lip and clutched his hair, squeezing his head with her thighs until the crashing wave melted the rest of her body and left her gasping for air, wondering what the hell had just happened.

Axel didn't wait for her to gather composure. He reared back and nudged her knees wider, took his hard and twitching cock in his fist and then stared down at her with the most wicked, masculine entitlement. It was pride she saw in his expression. Pride that he'd taken care of his woman, made her scream, and squirm, and pull his hair—even though he'd controlled the moment and taken his time. And if he continued to look at Daisy like that, she feared Parker would come running down from his penthouse wondering what the fuck was happening for there to be so much pride in the room.

She couldn't have that.

She lifted and pushed hard against his pecs. He fell back on the mat. The hunger returned to her system. Her body needed him again. It was an urge propelling her forward, wickedly whispering for her to join with him, to be one with him.

"My turn," she panted and fit herself over his length. "Time to go hard."

Before he could respond, she sank down until seated. They both shuddered at the sensations. Axel tossed his head back, the thick cord of his neck on display as he took her hips in his hands and squeezed, almost bruising her with his need.

"*Puta que pariu caralho filho da puta,*" he gritted out. "I'm going to fucking come before you even move."

With a smug sense of gratification, Daisy trailed her gaze down his body, enjoying the sheer sight of a powerful man beneath her, undone by her, knowing he would be like this every time. A slave to her whims and coming back for more. Because he revered her. Needed her.

Never judged her. Accepted her.

Wanted her.

He was never disgusted with her scars. Not the fresh jagged ones at her stomach, not the old silver spidery ones on her face, not the invisible ones inside. And she'd never cared about them because of it.

Daisy planted her palms on his sweaty chest and moved on him, sliding herself up and down his length. His brows slammed together, and he gave a strangled groan, holding back, not fully giving himself to the experience. She didn't like that. She wanted everything, like in the shower.

She raked her nails down his front, and said low and deep, "Look at me when I fuck you, Axel."

He hissed as she made marks on his skin. When his brown eyes hit hers, dark and hot with dangerous desire, she knew she had his attention.

"Watch me," she insisted.

His response was a sound caught between a groan and a purr. His upper lip curled and he slammed his hips up as she went down. The resounding clash sparked stars. She moaned her approval. Submitting to her lead, he turned their lovemaking hard and rough. He let his wild side out, gripped her hair and yanked her mouth down to his, clashing their teeth, pounding into her from beneath.

They rolled on the mat, heedless of the burn, using the rush to heighten their endorphins. He met her crazy, feral need to be close. He pushed her on the mat, dragged her leg up and over his shoulder, and then pounded into her until the vein in his forehead bulged, until sweat dripped down every bronzed crevice of his body, until he went red and furious with need.

Daisy loved the possessive, carnal look in his eyes as he watched where they intimately joined. No one had ever looked at her like that... and she couldn't quite place it. Not just lust, or need, or love... but ownership. Permanence. Never ending partnership. It sent her over the edge a second time. Watching her come had the same effect on him. He planted himself a final time, growled low into her neck, nipped her, and smothered her with his hard and sweaty body. He stayed seated long after he'd finished, raggedly breathing like an animal through his nose against her skin, holding her tight.

"I want to do that again," he proclaimed, mouth still squished against her skin. It tickled. "In our bed."

"Our bed?" she mumbled, frowning.

He looked at her as though she'd grown two heads. "Daisy. I'm moving in with you. I hope you know that. I'll fucking sell my apartment. Elena will—"

A cold bucket of water doused over them. The anguish in his eyes returned.

"She can stay as long as she wants," Daisy said, soothing him with her voice. She'd never wished more for Sloan's gift of affecting emotion. If she had it, she could gift him with peace.

Maybe he saw that in her eyes because he muttered, "I love you. You know that right?"

She felt the blush steal over her face as she looked away, but he drew her gaze back to his.

"You know that, right?" he repeated, his gaze turning hard.

"Sure."

"You need convincing." He gathered her clothes and tossed them to her. "Back to your room, and I'll start."

She snorted a laugh but that earned her another scowl.

"I'm fucking serious, Daisy. You need to understand how I feel for you, and if that means I leave an impression—physically—then I'll do it." He swallowed hard. "You're stuck with me."

"I…" She goddamned blushed again. "God… saying that word is hard for me. I've never…"

He hopped into his shorts and then crawled up the length of her body to kiss her in a deep, invading sort of way. His deep voice shimmied through her. "You don't like being vulnerable. I get it. But—" He kissed her again. "Get used to it. I'll be saying it a lot. And while I don't expect you to say it back to me now, eventually you will. A lot."

SOMETIME LATER THEY were in Daisy's bed, naked, and recovering from another round of enthusiastic love making. Axel traced his fingers over new marks—small bruises and red lines—he'd made on her body and kissed them apologetically.

"At least these will go away," he mumbled, his eyes turning dull in the dim light.

She captured his hand over her stomach and held it there… on the recent scars Julius's scientist had left. The bad kind.

"Is the person who did this to you dead?" he asked, voice rough.

She sensed his violence like the heat of a flame emanating from his skin in the dark. "I think the actual person who held the scalpel is. But Julius isn't." Her own vision blurred but her resolve hardened. "Before you say anything, or declare your violent, gallant intentions to track him down, I need you to know his life is mine to end. It's the only way I'll be at peace."

"How do you do it?" he asked. "How do you move on like that?" She sensed he had more to say so waited. "Will ending his life truly bring you peace?"

She shrugged. "No. But it's a start."

More silence. More tracing of the battle scars across her body, because that's what they were. War wounds. The roadmap to her life.

"When Elena goes..." He squished his face on her stomach and breathed against her flesh. "I won't have someone to blame. There will be no person to kill. I don't know how..."

She dragged his head up so she could see into his eyes. "I did it by finding joy in the little things, Axel. That's how you survive. That's how you stay whole. Whether it's a crack in the floor, a glimpse of sky, or a crushed daisy in my hand. I locked onto those small things and found peace in them. Now I'm here, finding joy in you."

"Elena is my joy," he said.

The haunted look he gave didn't bring her confidence. When Elena eventually succumbed to her disease, it could be Axel's unravelling. So long as Elena was alive, he had the strength to be the beacon of hope that had triggered their mating bond. The hope that Daisy needed.

As he fell asleep in her arms, she stared at the ceiling and wondered. She imagined the future. If they did get rid of Julius, what would life be like for them afterward? Would Axel just be a hollow shell, having served his purpose of triggering her gifts and being her mate? Daisy had been removed from her family, and the despair of it had broken her. She'd been turned into a killer. A monster. A villain, susceptible to the manipulations and machinations of a megalomaniac. Would Daisy be enough for Axel?

Was that even fair?

Or would he end up resenting her and leaving her. And she'd be in the same position she was in when Mary closed that fateful elevator door, shutting Daisy out, leaving her to burn in a building. Alone.

These were stupid, irrational fears that were hard to put to bed, no matter what logic told Daisy about her situation now. Because the simple dark truth of it was, the future would always be uncertain.

The only solid answer was the pain circling her heart like a prowling wolf every time she thought of Axel losing his last family member to an illness he couldn't control.

But maybe she could.

twenty-four

AXEL ALVARES

AXEL WOKE TO AN EMPTY BED. The first rays of dawn filtered through the open window. A cool breeze drifted in, kissing his face, cooling the sheets that had been warm and twisted around their bodies last night. Somewhere in the distant city, a cat meowed but no sounds of criminal activity assaulted him.

Perhaps the death of the city had taken a break, just like Elena's illness had stalled.

He hoped.

Daisy was probably down in the training room, getting back to what he'd interrupted last night. He scrubbed his face and cleared his throat and then checked his cell phone with trepidation for bad news from Mary. Nothing.

No news was good news, right?

He cleaned himself up, went to the bathroom, and then quickly made his way back to Mary's and Flint's apartment. The intelligent computer let him in. The apartment was quiet. Everyone must still be asleep. He tiptoed to Elena's room, holding his breath, hoping for a miracle.

When he entered, he almost did a double take, thinking he was still asleep and dreaming. Elena was sitting in the bed, awake, and with flushed and rosy cheeks.

"Ellie?" he gaped.

His surprise was echoed on her face.

"I just woke up," she said, eyes wide at him. "I feel… Axel! I feel amazing."

She threw her hands up in glee, but the IV cord caught and she winced. "Oh shit. I made myself bleed. I think there's blood back-wash in the line."

Axel went to her side to help. He'd done this once or twice both in his day job and helping his parents with their lines. But when he got to the skinny plastic tube, he jerked.

"This can't be right. It's not connected to the bag. It's connected to—" He trailed his finger under the line, followed it to the other side of the bed to—*Daisy on the floor!* Face down and in the narrow space between the bed and the wall. The truth quickly became evident. Daisy had hooked up a direct transfusion line from herself to Elena. She'd given her blood to a dying girl, and now was… unconscious… maybe—

"No," he choked out. He vaulted the bed, stumbled in the small space, and gathered her roughly, trying to lift her. "She's cold."

His heart stopped beating. He ripped out the canula from her arm. Blood kept oozing. Her blood, from both her arm and the tubing. It was also running down her nose. Dribbling from the corner of Daisy's mouth. Her ears.

"Pinch that," he barked at Elena, pointing at her tubing. "Or you'll lose blood."

Elena whimpered, panicked, but did as she was told. Axel didn't have time to deal with her. He bellowed, "HELP!" And lifted Daisy's lifeless body onto the bed, shoving his now perfectly healthy sister out of the way.

Holding her pinched blood-filled tubing, she scrambled away. "What's happening?"

"Daisy's—HELP!" His shout barely made it through his tight throat. He checked her pulse. It beat sluggishly against the pallid skin of her neck. Thank Christ. "She's given you her blood to heal. I think… I think she forced it into your body using her gift."

She'd gone too far. She was still weak herself, still recovering, still fragile.

"She what?" Mary ran in, her eyes wide and panicking.

"I woke up and she was gone." Axel's eyes burned.

"Call Parker," Mary said to Flint. "And Grace. And… everyone."

Then she came over to Daisy and checked her as Axel had. She found the same signs. Cold skin. Sluggish pulse. Labored breath almost too weak to keep her alive. Mary met Axel's eyes with a grim finality in her own.

"No." He pointed at her. "Don't you dare say it. So long as she's alive, there's hope."

"She's lost too much blood," Mary whispered.

"*No*," Axel choked, shaking his head. He gathered Daisy's limp body into his arms. He tugged her like a rag doll to his chest and held her tight, pressing her floppy head to his shoulder. "No, Daisy. Fight. Fight like you've always fought."

That she had done this… given her last to save his sister only proved she was someone who deserved to live. She wasn't a villain. She was a hero. She'd been a hero from the moment she was born. She'd survived a hellish life with a man who used and abused her. Yet she still had something left in the tank to give. *Please don't let it be all she has left.*

Mary found something crumpled in Daisy's fist. She covered her mouth with her hand as she read the note. Her eyes squeezed shut and she shook her head. Fuck.

Fuck!

If this strong, powerful matriarch was in tears, it meant only one thing. Axel shut his eyes and prayed.

"I'm sorry," Elena burst out. "I'm so sorry."

"It's not your fault, Ellie." He placed Daisy down gently. He smoothed her hair from her face. He reverently wiped the clotting blood from her nose. "What did the note say?"

Mary held it out to him but couldn't read it aloud herself.

The note was old. Had writing on both sides. One side said, *The answer is in your blood.* Beneath it, was a fresh message from Daisy. *This is me catching everyone. This is me leading from the heart.*

"What does that mean?" he asked, voice raw.

Mary swallowed, but it was Liza who answered as she entered the room.

"In the lab when we were children, Daisy and I used to play a game." Her voice was as raw as Axel felt. She looked over her sister's limp body with sad eyes. "She used to chase me and force me to cuddle her. I loved it. Once I climbed the table and slipped, but she was there to catch me. She said, 'I'll always be here to catch you.'" Liza scowled at her sister with glistening eyes. "You stupid girl. I told you it was our turn to catch *you.*"

Liza's jaw hardened, her bottom lip trembled, and she left. Thundering footsteps announced the arrival of more of her siblings. They crowded into the small room, one by one.

Parker's immense body was the first. From the satin pants, wild hair, and naked torso, he'd just woken up. Intelligent eyes swept the room, catching on Ellie in the corner, Daisy on the bed, and the paper in Axel's hand.

"She used her blood to save your sister," Parker said, nodding as he put two and two together. "When Max was poisoned, she left that note for Sloan. The answer is in your blood, meaning, as Sloan's mate, the regenerative power in her blood could transfer to him. This healing gift degrades if anyone else tries to use it... but... perhaps with a sibling with almost identical DNA, it still works. Daisy figured it out. She must have come in here and set up the transfusion line herself. It's a triage kit. The donor needs to be higher than the recipient. Was she on the bed, or—"

"She was on the floor when I got here," Axel said.

"That makes sense that she used her gift then. She didn't have the energy to stay standing, so she used her gift to push the blood into Elena. She did it until... *Fuck.*" Parker scrubbed his face, shaking his head. "We need her. She shouldn't have done that!"

"If I can take her blood, then she can take mine," Axel declared.

"Won't work," Parker said. "Not in the way you hope, anyway."

Elena's bottom lip wobbled and she pushed past everyone to run out of the room.

"I'll get her," Mary offered.

"This is your fault." Parker pointed at his mother with a dark scowl. "If you hadn't told her she had to lead with her heart, then this wouldn't have happened."

"The heart is how we win!" Mary shouted back.

"You know," Parker fired back. "If you had a problem with my leadership skills, you could have just told me. You didn't need to go putting ideas into a fragile woman's head."

Mary shook her head distraught. "It wasn't supposed to end like this for her. I saw her there in the end!"

"You should have told us about your vision," Parker accused. "Maybe if you weren't so secretive, this wouldn't have happened."

Tempers flared. Arguments ensued. And Axel was slowly losing his mind. He'd woken up this morning thinking one of the two people he loved was dying, and, although that person had changed, the fact still remained.

He was losing one.

twenty-five
JULIUS ALLCOTT

JULIUS HAD CUT ALL the hair on his head. He'd cut strips from his clothes until he wore nothing but shreds. The only thing left to cut as a reminder of his loved ones was his own skin. But there had to be something left of himself for his wife and daughter. Besides, he didn't need reminders anymore. The time had finally come.

"Do you have the items?" the voice whispered.

The clanking of old water pumps in this wastewater facility tried to hide her voice. It had ceased sounding like his wife days ago. But it was her. He knew it in his heart. Who else would want him so desperately to join her? His wife was the only person in the world who'd ever loved him enough.

"I have them," he replied.

He looked at the reason he'd gone back to his old home—the Fabergé egg and doll before him on the old, rusted table. These were the reason he'd stored the mates of all the Lazarus siblings there. And the reason he'd covered his tracks by setting a trap to burn the house down. But of course, he'd wanted to make sure they suffered the most. If they discovered the house, then he wanted the one who found the house to be within reach of rescuing their loved ones when they triggered the tripwire.

His upper lip curled. And if that person just so happened to be the Lazarus sibling who'd caused him the most pain, Despair, then all the better. He'd given half his life to that girl, to training her to be his soldier, to being his right hand… and what did she give him in return? Betrayal.

That's why he secretly hoped no one would rescue the kidnapped mates. He hoped they'd all die a slow and agonizing death in that attic.

Despair thought she had taken his only chance of replicating his dead wife and daughter. Well—he gingerly touched the items—the joke was on her. Julius was still bringing them back.

And—he checked the iPad winking at him, ready for the execute directive—he was still going to eradicate the sinners of the world as per his original plan. His wife and daughter needed a safe place to live in when they returned, after all.

All he had to do was hit that button and every contingency he had was released. From replicates, to plant monsters, to greed serum dispersed into the city's drinking water supply, to mech suits handed to his Faithful.

"Then we can start the ritual," his wife said, her voice hissing like a snake. *"You know where you must go."*

Julius shook his head. It must be hard for her voice to reach him from the afterlife. That must be why it hissed so badly. With the shake of his head, he caught sight of a person standing before him… talking. One of the Faithful. How long had he been there watching Julius?

"What?" Julius spat.

The Faithful blinked. His white robe was dirty at the feet. His white mask was pushed up to rest on top of his head. The scars on his face indicated he was one of the herd who desperately wanted a new, perfect life. Julius had found those were the best of his flock—so eager to please. So dumb.

"You said something," Julius pointed out. "What?"

"I... um... it's just that you asked me to give you an update on the situation with the Deadly Seven."

"And?"

"They got out of the house alive. Everyone did."

Julius's blood ran cold. "They survived?"

The Faithful nodded. "And... um..."

"Spit it out!"

"The train of supplies was run into the sea." He shook his head in disbelief. "I don't know if we have enough for what you planned."

Julius's nostrils flared and he breathed hard like a bull for a long, hot minute. The voice of his wife whispered obscenities in his ear. Cursing the day this Faithful was born. Promising dark, torturous punishment for his impudence. Part of Julius knew his wife would never speak so harshly. But part of him shut out that doubt. He was too close. Too close to have those kinds of thoughts.

"It's fine," he mumbled, tapping his chin. "It's fine. We can still work with this. We have the replicates. We have *some* animals, right? *Some* plants?"

The Faithful shrugged.

Fuck.

Julius scrubbed his face. So, then, maybe the entire city wouldn't be destroyed. Maybe the Deadly Seven had their mates to balance them. But he had powered replicates still waiting to be unleashed. And he had the greed serum ready to pour into the water supply. Theoretically, that would turn any civilian drinking the water into a monster themselves. All he really needed was for the Sinners guarding the gate to the afterlife to be distracted so he had time to complete the ritual and bring his family home to him.

At the end of the day, that's all that mattered.

"Their reunion will distract them," his wife hissed. *"We must do this now."*

Yes. Of course, she was right. Even though the mates were still alive, every single one of the Deadly Seven would be a slave to their emotions right now. They would be spending time reuniting with their loved ones, just as he would when he found his.

"We do this now," he echoed, and he pressed the red button on the iPad. "While they're distracted."

twenty-six

EVAN LAZARUS

EVAN LAZARUS STARED at the wall of his artwork in the training room. He'd come down after checking in on Daisy and pinned his latest dream sketches straight to the wall. Then he stood back, his arms folded, and stared.

This was his life.

Wall to wall, messy charcoal lines. Some of them made sense. Some of them were just black holes in his head. Feelings. Vibes. Senses. Before Daisy had brought Grace back to him, in his sheer and utter desperation, all he'd dreamed was of his mate in a dark place, a single glimpse of the sky through a window. The dreams had come in broken segments, and none of them had been helpful.

And last night, after he'd spent a glorious few hours feeding his mate, washing her, massaging her, making her feel safe... they'd made love on the fresh chevron sheets he'd fitted to his bed, the same sheets they'd slept on when she'd first come to live with him two years earlier.

He'd slept soundly for the first night in a long time. Until he was awoken this morning by the shouts of his brother. But there had been a second—a split second moment where he'd been caught between sleep and awake that he'd had the vision.

His eyes tracked to the newest sketch he'd pinned.

Daisy. Not dead. But with lightning in her eyes, her hair lit up like it was radioactive, fangs in her mouth, her veins on fire. Maybe she was dead. Maybe that strange rendition of her was from another life. Maybe another universe.

"Hey, honey." Grace walked into the room.

His reason for living had her long, dark hair tied back in a braid. She would be in civilian clothes until she recovered from her kidnapping ordeal. He simply refused to let her out of his sight, and back to surgery, until all this mess with Julius was over. She'd already mentioned that she could be of use at the hospital with the state of the city, but no. She had to stay here. His heart simply wouldn't take another scare.

Unlike some of his siblings who'd fallen completely apart, Evan had always had a feeling. It had been a calm spot in the storm of fear constantly barreling through his body. He'd told himself it was part of his precognition that put the feeling there. It meant they would find their mates. And that they would be safe.

That feeling was gone now, even when he thought of his eldest sister in a bed, dying.

He gathered Grace into his arms and kissed her long, hard and deep. She moaned appreciatively into his mouth, telling him with her sounds that she missed him too.

"How's the patient, Doc?" he asked roughly.

Grace's eyes dimmed and she shook her head. "Axel has been trying to get me to give his blood to Daisy, but I keep telling him it doesn't work the same way as hers does to him. His won't heal her enough. And she's far too damaged. Julius took too much of her spinal fluid. I'm surprised she was able to function."

"She's incredibly tough."

Grace blinked away tears. "She deserves so much more."

"And one of us can't transfuse our blood to her?"

Again, Grace shook her head. "She's lost so much blood that even if she doesn't reject the transfusion, it will leave the donor in the same position she's in. And then there's the fact that if you donate your blood, and I get injured, you'll have nothing left to help me, and then we'll be back in the position Griffin just was in. If you survive, you'll be unbalanced. I'll be dead. Which of you will do that, because I might be a selfish bitch for saying this, but I refuse to let it be you."

He smoothed his thumb over her cheek to rub the spilled tear away. His heart ached, because he felt the same way. He loved Daisy... but enough to die in her place? Enough to leave Grace behind? Enough to risk going dark? And for what, a *chance* for Daisy to survive?

He was a bastard for thinking of it. Maybe it was why he was hiding out here in the basement. He cupped the back of Grace's head and tugged her to his chest, holding her tight against the beating of his heart. His eyes skipped to the wall, unsure why he kept coming down here to look at it all. He settled on the recent sketch, wondering why Daisy looked so different, and then he saw it.

The electric eyes. The fangs. The veins on fire.

"Holy shit," he murmured.

"What?" Grace pulled back with a strangled sob. She wiped her eyes when she caught Evan's intense gaze on the wall. "What is it?"

"You said Daisy's lost too much blood, and one of us won't have enough to donate safely without harming ourselves... but what if we all donate a little. Would that work?"

"Multiple donors are risky at the best of times. And Daisy's blood cell count is so low. I suppose if it's coming fresh from a vein then there's no chance of the preservatives normally used to create complications. How many are we talking?"

"All seven of us." He pointed at the sketch. "I had a flash of that in my mind before I woke this morning. Call me crazy, but it looks like she's exhibiting our powers. Look—fangs. That's Parker. Fire in the veins—that's from Tony. Electric eyes—me." He thought hard about that image he'd seen. "Come to think of it, there may have been smoke like Liza's poison. And I wouldn't have seen Sloan's or Wyatt's gift visually."

She canted her head. "You think by donating your blood, you'll also be donating your gifts?"

He shrugged. "I don't know. Maybe. Maybe it's just a sign for all of us to give her something."

Grace rubbed her chin. "I mean... multiple donors are not something anyone would recommend, but none of you are normal. It could work if we do it a little at a time over twenty-four hours. We've done that after surgery once. Give her a chance to accept the donation before moving onto the next."

"So... yes?"

"Evan, I don't know. There's still a risk of embolisms, hypothermia, and then there's the unique properties in someone like Liza's blood who might have more acid than normal to combat her tetrodotoxin capacities. It could overload Daisy's system and kill her faster."

"That's not a no."

She frowned and stared at the sketch. "Maybe if we start with the less lethal blood types. Wyatt's. Parker's. And so on. Theoretically, she would gain strength as we go along, and *theoretically*, she would be able to receive her siblings' blood as it would have enough similar DNA markers as the donor." She shot hopeful eyes to him. "I think there's a chance it could work."

Evan whooped loudly and clapped his hands. Grace grinned. And then the foundations rocked beneath their feet. Crumbs of concrete and dust fell from the ceiling. Evan grabbed Grace and pulled her to a doorway where he covered her head with his hands, turned, and sheltered her with his body. The rocking stopped.

"What was that?" Grace asked, eyes wide.

"I don't know."

Evan took Grace's hand and jogged to the operations room, only feet away.

"AIMI," he shouted. "What happened to the building?"

The wall of flat screens flickered to life. Each depicted different news networks. Some had footage feeding from their CCTV building cameras at street level.

"It appears the building is under attack," AIMI replied. "Hostiles have been spotted on the street outside Lazarus House. Parker has been notified. The team is assembling." AIMI paused. "Incoming footage on screens one and two... more attacks have been reported around the city."

Through the dust clouds and flickering, silhouettes of hostile bodies moved with menace. Replicates. They encroached on popular landmarks around the city, using whatever gift they'd been graced with to damage.

"That's the municipal district. The Quadrant. Syndicate Tower." He frowned as he said those last words. "Julius is attacking his own tower?"

"He destroyed his own childhood home," Parker said, coming up behind Evan. "Why not his tower?"

He went straight for the glass cabinet housing his Deadly battle gear and started dressing. Evan hesitated to follow suit. Others jogged into the room. Wyatt, Liza, Sloan, Tony, Griffin.

They were all there and changing into their battle gear. Parker noticed Evan's hesitance.

"Gear up," Parker said. "This is it."

Evan shook his head and shared a look with Grace. "We thought of something that will help Daisy."

He explained his vision-sketch and what they'd deduced. Parker hit the form fitting Deadly Seven emblem on his breast pocket. Air whooshed out of the arms and legs in his suit, sucking the bullet proof fabric against his muscular frame. His eyes were bright gold, already flickering with evidence of the beast that prowled beneath his skin.

"Grace, you believe this could work?" he asked, voice a low rumble.

"There are risks," she replied and then swallowed, betraying her nerves.

Evan could already see the doubt enter Parker's eyes as he checked the situation of the city on the screens. Chaos. Pure, utter, madness.

"The Sinners are in trouble," he said. "We'll be spread thin. We don't have time to sit here and spend hours transfusing our blood into Daisy."

"Mary said it wasn't supposed to end this way for Daisy," Evan growled. "I believe her. Don't you?"

Parker's hard, contemplating gaze pierced Evan and, for a moment, Evan considered what he'd have to do if Parker said no. Would he go upstairs and donate his blood anyway. Would he go against orders?

"We're all too cowardly to sacrifice ourselves for her," he snarled, giving voice to his own fear. He tugged Grace to his body and hated that he couldn't give her up, because that's what could happen if one of them donated enough blood to bring Daisy back. That Lazarus sibling might take her place, or at the very least be out of commission. And he was terrified of not being there to protect Grace.

Multiple pairs of guilty eyes darted to him, and then looked away as they no doubt felt the same thing. He opened his mouth to say more, but then Liza ran to a screen and pointed at figures milling about in the Quadrant Park. "Somethings wrong with them."

"And here," Griffin added, pointing to another screen where people were attacking one another like animals. He frowned. "They're acting like... no... that's too weird."

"Like what?" Parker asked.

"They're acting like Doppenger acted when he took the greed serum. Could it be they've been infected?"

"All of them?" Liza gaped, and then raised her voice. "AIMI, show us CCTV footage from random cameras at busy spots around the city."

One by one the screens flicked over. People were attacking people.

"What the fuck?" Wyatt growled, his eyes wide.

"It must be the greed serum," Griffin said. "But how has it infected everyone?"

"Air?" Sloan asked, frowning. "Or—"

"Water supply," multiple voices said in unison.

"Shit," Parker cursed. "AIMI, broadcast to the entire building not to drink from the faucets, and not to go outside. Close-filter air back through the building, just in case. And—" His face paled. He looked up suddenly, eyes wide. "Alice went to check on the Sinners because they weren't answering her calls. I have to get down there." He went to leave, but Evan stopped him with a question in his eyes.

Parker scrubbed his beard with his good hand before returning his gaze to Grace. "Do it. Set up a roster so that over the next twenty-four hours, we each donate blood to Daisy. She's our sister, a Lazarus, and we won't let her quit." He snarled, his fangs elongated, and his claws distended from his fingertips—one metal set, one natural. "Everyone else, split up and do what you can to contain the replicates. Put them down as quickly as possible."

"What about the infected civilians?" Tony asked.

"Don't hurt them," Griffin pleaded. "As long as they've had a mild dose, the serum will wear off. Doppenger only turned into a beast when he overdosed."

"Go," Parker said to everyone. "Wyatt, you donate first. Everyone else keep your communicator watches on and your lines open in the suits. Be ready to come back for your shift. Coming home will also serve as a chance for us to reset our balance before heading out again into the streets. Keep an eye on your tattoos."

"And if we come across Julius?" Liza asked, lifting her chin.

"If he's dumb enough to show his face, take him down. For Daisy."

"For Daisy," they all echoed.

IN MARY'S KITCHEN, Axel helped his sister prepare lunch. It was the least they could do after everything. He rinsed lettuce under a stream of bottled water and gave his sister the side-eye as she chopped tomatoes for the salad. The color had returned to her face. The brightness to her eyes. The spring in her step. All signs pointed to recovery, and dare he hoped, remission.

He'd thoroughly checked her over the minute he'd had a chance, and she'd told him she'd never felt better. Like a new person. Like sick wasn't even a word in her vocabulary. There was guilt in her eyes, and he hated that if things went south with Daisy, she would live with it forever.

But things wouldn't go south.

If she was alive, there was hope. Hope that Daisy would survive. Hope that Elena's illness wouldn't come back. Just goddamned hope. He goddamned deserved this after all the hardship he'd suffered. He was owed it.

Axel kept a brave face on as he continued prepping food.

Less than an hour ago, Evan and Grace had come running into

226

the apartment with Wyatt, claiming to have a plan to bring Daisy back. Since each of the siblings could donate blood to their mates—and in Elena's case, their mate's sibling—they assumed they could donate blood to each other as well. So they'd set up a roster to donate a little at a time from each Lazarus sibling and then monitor Daisy for reactions and complications.

She was on death's door, her heart weak, her body drained dry of nutrients. But her family was rallying to give it all back to her.

Wyatt's turn was almost done. But since Wyatt's skin was invulnerable, setting up the line had taken longer than they'd expected. Grace had to get creative. So Axel had come out here to give Elena something to do. Her boundless energy made Misha and the baby restless, and on more than one occasion Lilo had told her to sit down and be still while she spoke on the phone to her news network contacts about the contaminated water supply.

Elena finished cutting tomatoes. Axel added them to the enormous salad bowl then took it to the long, family dining table by the window where Mary sat writing something. Sheer curtains gave them a view of the city, of the smoke billowing from random places. Every so often, sirens filtered in as Cardinal City's finest joined the heroic family with their efforts. A lot of good people were going to die today.

Axel should be out there helping his crew. They'd be wondering where he was. He gritted his teeth and turned back to the table.

"Sorry," he mumbled as he placed napkins near Mary as she wrote.

She glanced up. "I'm almost done."

He went back to the kitchen, just as Grace joined them.

"How is she?" he asked.

"So far so good." Grace bit her bottom lip.

"But…"

"There's something we didn't think about by putting Wyatt first." She took one of the many bottles of water and unscrewed the cap. "In Evan's dream-sketch, Daisy exhibited powers that weren't hers."

Axel's heart stopped as the implications hit. "You're saying we should have put Wyatt last."

She nodded. "Because his epidermis is invulnerable, I had to go through his mouth to access a vein that could bleed. And… it wasn't pretty. He's extremely brave to have allowed me to do what I did."

"Do I want to know?"

"Not unless you want me to detail exploratory surg—" She clamped her lips shut as she noticed Misha coming over to the dining table with Amari. Grace met Axel's eyes. "You don't want to know."

Misha bounced the baby on her hip. "Is everything okay?"

"It's fine," Grace answered. "Wyatt is set up and Daisy is taking his blood. I'll go in and check in a few minutes to make sure it's all going according to plan." She paused. "Maybe stay out here for the duration. I'll keep you updated."

Misha nodded and forced a smile on her face. Axel and Elena finished setting the table. Soon, Lilo came over and helped.

"Will Flint be coming?" Axel asked.

Mary gave him a tight look as she gathered her papers. "He's running comms in the basement. I'll bring him a plate."

Just as Axel placed the plate down, an explosion in the streets rocked the building. At least, Axel thought it was in the street. An alarm went off. The baby started crying, and AIMI announced over the speaker system that the building was under attack again.

"I thought Nightingale Security was down there," Axel stated, worried. The rest of the family had dealt with the earlier disturbance and set up Max, Bailey, and their team to man the front entrance in case more Faithful, replicates, or drugged civilians arrived while the Seven headed into the city and hunted down the worst of the sinners.

"They are," Mary replied grimly.

"If they're in trouble, Wyatt should go down," Misha said, eyes wide.

"He's about done," Grace blurted. "I'll go and take his line out."

She jogged down the hallway and returned a few minutes later with a grumpy looking Wyatt. He was already in his battle suit, ready to go. He checked to see that his mate and daughter were safe, then strode over and kissed them both on the head before saying, "I'll go sort this shit out."

"Be careful," Misha blurted.

He gave her a wry smile and it was the only time Axel had seen that wickedly mischievous glint in his eyes.

Misha smirked back. "I know... you're invulnerable. I'm still allowed to worry."

"As long as you're both safe, I'll be fine." He turned to Axel. "Take care of them. I could be out there for a while. Days, even. Keep us updated on Daisy's condition."

Axel gave a curt nod and watched Wyatt leave. A strange squirming sensation entered his gut. Long after the door had closed, he realized it was pride. Wyatt trusted him to look after the most precious people in the world to him—his only weaknesses.

But Axel was a fireman. He should be out there, like them. He needed to help or the guilt would weigh him down.

Elena knew exactly what he was thinking and raised her brow at him.

"Maybe you should go too, Axel."

"Daisy needs me."

"We got her."

"But what if she reacts badly to the—"

"She won't."

"No." He dug his heels in. Wyatt would kill him if something

229

happened to his family. All of them would. And the last time he'd taken his eyes off Daisy, she'd gone and donated almost every blood cell in her body to his sister. If she'd told him her plan, he was sure they could have found a smarter way to do what she did. They could have done it the right way.

The way that didn't risk her life.

He nodded at the table. "Go eat with the others, Ellie."

She cast a worried glance down the hallway.

"I'll let you know how she is," he said. "Don't worry."

twenty-eight

DAISY LAZARUS

DAISY WOKE up groggily to Mary sitting at her bedside.

Her body felt weird. It was strange that she was awake at all. The last thing she remembered; Elena was lying in the bed, not her.

After seeing how much pain Axel had been in about his sister's terminal condition, Daisy knew two things. One, she couldn't be the one left behind again. If Elena died—and Axel resented Daisy for it—her fragile heart, only just pieced back together, would crumble into dust.

The second reason was Elena's hug, back when they'd broken into the baseball batting cages. Elena had reminded Daisy what hugs were meant to be—a spontaneous thank you, a sharing of joy, a connection.

A small act of kindness to a stranger had the power to change the world.

"How is Elena?" Daisy croaked.

Mary, who'd been reading a book, looked up suddenly. Her facial expression lifted, and Daisy sensed a hit of joy. But then Mary's eyes narrowed.

"That was a very stupid thing to do, *mija*. There have been consequences."

Daisy plonked her head back on the pillow and stared at the ceiling. "Well, I never expected to be here to deal with said consequences."

Daisy blinked the burn from her eyes. She'd known her actions would piss off her family. She knew some of them might call her selfish. That's why she'd written the note. She wanted them to know that it had been because of them, because she wanted to show that anyone —not just immediate family—deserved to have someone in their corner, sacrificing and giving them their all.

But it seemed she couldn't do anything right. She'd tried to be a hero, but she didn't feel like one. She felt like crap. Wrung out and dry. God, even her mouth was dry. She licked her parched lips. Mary brought a cup of water to her lips. Daisy drank deeply, the heat of Mary's disapproval scorching her skin.

"Is Elena okay?" Daisy asked when finished.

"She's more than okay," Mary gritted out as she put the cup back on the bedside table. "She's the picture of health."

Elation soared in Daisy's chest. "So, she's healed?"

"For how long, we don't know." Mary's voice softened. "You came so close, *mija*. Your skin had gone cold. Blood came out of your nose, mouth, and ears. Axel was…"

Axel.

Daisy screwed up her face as the hit of emotion tried to strangle her. "Is he okay?"

"Look beside you."

Daisy glanced down to the opposite side of the bed. Axel was asleep on the floor. Daisy's face crumpled again. He hadn't left her.

"What is it going to take to teach you that you deserve to be here?" Mary asked quietly, pain in her eyes. "I don't know what else to do. I don't know how to show you that leaving you was a mistake. It wasn't personal. It was a black and white decision I made with a shitty outcome."

"As was this," Daisy replied. "I knew Axel wouldn't survive the loss of his last remaining family member. I knew I could help. That was it." She scowled at Mary. "You asked me to lead with my heart. Why are you so angry at this?"

"Because I don't want to lose you," she choked out. "None of us do."

Daisy wasn't sure if she was ever here for them to lose. Sometimes she felt like she watched herself from a distance. Sometimes—she glanced down at Axel—sometimes she didn't. She felt whole. But it was so new, she wasn't sure how to accept it. She guessed she would get used to it over time, and maybe one day, that distance would disappear completely.

She hoped.

"Don't do that again," Mary said, standing up. Her eyes hardened. "As the eldest in this family, you have responsibilities. *Don't die* being chief among them."

With that, Mary left the room and Daisy was left with her self-destructive thoughts and Axel still snoozing on the floor. He must have been tired to sleep through the argument. And if he was here, instead of with Elena, he must have been worried about Daisy. More guilt sliced through her, and she screwed up her nose. No matter what she did, she hurt someone, but maybe that was just part of life.

Daisy must have dozed off because the next time she woke, Axel was sitting in Mary's vacated chair, his head in his hands, eyelashes drooping.

"Hey," she rasped. Dry throat again.

His lashes lifted and it was a hit to the solar plexus. What little breath Daisy had in her body vaporized as he ensnared her with those gorgeous eyes. It was more than the aesthetics of them, it was the way they stared at her with longing, need, and consuming love. Or maybe that was her own emotions.

"Hey yourself," he said softly, and brought the water to her lips.

While she drank, she marked the changes in him. His stubble had grown to a beard. His hair was messy. He looked more disheveled than when she'd found him by Elena's bed side.

"How are you feeling?" he croaked, and then cleared his throat.

"To be honest, a little weird inside."

He frowned. "Like how weird? Your blood pressure dropped a few times. You've been out for a day. Should I call Grace?"

"A whole day?" She blinked. Then squirmed. She couldn't explain the weirdness. Her body just felt off. Must be the loss of blood still. "Don't call Grace."

She couldn't take it if she got another lecture about how reckless she'd behaved.

Axel took Daisy's hand. "Each of your family donated blood to you to make up for what you gave Elena."

"They did?" She stilled.

He nodded. "They weren't sure it would work but donated a little at a time over a day. You look good."

The corner of her lips lifted in a hesitant smile, then dropped when she caught the anguish on Axel's face.

"What you did," he said, voice low.

Daisy braced for the lecture, but it never came.

"I can't thank you enough, Daisy."

"You're not angry?"

"Angry?" He shook his head. "I'm fucking beside myself. I'm..."

He couldn't seem to get the words out.

"You *are* angry," Daisy said, slumping.

His expression hardened in a way she'd never seen before. "After the best sex of my life, with the most incredible woman who I trusted implicitly, I woke up, Daisy, and you were gone." He swallowed. "I've seen some shit in my job, but I'll never forget the image of you on the floor, bleeding out of your nose and ears… cold. Lifeless." His bronze skin turned green, and he couldn't look at Daisy. "It should have been a happy moment. Elena was better. But all I could see was your face all slack and… it scared the shit out of me. I've never felt this way."

"I'm sorry."

"I'm not angry at you. I'm angry at me." He shook his head, and scrubbed his hand through his hair, getting more worked up with each passing second. "Daisy, I love you, but you can't risk yourself like that. I don't know what I said or did to make you feel like that was the only answer."

"You didn't *make* me do it."

"I know that. I just… I never thought I'd feel this way again. My parents' illness came on a lot faster than Elena's, and in some ways, it was a shock to my system. With Elena, I've been praying and hoping and refusing to admit defeat… but there you were suddenly at death's door and I wasn't prepared." He cleared his throat and stood. "I'm glad you're feeling better."

That sounded cold. Clipped. Final. Daisy didn't like it. She tried to get up, to reach for him, but he stepped back. He put his hands in his pockets. Still couldn't look her in the eye.

"The city is falling apart." He glanced out the window. "Now that you're okay, and Elena is okay, I need to clean up my karma and get back to work."

"Wait." She tried to get out of bed.

"Don't," he said, eyes softening. "Please don't. You need to properly heal this time. I need time to think. I have to… feel like I have a bit of control in my life or something. I have to go. Let the transfusions do their job. Stay and rest. Promise me that?"

Dumbfounded, Daisy could only nod. The lost look in his eyes was too much. What was happening? Was he leaving? She opened her mouth to speak, but he walked out.

twenty-nine

DAISY LAZARUS

DAISY'S FINGERS fisted in the sheets. To keep tears from spilling, she stared at the potted plants she'd put in the room for Elena. They now looked dull and limp.

She wasn't sure why she was so emotional. Axel had a job. He had a life. She couldn't expect him to stay with her.

I need time to think, he'd said. There were no strings of Portuguese curses mumbled under his breath. At least if he'd been angry at her, then at least she knew he felt something. But he'd been angry at himself. And then he'd looked dejected. Cold.

And Daisy knew that detachment was worse than anything else.

A million logical reasons danced around her head, but the only one that stood out was the irrational one. That this was the start of her being left behind. And this time, she only had herself to blame. That she hated life with its messy love.

A knock came at the door. Elena poked her head through.

"Hi," she said, a broad smile on her face.

She still wore her beanie to cover her bald head, but her complexion truly glowed. Daisy had never seen her so beautiful and full of life. It was remarkable. Her spirits lifted, if only for a little while, and all the stupid things she'd just thought hurt her head.

Feelings were confusing.

Too hard.

"I brought you soup," Elena said and showed a bowl of steaming liquid. "I hope you like it. I wasn't sure what your favorite was so made you mine. Apparently *minha mãe*—my mother—used to make it. Since I was so little when they died, Axel taught me." Her brows lifted. "He taught me many things, chiefly the naughty words in Portuguese."

Elena waited expectantly at the threshold and Daisy didn't have the heart to turn her away.

"Come in," Daisy said.

It was only meant as appeasement, but the moment the mouth-watering aroma of chicken soup hit Daisy's nose, her stomach grumbled, and she groaned. "That smells good."

"It's *Canja*. You'll love it. Trust me." Elena lifted a small bed tray from the floor and placed it over Daisy's legs. Then she set the bowl down and handed Daisy a spoon. "I hope you don't mind that I cooked it. I wanted to say thank you and Doctor Grace said that if you woke to feed you proper food." She blushed. "So stupid to think a bowl of soup will ever measure up to your gesture but, like Axel, I'm kind of like a bad smell. I won't go away."

Daisy hoped that was true of her brother. She hoped her manic thoughts were just her own stupid fears and irrational insecurities. But after the life she'd lived, decades of self-destructive thoughts were hard to correct. Elena perched on the bed near Daisy's feet and stared.

"You're just going to watch me eat?"

"Yep."

"Did Axel tell you to watch me?"

"Nope."

Daisy slurped the soup. "This is good."

"Told you." Elena beamed.

In the next two minutes, Daisy ingested the entire bowl while Elena watered the plants and hummed a song that sounded remarkably like *You Are My Sunshine.* It was nice.

Daisy hadn't even known she was hungry until she'd tasted it. A bit like Axel, she realized. She hadn't known how bad she missed him until he was gone.

"Does he hate me?" she asked quietly.

Elena stopped watering. "Of course not."

"I think I messed up."

"Why?"

"I guess I should have asked him to help when I helped you." She bit her lip. "Mary is also angry. I would have thought saving you was a good thing, but they both acted like I was being selfish."

Elena came back to sit on the bed by Daisy's legs. "They're angry because they care for you."

"I still don't get it."

"It's a good thing."

"How?"

"They don't want you to die, and to be honest, seeing the way my brother reacted, I know he's in love with you. If you died…" Elena blinked rapidly then sniffed. "He'd be a complete *filho da puta,* if you know what I mean."

"No, I don't. He really loves me?"

"Of course he does." Elena's glistening eyes slid to Daisy's. "He deserves to have someone he cares about in his life. Someone who cares back."

"I don't know if I'm that person."

Elena let loose a string of Portuguese curses, just like she'd heard Axel do, and it made her smile.

"Duh," Elena said, brow furrowing. "Yes, you are that person. You almost died so his sister could live. If that's not caring back, then I don't know what is."

Daisy bit her lip, smiling at Elena.

"So, he'll be back?" Daisy asked.

"Double duh." Elena collected the bowl from Daisy. "You guys talk the same language. Of course, he'll be back. Now, you get some rest. Just give us a shout if you need anything. Oh, and I almost forgot."

Elena pulled a small card out of her pocket. She placed it before Daisy on the bed with a shy smile. "I made you this. Maybe when you're better, we can finish it."

It was a card with a likeness of Daisy's face on it with the word Despair and some numbers.

"What is this?" she asked.

"It's a collector's card. Kind of like baseball cards. I was working on some before I met you all. Alek and I were talking before about what kind of stats each of you would have." She pointed at the numbers in the corner. "See? There's power, dexterity, and heart. Since we've not really seen your gift in action, we weren't sure what to put for those."

"It says three thousand next to heart." Daisy blinked.

"It's the most of them all. Anyway, I'll leave you to rest." She gave Daisy a shy wave and then rushed out as though embarrassed.

After she left, Daisy stared at the ceiling for a long time. The most heart of them all. Tears burned her eyes and she blinked fast so they didn't flow over.

So... having people angry that she almost died meant they cared deeply for her. It had confused her because Julius used to also get angry at her if she put herself at risk. But it had always been because losing her jeopardized his plans. He would withhold affection and lord it over her like bait. He would lock her in the attic and take away her privileges.

But Mary and Axel were just angry. As Flint once said to her, people were entitled to their emotions. It was annoying, but she guessed, that was what family was—a safe place to let loose emotions. That was what being loved meant.

We make mistakes together.

Axel had just wanted to be a part of Daisy's life, the good and the bad.

LIZA AND SLOAN were Daisy's next visitors. Both were freshly showered and looking a little worse for wear, as though they'd been out fighting. Probably had. Daisy could still hear police sirens outside every now and then and drifting in and out of sleep so often, she lost track of time.

"Hey," Liza said as she knocked on the doorframe.

"How you feeling?" Sloan asked.

Liza sprawled in the chair by the bed. Sloan perched on the edge of the bed near Daisy's feet.

"I'm okay," she admitted. "Feeling better by the hour."

Silence descended and Daisy knew they felt the same awkwardness she did. Not only was Daisy not a girly-girl, but she'd missed out on sister bonding with these two growing up. She wondered how close they'd all have become if things were different. Sloan popped the end of her dark braid into her mouth and chewed the end. Liza scowled at her as though it was a common habit but didn't say anything. Then she turned her scowl on Daisy.

"You shouldn't have done that, Daisy," Liza clipped, her eyes wide. "For fuck's sake. I know you're our big sister, but for once will you do as you're told and stop making the sacrifice play?"

"Sorry," she mumbled.

"Promise." Liza punched Daisy in the arm.

It hurt. "Ow."

"Promise," Sloan added, and gave Daisy a look that said she would punch Daisy too.

"Fine, I promise."

"Good," they both said.

Then more silence descended and Daisy fiddled with the blanket.

"You bored?" Sloan asked, straightening as though a great idea had hit. "I could get my gaming system for you and hook it up in here."

Daisy gave her a small smile. "No thank you. I wouldn't know where to begin."

"You shitting me?" Sloan blurted. "You mean you've never gamed?"

"Wasn't really allowed."

"Fucking Julius," Sloan snapped. "What a dickwad. Well, after all this, I'm going to show you how."

Liza scoffed. "You can say no to that too."

Sloan mocked her, "*You can say no to that too.* Mind your own beeswax, Liza."

Liza rolled her eyes and then asked Daisy, "Where's Axel?"

Whatever humor had danced in the air dissipated.

"I think he's gone back to work," Daisy mumbled.

Perhaps Liza could see the worry in Daisy's eyes because her voice softened. "He'll be fine. If he's anything like Joe—"

"Or Max," Sloan offered.

Liza glared at Sloan. "You didn't even know what I was going to say."

Sloan tossed some lint at Liza. "Just say it then."

Daisy tried to hide her smile. She liked this ease between them. She liked it even more that they were including her and had the sense that in a few months time, if things ever settled down, Daisy would joke around with them just as much as they did now.

"What I was saying," Liza continued. "Before I was rudely interrupted is that if Axel is anything like Joe, then he'll need to feel useful."

"That's exactly what I thought you'd say," Sloan snorted.

Liza met Daisy's eyes. "Being the mate to a powerful woman isn't easy. There are times Joe can be a real dick."

"I'm more worried about his safety."

"He'll be fine. But, yeah, if anyone understands about the worry, it's us. Also you should know, that even though we're as gifted as we are, our mates can all be alphaholes sometimes. They blame it on our pheromones. Dicks. Point is, if you ever need to borrow my handcuffs to teach him a lesson, just let me know."

"You're serious?"

"Deadly." Liza smirked. "Especially if you use them in the bedroom, if you know what I mean. He'll learn his lesson real quick then."

"Ew," Sloan said. "I don't need to hear about your sex-capades. But for reals, Daze. If he's an asshole about anything, you let us know."

"Thanks," Daisy replied, amusement warming her soul. "But I hope I have it sorted. He's a good guy."

"Bit younger than you, am-I-right?" Sloan teased, waggling his eyebrows. "You clearly still have it."

Daisy deadpanned. "Are you calling me old?"

Both her sisters blanked. Sloan's mouth opened and shut like a fish.

"Um…" Liza's eyes widened.

Then Daisy laughed and snorted. "Got you."

Everyone sighed at once, then her sisters joined Daisy in chuckling before finally standing.

"Right, well, while we thoroughly enjoy having our big sister dish out snappy comebacks, you need to rest." Liza dragged Sloan up by the arm.

"But I wanna set up the Xbox and game." Sloan whined, but then caught the glare on Liza's face. "Right. We gotta go."

They both gave Daisy a quick squeeze on the arm, then left. The next time Daisy drifted to sleep, it was with a smile on her face.

DAISY COULDN'T SLEEP.

After she'd eaten the soup, and Liza and Sloan visited, her energy came back in surges. Tony had also popped in at one point with Bailey and offered to make more food, to which she politely accepted, ate, and then went back to sleep. But now… now she felt like she'd been sleeping for weeks.

It had only been a day, surely.

Daisy didn't want to piss off anyone so stayed in bed. She practiced using her gift, finding it easier to call to the surface. First, she'd started by fluttering the leaves on the plants. Then she moved entire objects. She finally got to the point where she could lift multiple plants in the air and not feel drained.

No blood leaked from her nose. Not even a sniffle.

In fact, she felt energized. So much so that when she heard Parker's and Alice's voice in the main living room, she ripped the IV drip from her arm and tossed off the coverlet.

She was done lying around.

What the hell am I wearing?

Glancing down, she found she was in some kind of boy-short underwear and a singlet. How had she not noticed wearing that when going to the bathroom? She didn't even want to know who put that on her, or where the items had come from. Daisy pulled the thin coverlet off the bed and wrapped it around her, then went out to greet her brother.

He was in the kitchen, guzzling water. Still in his Deadly suit. Alice was next to him, her head down. When they looked at Daisy, she gasped. Both had injuries and blood over their features.

"What happened?"

They became confused.

Parker asked, "What do you mean?"

"I mean, you're injured."

"Not as bad as some of the others."

"What?" she gaped. "What the hell is happening?"

"I thought someone told you?"

"Told me what?" She glared, her heart racing a million miles an hour.

"That shit has hit the fan," Alice replied. "Out there. It's like Julius unleashed every weapon in his arsenal. We've been non-stop fighting since you—" Her gaze snapped to where Elena watched them from the couch. "Since you almost died."

"Why didn't someone tell me?"

"You needed rest," Parker shot back with a growl. "You still need rest. What are you doing out of bed?"

"I feel good. Better than good. Get me some clothes and I'll get out there. Surely Julius is running out of people to fight for him by now."

Alice's expression turned bleak. Her freckles seemed to melt away.

"That's why he poisoned the water supply. We're still trying to work with the Mayor's office to flush it out."

Daisy's blood went cold as she realized Axel was out there. Before she could speak, Parker seemed to know her question.

"He knows to be careful," he said.

Alice's cell phone rang. She stepped away to take it.

Parker asked, "Where's Mary?"

"Here." She came from down the hallway where her room was.

Strangely, she was dressed in her old Sinner uniform. Black assassin attire. Skintight. Hooded. With a red face scarf that was pulled down around her neck. Her long dark, silvershot hair was pulled back into a tight braid. But the most alarming thing was the look in her eyes. Daisy had seen that look before—just before Mary had punched the close button on the elevator door almost thirty years ago.

Surely Daisy was imagining things.

All the warmth leaked out of the room.

"What are you doing?" Parker asked, straightening.

Mary didn't answer. She turned in the direction Alice had headed and stared. Two seconds later, Alice returned with a grim set to her lips and jaw.

"What the fuck is going on here?" Parker asked, golden eyes darting between his mother and fiancée.

"That was Thea, one of the Sinners."

"Are they okay?"

Alice shook her head, her clever eyes sliding to Mary who only lifted her chin with a stony resolution hardening her eyes. "You know, don't you?"

"I had a vision."

"Why didn't you say something?"

"It won't change the outcome."

Parker slammed his metal palm on the counter, rattling the foundations. "What the fuck is going on?"

Alice folded her arms and shot him a look that said, *Don't take that tone with me.* She waited a moment before answering.

"Syndicate Tower is under attack," she explained. "And it's not random, like the rest of the chaos is. This seems targeted."

"He's going for that spot," Parker said. "Truly?"

Daisy swallowed. Julius believed, as did the Sinners, that the replicates when uncontrolled tried to get to the strongest concentration of sin. They'd tried to dig through a spot in the Tower's sewers. The Hildegard Sisterhood thought if the replicates got their way, they'd open a portal to another dimension—a hell dimension. Parker said it was rubbish. Daisy didn't know what to believe.

Opening some kind of worm hole portal had never been part of Julius's original plans, but since Daisy had destroyed his only viable biological samples of his wife and daughter to replicate, he'd gone crazy. Nothing he did made sense.

Daisy just knew one thing. If there was an attack there, then Julius wasn't far away. She could go down there, hunt him down, and end things once and for all.

"I'm coming with you," Mary said.

"Don't be silly," Parker shot back. "You know you'll just hurt yourself."

"I know how to take care of myself," Mary replied coolly. She stared at Daisy for a moment, seemingly wanting to say something but holding it back. Daisy wanted to say something herself. She wanted to tell Mary she understood now. She knew why Mary was angry at Daisy all the time, just as Daisy knew why she was angry at Mary.

They cared deeply for each other. Always had.

Parker gave his mate an exasperated look, but Alice only shrugged. "We're exhausted. We need all the help we can get."

"Then get me something to wear, too," Daisy returned.

Both Mary and Parker tried to refuse her, but she shot back, "If Mary goes, I go."

Mary lifted her chin. "And I won't go without Daisy."

Alice said, "Fine with me."

"*Women*," Parker cursed and stormed off.

The smile on Daisy's face was the first she'd shared with Mary. One of many, she hoped.

thirty

"YES, YES, YES," Julius cackled as he placed the personal items belonging to his wife and daughter around the underground sewer beneath Syndicate Tower.

His replicates and Faithful had drawn the Sinners out. He could hear them fighting as he set up the ritual. He was running out of time.

"Get the chalk," the voice hissed. *"Make the circle like I showed you."*

"There's still too much water," he replied and frowned at the puddled concrete culvert.

He'd let loose a few sentient plants in the sewage system to drink up the water so he had a clear view to the surface below. He'd been planning how to do this for days. He pulled what remained of his shredded trousers off and mopped up the mess around the gouge marks the replicates had made when digging.

"Hurry," the voice urged.

Julius scratched the arcane symbols into the concrete with shaking fingers. He couldn't believe he was about to see his family. Finally. He was bringing them home.

He tapped his chest with a chalk-stained finger. "Almost time, my loves. Almost time."

thirty-one
DAISY LAZARUS

DAISY WAS IN *THE* SUIT.

In all her years, in all her time, she'd never expected to be wearing it. She still didn't like it. It was temporary and only to get Parker off her case about needing the Kevlar-like protection. She scowled at him from across the operations room table as he vehemently argued with Flint and Mary about her staying at Lazarus House until she was recovered.

She appreciated him wanting to protect her, but she knew her own limits, and was about to tell him so when her cell phone rang. She picked it up from the operations table and walked into the weapon's room, ready to sync a katana to her back. Alice had already left to help her Sinner sisters with the attack at Syndicate Tower.

"Hello?"

"Daze." Axel's voice came through with loud background noise. Banging. Shouting. She went on high alert.

"Axel? Are you okay? Where are you calling from?"

"I'm fine." A drilling noise. He cursed then shouted at someone to wait two seconds before returning to her. "Elena texted and said you're heading out. I told you to stay. You almost died. Why can't you just stay and—"

"I'll be fine. I'm finally in a place where I have the freedom to do what I want and feel good about it. They need me."

He growled, "Then wait for me to come to you."

"Don't come. Your people need you."

"Daisy!" he snapped. "*You're* my people."

Parker tapped her on the shoulder, eyes fiery, jaw flexing. So the argument didn't go well, and from the look of restraint on his face, he'd heard her declaration to Axel. She waited for Parker's bossy demand to stay, but he surprised her. "Let's go. Griffin and Wyatt have already left. The rest should be there."

She nodded then found a katana on the rack as she returned to Axel. "I have to go. I love you."

Silence.

"Did you hear me?" she blurted. "I love you."

"Why are you saying that now?" His tone was tight.

"I have to go. Be safe."

She cut the call. The last thing she needed was for her mate to be where the danger was thickest. It was good he was at his job. He was doing something worthy. She synced the sword to her back, grabbed a bullwhip, and added a few shuriken and daggers to the utility belt at her hip. Pigeon had done well with the suit design and tech. She had to admit the suit was handy and even considered bringing her baseball bat. Someone had put it in the weapon's room. But it was time to be the villain again—the villain in Julius's world. She would not be pulling any punches.

"Hurry up!" Parker bellowed from the hallway.

"I'm coming." She jogged out, but Mary blocked her.

Daisy pulled up short.

"I have to be there," Mary said with urgency.

"So go."

Mary's eyes flashed. "He can't make me stay. Flint understands."

Daisy's eyes narrowed. Why was Mary telling her this? It was weird. Since when did Mary need permission. And then Daisy remembered the look in Mary's eyes when they'd been upstairs.

"You saw something in your vision," she said. "You didn't elaborate upstairs, and Parker thinks it's something to do with the Sinners, but it's not, is it? Just promise me one thing… none of us are getting left behind this time."

Mary's eyes glistened and she nodded. "You have my word. Everyone you love will be safe."

"Then you have to be there," Daisy agreed. "To do what you need to do. I'll back you up."

The garage door burst open, and in rushed two of her siblings. Evan held Tony as they limped in. Blood and dirt on their faces.

"Get Doc," Evan clipped, his eyes pinched. He also looked pale.

"What happened?" Mary asked as she rushed over. She gestured to Flint who picked up the phone, presumably to call Grace down.

Evan's green eyes skated to Daisy. "He gave too much blood. He's injured. Not healing fast enough."

"Where is he hurt?" she asked.

"His leg. I cauterized it." Evan peeled back the fabric on Tony's thigh. Red messy flesh greeted them. "His fire stopped working."

Tony winced. "I'm fine."

Daisy noticed Evan had wounds on his neck. His tattoo was all deformed. That meant the skin had been ruptured but she couldn't see details. "What's that from?"

Evan dabbed his neck. His fingers came away red. "Powered replicates. They've surrounded Syndicate Tower. Half the Sinners are down. Griffin is—"

The sound of tires skidding echoed through the garage door. Parker. His impatience had won and he'd left to join his mate. Shit.

"I have to go," Daisy blurted as Grace entered the room with her physician's kit in tow.

The doctor's alarmed eyes went to her mate, but Evan forced her to tend Tony. Daisy left them and jogged to the garage. She tried not to think about Evan's wounded neck. It was still bleeding. She tried even more not to think about what Evan said. Tony's fire had stopped working.

Had Daisy doomed them all when they'd donated their blood?

BEFORE DAISY COULD HALT her motorcycle at the Syndicate Tower battlefront, something hit her and flung her from the seat. She landed hard on the road and skidded. Friction warmed her side but the suit saved her from burns. Rolling like a cat, she grabbed a dagger from her belt and stabbed the asphalt to slow her trajectory.

Her blade went so deep it dug up rock. *Weird.*

She had only a moment to think, maybe the workmanship was dodgy and that's why she was strong enough to gouge it, then she was on her feet, wind blasting her face as she surveyed the scene. A setting sun crested the building, casting glare on a myriad of city windows. Mindless replicates fought the Deadly Seven on all sides—replicates seemed to be everywhere. At least three Sinners joined in. One redhead, two others. Their hoods had fallen back and, too exhausted from the battle, or too busy, they'd not lifted them again. From the way Parker roared as his bionic arm went through a replicate attacking another dark-suited woman, Daisy guessed it was Alice he protected.

Yanking his bloody hand out of the chest cavity, Parker barked something at the woman and pointed to the building, to presumable safety. She flipped him the bird and then dove headfirst back into battle with the other Sinners—none of which had the protection of a bulletproof suit. Definitely Alice. Daisy grinned.

The Sinners moved like synchronized dancers as they twirled and stabbed anything that came their way. It wasn't just replicates that attacked, but other Syndicate monsters—Daisy only needed to swivel her head and she found dozens more. Rabid animals. Humans with red eyes—drugged up on greed serum. A solitary Faithful piloted a mech suit—his white face mask flashed deep inside the robotic monster as it laid waste to a brick and mortar building.

The robotic arm halted mid air. Then the mech punched itself and fell backward. Daisy located Griffin standing twenty feet away, chasing down the Faithful before using his gift to pry open the cockpit and yanking the pilot out. Two seconds later, the mech suit sizzled as wires were cut.

While he was busy pulling out the mech suit wires, a shadow converged on him. Daisy had a split second to recognize a replicate with beastly claws about to strike down her brother fifty feet away. If she shouted, he might not hear her warning. A wave of instinct built inside her and she followed the need, she let it scorch through her body until she connected with the atoms between her and the beast. Then she squeezed.

As though an invisible rope lassoed around the replicate, he jerked toward Daisy, his feet dragging on the floor. Griffin looked up, saw what had just come after him and where it was now headed—to Daisy. Their eyes met over the distance, then he gave chase. His bo-staff flew from his hand, hit the beastly replicate in the head and took him down before Daisy could drag him more than twenty feet. Their eyes met again and then he nodded before collecting his bo-staff and finishing the job.

Daisy let go of her gift and wondered if maybe she found high ground she could be of better use. But the replicates seemed rabid. Insatiable. Even the one Parker had put his fist through tried to get up and fight. It was that serum. It made them mindless zombies with a taste for sin.

Closer to her, Daisy zeroed in on Wyatt near a hydrant as three replicates jumped him like cubs on a lion. He went down. She pushed effort into her legs and marked how good she felt. Energy crackled from her skin. She buzzed with adrenaline. Alert. Alive.

An arrow whizzed past Daisy's face and lodged in one of the replicates attacking Wyatt. Daisy unleashed her katana and took the second down. Sliced his head clean off. Wyatt broke the third in half. Blood sprayed Daisy's face, sinking into her mask.

She yanked it down to breathe. Didn't really like the mask anyway.

Fury contorted Wyatt's red-streaked face as he pushed the body parts off him as he got to his feet and yanked his own mask down. Blue eyes looked stark against the macabre war paint. He lifted his chin in greeting, then reached behind Daisy—no, he punched. His fist grazed her cheek but crunched bone behind her. Pivoting, Daisy discovered a replicate had stalked her. Wyatt shared a meeting of the eyes with Daisy and then ran down the street as he no doubt located another threat—probably sensing wrath.

The sense of rightness bloomed in Daisy's chest. This was her family. They had each other's backs. This was where she belonged, fighting alongside them.

It was also the doomsday Julius had hoped for. The moment they felled one attacker, another rose in its place. And the people, the poor infected people, were getting hurt.

Sirens blared as local police and SWAT turned up. Parker lifted his head from where he crouched at the ground, dragging an unconscious civilian to the side. His mask had also been torn from his face as he fought. Golden eyes met Daisy's then continued searching until he sourced Liza, still with her fuchsia face mask up and hiding her identity.

Liza's ungloved hands covered the mouth of a replicate as they wrestled on the ground. Within seconds her opponent went limp. When she removed her hands, foam bubbled at his mouth. Poisoned.

"Get them out of here," Parker bellowed, pointing to the new arrivals. "The last thing we need is for cops to get injured."

Or their identities exposed. Liza jumped up, nodded, then jogged to the police.

Her feet dragged. Tired. They all were, Daisy realized. Her family was running out of juice. She slid her gaze to Syndicate Tower, her old home. So many memories tried to push in. None of them good except the night Axel had shared with her.

The fight was out here because Julius was in there.

Someone grabbed Daisy's arm. She whipped around to see a Sinner. Not Alice. The other redhead.

She pulled down her red mask to reveal a pretty face.

"You," she panted. "We've been waiting for you."

"What?"

"Raven foresaw it had to be you to stop Julius from opening the hell gate."

"I just want to stop *him*."

"Whatever you believe, it's you."

"Mercy!" Another Sinner tossed a dagger at them.

It whizzed by their heads and embedded in the chest of a Faithful running closer. Two more emerged from behind as the first fell to the floor. Daisy's hand whipped out, intending to use her telekinesis, but a flush of fire laced with lightning shot from her hand. The stream hit the Faithful on the left in the chest, both igniting him on the outside and electrifying his insides. He was dead before he landed. His corpse sizzled. His white Halloween mask had melted to his face.

The third Faithful stopped suddenly, staring at the fate of his companion, then backed up and ran for his life.

Mercy gaped, "What the fuck was that?"

From around the street, Daisy felt the eyes of her siblings on her.

Parker shouted out, "You've taken on our traits through the blood exchange."

His words snapped Mercy into action. She gripped Daisy by the scruff and snarled in her face, shocking with her vehemence, "You're the only one who can stop him."

As if to punctuate her claim, the ground shook beneath their feet, setting off car and building alarms in the vicinity.

"That's him," Mercy blurted, her eyes wide. "You need to go *now*."

She shoved Daisy toward the building. Daisy jogged as her mind caught up. The earthquake was caused by whatever Julius was doing in the basement. And that extra energy Daisy had felt, it wasn't just some kind of advanced healing. It was each of her siblings' gifts simmering inside her, blending with hers. But for how long? At what cost?

Maybe Mercy was right. Maybe this was Daisy's fate.

It started with her; it would end with her.

She turned to Parker as she arrived at the Tower double glass doors, tapped her hood and activated the microphone to broadcast her next words, "Pigeon, I'm going after Julius. Don't wait up."

thirty-two

DAISY LAZARUS

INSIDE THE TOWER was as much of a war zone as outside. Daisy picked through the destruction of the lobby and then hurtled herself down the stairwell. This was all happening so fast. She burst into the basement and forced herself to quiet her mind.

Just as she had when she'd become the Falcon, she pushed out anything that made her human. Her new found love for her family. For Axel. She couldn't afford distractions. The time for ruthlessness was here. An ominous sense of doom clung to the air when she entered the laboratory the Sinners had been guarding.

Live wires hung from the ceiling where panels and lights had been scorched during what was probably a powered replicate battle. Lab equipment, that had already been damaged, was now destroyed. Tables were overturned. A wet substance was on the floor. She couldn't tell what it was.

The only light came from the ghostly hole in the wall that led to the sewer. Flickering light. Like candles.

Daisy still had her katana in her hand but decided in the small space she'd be better off with a knife. She swapped the weapons.

Parker's voice shouted at her through the hood's microphone.

"Despair, don't be stupid." He breathed and grunted hard as though he still battled. *"Come back and help us sort this shit out and then we do this together."*

"This was how it was always going to be," she whispered back as she surveyed the dark room, noting her eyesight had improved in the darkness—must be from Parker's blood. "Falcons hunt best when they're alone."

No hostiles here. Just the flickering light beyond and through the hole in the wall.

"You're not that person anymore," Parker shot back. *"Wait."*

She wanted to say that she'd learned her lesson about going off alone. That she'd learned she was a valued part of this incredible family. That mistakes were meant to be made together. But she knew. She knew with absolute certainty that this fight was hers, and hers alone. It always had been. From the moment she'd been left behind, she'd been groomed to fight alone.

It might have been Julius who did the grooming, but it was her family that taught her how to trust her instincts.

If what Mercy said was true, that Julius was about to rip open a gate to another dimension, then none of what happened on the street mattered. And Daisy was the only one powered up with enough juice to stop it. Her reuniting with her family, gaining their love and gifts, had led her to this moment.

Parker barked more orders, and her siblings joined him in berating her—trying to get her to wait, to do this as a team.

But she pulled the hood off so their voices dulled. They didn't understand the teamwork part was over.

DAISY CREPT through the destroyed lab, using Parker's sharp eyesight to navigate without alerting whoever was in the sewer. Smells assaulted her keen nose, and she couldn't distinguish what was what. Sulfur? Dirt. Water. Mold. Sweat. Some kind of fruity perfume that might have been shampoo. She wanted to sneeze, to get it all out, but forced herself to breathe slowly and calmly.

She had no idea how long these borrowed abilities would last. Her molecular biology might burn through the donated blood in hours, or... she could be stuck like this forever and end up with more complications. All she knew was that she had to be quick—get this over and done with.

With a dagger in her fist, her eyes on the flickering light, and her ears straining toward the low-pitched voice coming through the hole, she didn't notice the person hiding behind a fallen stainless steel table. A hand wrapped around Daisy's ankle. Her dagger was down and at the throat of the intruder before she registered who it was.

A Sinner. Black long hair, rainbow tips, stark brown eyes. Latino heritage.

"I'm Raven," she said. "I've been waiting for you."

Daisy crouched to get low. Raven winced and checked a wound at her ribs.

"Are you hurt?" Daisy asked.

"I'll live," she gritted out. "But we couldn't keep him away. He's in there now setting up the ritual."

"I don't care about that," Daisy said, straightening. But Raven tugged her back down.

"You should, because he's going to get it open."

"Then why aren't you letting me get to him now?"

"It's too late."

Like it was scripted, a hissing sound, a flare of light, and a cackle of a madman burst from the sewer and echoed off the walls. Two seconds later, another tremor rocked their feet. Daisy's eyes widened. Sulfur and burned candle wax bloomed.

"What the fuck?" she whispered to Raven.

"He's completed the ritual. It's happening."

"You can't be serious."

"Deadly. Listen carefully." She dragged Daisy down so they were face to face. Raven's eyes turned white. Her voice turned deep, and unearthly. "Two gates will open. Two afterlives. Heaven. Hell. Yin. Yang. One cannot close without the other. Balance must be maintained. One cannot exist without the other. And we cannot exist with them."

She slumped and breathed hard. When she slid her eyes back to Daisy, hers had returned to their normal shade. Hairs on the back of Daisy's neck lifted as though the weight of this moment was too heavy for reality.

"You need to hold the gates until Mary arrives," Raven explained. "She will know what to do."

What did Mary have to do with this? "This is madness."

"This is what we've been telling you all along." Raven's jaw hardened. "The fact that none of you believed us is not on us. But we *will* do everything in our power to make this work. Now go. Hold the gate."

Raven shoved Daisy toward the hole in the wall. Hold the gate. Whatever the fuck that meant. Her mind was awhirl with what she'd learned.

The state of her being was in such a flurry that she couldn't control the power leaking from her body. It seemed once she'd triggered them outside, the rest wanted to come out to play. Electricity skipped from her fingertips. Metal objects in the lab rattled. Yellow poison itched her palms, and as she got to the wall, claws ripped out of her fingertips.

What the fuck? How was this even possible? All she'd taken was their blood.

Parker had said their maker, their biological mother Gloria started with perfect when she'd created Daisy. Gloria herself had said she was special.

Daisy had thought it was because she could sense both virtue and sin... but... maybe Daisy had these gifts all along? Maybe she'd always had the extra organs inside her body.

When she arrived at the hole and peeked through, she wished she hadn't. Inside, where sewage water used to run in a culvert, the way was empty. Damp, scratched-out gouge marks had dug into the concrete. Hadn't the replicates done that with their fingers?

But it wasn't the scratch marks that worried her. It was the ritualistic dual circles next to each other sketched out with chalk into a warped ven diagram. A five-pointed star inside each. At the apex of each star sat an item. On one circle, Daisy recognized items from Julius's home. Those strange dust free marks on the furniture. Now she remembered what had been there. A Fabergé egg that belonged to Julius's wife. He'd told Daisy it was her most prized possession. At another point on the star was a doll. A candle, a jewelry box, and a stuffed animal missing an eye finished the star. On the other circle were disgusting objects. The carcass of a chicken, freshly killed. Bones. Some kind of eel. Human teeth. Another candle, this one sputtering and made from black wax. Bridging the middle of the circles, one foot inside each, Julius stood facing the opposite curved brick wall with his hands in the air. He chanted some stupid occultist shit that made no sense. It was probably gibberish.

He wore no pants.

His hair had been hacked down to the scalp.

He was insane.

Daisy straightened when she realized that's all he was, a madman without pants. It almost felt wrong to put him down.

"I can't believe I looked up to you once," she sneered.

He faced her and his eyes weren't his own. Two demonic black eyes looked back at her. Daisy gasped. The shock to her system made her realize other senses were firing in her body—telling her something wasn't quite right. That telekinesis sense that could fit between atoms went haywire. It was as though the atmosphere was changing. Popping. Equalizing… or the opposite. Imbalance.

The hairs on her arms lifted beneath her suit, making her skin feel tight.

Something evil was coming. Knowing this could be part of Evan's precognitive skill, she acted immediately. She trusted her gut and threw the knife at Julius, aiming for his neck—just as a long crack rent the ground, splitting the ritualistic circles in half.

Her knife went sideways and hit a solid wall of air and clattered to the ground. Two holes opened up in the ground on either side of the thing that wasn't Julius and he grinned.

thirty-three

DAISY LAZARUS

DAISY LEAPED BACKWARD AS two holes opened up in the ground, one on each side of Julius. She felt the rip in the atmosphere as though it happened through her body.

Wrong.

Everything felt wrong.

It was as though she existed upside down but was still standing on her feet. The tunnel became a space that existed between time. The air thickened and sizzled with power. Wind buffeted her face. Light and shadow burst from the ruptures—tendrils from each fighting for supremacy.

Julius's laugh turned into a cackle. "It's happening! It's finally happening."

His voice warped between his own and that other deep monstrous side. This was beyond anything Daisy had ever trained for and she could only stand there stunned, watching it all unfurl before her eyes like a nightmare made flesh.

From the middle, Julius crouched and dipped his hands into the chasms beside him—one into each hole. He heaved and pulled some-

265

thing out, *someone* out. Deafening screams hit Daisy's sensitive ears. She clamped her hands over them, trying to focus through the piercing sound. It wasn't only the sound, it was the sense of despair clawing at her gut—it came from the dark hole. And the flutters of joy came from the light. The resulting turmoil inside her took long gulps of air to control.

Biting her lip, she knew she had to do something. Anything. She couldn't stand there like a statue and freak out. She was better than this. So she pulled her katana from its sheath, braced herself against the wind, and stabbed in Julius's direction. All she could think was that if she could get to him, then everything else would work itself out. He'd started it all. He would be the end. But her sword hit an invisible wall. Her wrist jarred painfully and she involuntarily dropped it. Metal clanked on the tunnel's concrete floor.

"What the—?" she gasped.

She tested the air before her, with both her hands and her gift. Like a mime, she placed her palms about the space. It felt solid to the touch, despite being able to see through.

While Daisy stood helpless on one side of the barrier, Julius dragged a woman out of the light cavern. An echo of his action on the dark side oozed a shadow creature out. It was dark. Four legs. Monstrous with red eyes and a dripping maw.

Daisy couldn't see it properly. Couldn't decipher what it looked like beyond the shadow, but she *felt* it. Pure despicable evil. It was a thing of indiscriminate nightmares. Sin coming to life. While on the lighter side she sensed only joy and happiness. Comfort. Peace. It called to her most basic desires to belong.

She glanced down at her Yin-Yang wrist tattoo. Light and dark. Heaven and Hell.

It must be.

Panic like no other filled her to the brink. Goosebumps erupted over her flesh and she pushed every ounce of power from her body at the invisible wall, hammering it with her need to protect.

In her mind, all she could see were her loved ones. Her brothers and sisters outside fighting against beings of flesh and blood, winning when it might not even matter. Axel somewhere in the distance, rescuing those who needed it... Elena, freshly recovered and finally looking forward to a life. Mary. Flint. Daisy's family.

The world could be ripping apart, right here.

"Focus on the barrier," Raven shouted from behind Daisy. "Use your gift to find a weak spot. This might help."

The Sinner limped up beside Daisy and tossed something wet at the the invisible boundary. Everywhere the water touched, it sizzled like acid. Daisy had no idea what Raven had tossed, but as soon as the droplets hit the ritual boundary, she sensed it weaken. The psychic must know what they were dealing with. Daisy had to trust her.

She shoved her gift into those tiny droplet spaces and expanded, hating that this was all she could do while watching Julius pull a second, smaller figure from the hole. She almost lost the contents of her stomach as another twisted creature emerged on the dark side—as though that hole was a horrific mirror reflecting the pure souls coming from the light.

"My loves, my loves," Julius cried, tears in his manic eyes. He sounded more like himself now. Less like the thing occupying his body when Daisy had arrived.

Julius gathered the two stunned females into his arms. His wife—a dark skinned beauty. His pre-teen daughter—the perfect blend of both parents. They looked just as bewildered and afraid as Daisy.

"What have you done?" his wife murmured, tears streaming down her face.

Their daughter cried and grasped onto her mother's ethereal dress as it solidified.

"I brought you back, my darlings. You're safe here with me!"

"But we were happy," his wife accused, her anguish crumpling her features. "We were happy!"

Julius blinked. Stunned. As though he'd never once imagined this would be her reaction. Then he hit his temple, and growled, "No. You *will* be happy now that you're back with me."

His jaw set as he tried to drag them to the side so they wouldn't fall back into the hole, but they rejected him. His daughter's cries worsened to a wail. His wife kept shouting and shoving Julius off her.

"No, no, no," she cried. "Let us go back."

Daisy shouted at Raven, "I need more of that liquid!"

"Holy water. This is the last of it."

She tossed a small vial to Daisy who smashed the glass bottle on the invisible barrier. Holy water ruptured the block. Daisy forced her gift into the weak points and then expanded it. Feeling the gap widen, she added everything she could. She pushed in electricity from Evan, magnetism from Griffin, fire from Tony until burning embers surrounded the perimeter of the opening she created. It burned wider, bringing with it the smell of ozone and the foul stench from within. Whether the stink came from the macabre ritualistic pieces, the sewer, or the holes in the ground, she wasn't sure.

But she was gaining access. With the weakening barrier, the mind-numbing, gut curdling sense of despair worsened. More came from the dark place the creatures had come from. They prowled around the dark hole, sniffing the shadows and pawing at it. There were more of its kind behind the shadows, Daisy could sense it. All it took was for them to find a way to pull their friends through and then they'd be overrun with the monsters.

Follow my instincts.

That's what everyone kept telling Daisy.

Just let go, Axel had once told her.

Stop thinking about it. Just do it.

So she became what monster's ran from. She summoned the worst she'd ever felt, called on Sloan's gift and projected despair, fear, horror, and helplessness. She speared it through the gap in the barrier, toward Julius, toward his family, toward the creatures. She flung it through until the two women screamed in terror and the twisted creatures cowered. Julius's family ran—right out of the arcane circles.

"No!" Julius bellowed, chasing them. "We're not ready—"

But the moment their feet stepped outside of the circle, the invisible barrier holding Daisy back broke, and with it collapsed whatever force held Julius's wife's and daughter's corporeal forms together. They became ghostlike. Their screams became distant. The candles inside the ritual circles winked out. Then, like falling grains of sand, the last of their light spilled onto the ground in a cascade and Julius's original family was no more.

Daisy sensed nothing from them, and in horror realized that they hadn't returned to their happy place. Their existence was over. Daisy had interrupted his ritual before it had a chance to completely bring them back... or they needed more time to fully solidify.

Julius wailed and fell to his knees, desperately trying to gather the sand left over from their forms but it spilled through his fingers.

Daisy wanted to gloat, to laugh at him and say, "After all that, your greed has left you with nothing. You ruined your family's happiness by bringing them here."

But despair from the pit of the dark hole thickened. It pulsed. Unlike the light side, where Daisy sensed joy and happiness, things tried to crawl through from the darkness.

"Now," Raven cried and limped to pick up Daisy's katana to spear at the shadow creatures, still cowering and pawing at the shadow hole. "Help me get them back where they belong. They're fully formed so they have to go back. Don't let more out."

"Hold it closed," Daisy murmured, her eyes wide as she stared at the pulsing shadow. That's what Raven had told Daisy to do when she'd first arrived. Raven's eyes had gone white. It had been a vision, just like Mary's.

If this is what Mary faced when she had visions, then Daisy understood why she made the choice she did to leave Daisy behind that fateful day when she was a child. Sometimes risks had to be made for the good of everyone. For loved ones.

Daisy stepped toward the holes, placed herself between the two and reached into the pit of despair. The instant she touched shadow, she felt it crawl up her arms like spiders. But she was ready for it. She opened herself up. She let the shadows see she *was* despair. She was like them. Once they recognized her, the gate's defenses eased enough to let her awareness in. She latched onto the metaphysical opening with her mind, and like a handle on a door, she mentally grasped it and held against the pull of beings on the other side.

They didn't like that. And the black twisted creatures also didn't like that. Guttural snarls filled the air. Mounting pressure, moans and groans, cries and shrieks, pulsed against her, forcing her to hold more until tears burned her eyes and she screamed against the strain.

"I'm holding it! Now how do we close it?"

"Balance," Raven said as she booted one of the creatures. It fell writhing and howling into the dark hole, disappearing into the shadow and smoke. "Each side needs their souls returned."

The last twisted creature launched at Raven, dripping fangs snapping.

"Shit," Raven blurted, dodging. She hit a tunnel wall, jarring her shoulder.

She was completely vulnerable, soft and mortal, unlike Daisy.

"Get out," Daisy shouted. "Leave this to me."

"You can't do it on your own." Brave words from Raven weren't reflected on her face as she flattened herself against the wall as the monster prowled closer.

A dagger whizzed past Daisy's cheek from somewhere behind in the lab. It embedded in the shadowed shoulder of the creature. The hilt stuck, wobbled. Not all shadow after all. *Fully formed,* Raven had said. It turned and faced Daisy, thinking she'd thrown the dagger. Another dagger flew. And another.

No, not dagger. Shuriken. A throwing star.

Daisy glanced over her shoulder to the lab. Standing there in the middle of the hole in the wall, with her husband at her back, was Mary. Wind from the gates blew her long braid. In her hands, she had more shuriken loaded and ready to loose.

"Duck!" Mary shouted, then threw.

Blades whizzed by Daisy. Each target hit home. The creature jolted back a step. Mary was almost sixty, yet she'd not lost her touch. Flint darted about the broken lab behind Mary, collecting items, doing something with a determined look on his face.

"Concentrate on holding the gate," Raven demanded, drawing Daisy's attention back. "And I'll—"

The creature lashed out. It's claws shredded Raven's shirt at the stomach.

"Get back!" Flint bellowed, barging past Mary. He used a lighter to set fire to a rag sticking out of a bottle then tossed it. It hit the creature. The glass broke. And chemical flames enveloped the being. Holding her bleeding middle, Raven booted the beast. It fell backward screaming into the black hole.

Daisy felt the atmosphere lighten a little, almost as though she was returning to normal—not upside down but half way.

"You sense that?" Raven's eyes shot to Daisy. "The mystical energy is shifting."

Panting and sweating, she stumbled to the wall beside Daisy

where she collapsed. Her complexion was pasty as she met Daisy's eyes.

"When balance is restored, do your thing," she rasped.

Raven's eyelashes fluttered. Her eyes rolled.

"Help her!" Daisy shouted to Mary, but the woman was already racing forward. She checked Raven's wounds. Shredded claw marks ripped across the old wounds on her stomach. Daisy flinched at the glimpse of raw flesh.

"Get help," Daisy said through her gritted teeth.

"The Sinners won't let anyone else in," Mary said, coming to her feet.

Daisy went cold. That tingling precognition sense she'd borrowed from Evan went haywire.

Wrong.

She almost lost her mental grip on the gate, but grasped it again as beings beyond pulsed and pushed at her.

It only occurred to her now that it was strange the Sinners had said to wait for Mary and Flint, and not the rest of her siblings. Not the Sinners, nor a priest, or someone else who could fight this evil trying to come through.

"Why won't they let anyone in?" Daisy shouted.

Flint placed a calming hand on Daisy's shoulder. "You know why."

Her wild gaze darted to Flint, Mary, then to Julius still blubbering over a pile of sand. She looked at her hands stretched wide toward the gates. The yin-yang tattoo on her inner wrist glared at her. Balance must be restored. They'd removed two souls from each hole, but only the dark monsters had returned. And with Julius's wife and daughter a pile of sand, two souls needed to go through the light gate in order to close it all.

"We couldn't tell them because they would have found a way to stop us," Mary explained. "And this way had the highest chance of success."

Tears burned Daisy's eyes and she shot accusatory eyes at Mary, who had clearly seen this in her visions. Why else had she been so determined to come?

"You promised," Daisy accused. "You said no one would get left behind!"

Mary lifted her chin and took Flint's hand. "I promised that no one you loved would get left behind. And, *mija*, despite our efforts, you don't love us. Not the way you're learning to love your siblings and I accept full responsibility for that."

"We need to do this, Daisy," Flint's deep voice rumbled, just louder than the moans and wails coming from the dark hole. "We've lived a full life, something that was robbed from you. We need to show you how much you mean to this family."

"No," she whispered, shaking her head. "Don't do this. Two others can be sacrificed. I'll be one, Julius can be the other."

"It needs to be us." Mary came up to Daisy, knowing full well Daisy could do nothing to stop her unless she released her hold on the gate. "I owe you this, *mija*. And Flint won't let me do it alone. We decided together."

Flint nodded, and tightened his grip on Mary's hand. "This is our choice, Daisy. We're making it willingly and we're doing it out of love."

"Family first," Mary said. "Is something I always drilled into your siblings while they were growing up. It means the unit before the individual. You're a part of that family, Daisy."

"So are you!" she countered.

Loud banging, walls shaking, and shouts came from within the lab. When Daisy checked over her shoulder, she saw through to the lab where the Sinners, all worse for wear and torn and bleeding, held a line on this side of the glass doors. Beyond the doors were the Seven. Parker's gold eyes were bleak as Alice held him back from tearing everything down. Metal in the lab lifted and hovered as Griffin worked to overpower them—but his hold was weak. They were all tired. Liza threw her shoulder against the glass. Sloan's palm plastered to the door, tears running tracks down her dirty face. Tony's fire spluttered somewhere behind the group and they all made way for him. Evan was the only one standing and staring as though, perhaps, he had also seen Mary's and Flint's fate and expected this. Or maybe he was finally piecing it together.

Julius, sitting in the dark with his failures, laughed and hiccuped between his tears.

"It should be him!" Daisy choked out as she glared at him. The force of holding the gate sent a warm trickle running from her nose. Blood. She wouldn't be able to hold for much longer.

Mary kissed Daisy on the cheek, through the wet tears sliding down her face.

"It can't be Julius," she explained as she looked at the illuminated hole in the ground. "We don't want to send him to an afterlife full of joy, and that's what it is, you must sense it by now." She was right. Daisy knew this, deep in her gut. One side was despair and sadness, the other joy and light.

"It has to be us," Mary insisted. "It's the only way you'll see that you're worth it, *mija*."

Flint kissed Daisy on the other cheek and patted her shoulder.

"Remember what I told you when Mary had passed out?" he asked her softly.

"You said, when you love someone, you keep the faith."

"Good girl." He coughed in the manly way fathers do when trying to hide their feelings, but then he added, "Remember to remind your siblings of that when we're gone."

Daisy sobbed, fell to one knee, and the dark pulsing shadows pushed out, testing her hold. She screamed with the pain of reining her control back in. More wetness trickled onto her upper lip. Just as Mary and Flint walked toward the hole filled with light, just as they were about to step in, Daisy shouted at their backs, "You're wrong. I do love you. I never stopped."

That's why it hurt so bad.

Mary's liquid gaze filled with forlorn anguish. "Then you understand why we're doing this. And you know what must be done afterward. We are grateful for you, Daisy. Family first."

With that, they stepped into the beyond. Light swallowed them. Gone.

There were no screams of terror, no sensed despair, only flutters of joy. Then the pressure in the atmosphere equalized. *Balance.* The malicious forces pushing against her hold on the dark gate eased. The pulsing shadows lessened. All light in the tunnel winked out.

The gates were closed.

Daisy scrambled to the hole Mary and Flint had stepped into, but the bottomless pit was gone. Only a ditch of dirt and rock remained. She dug around with her fingers, desperate to find them. Nothing.

Julius's laughter spurred her on.

"You did this," Daisy blurted, aiming her fury and pain at the location his laughter came from. It was hard to see in the darkness, the only light coming from the hole in the wall leading to the broken lab. She wasn't sure if her borrowed gifts were weakening, or if it was the light blinding her. "You took them from me, not once, but twice."

"*You* did this," he shot back. "You ruin everything. Always have! Ever since the first moment your mother birthed you, and she looked into your eyes and changed her promise to me." He put on a mocking tone, "*Ooh Julius, we've done something wrong. We can't make murderers of these beautiful creatures. We can't!*"

While Julius descended into mumbled curses and conversations with a dead woman not there, cold fury stole through Daisy's being. Her katana scraped along the concrete as she picked it up and stood.

"I'm not a helpless child anymore, Julius. I don't fall for those cowardly remarks. You lost. Face it."

Evil eyes stared back at Daisy in the gloom. For a moment, she thought the being that had invaded him before still existed, but then dismissed it. This was all despicable Julius.

He tossed the sand of his loved ones into Daisy's eyes and escaped into the sewer.

WIPING TEARS FROM HER EYES, Daisy's bottom lip trembled. The sounds of her family breaking through the lab door only punctuated her pain.

Mary didn't think Daisy loved her, and that's why she'd offered herself up. Flint went because he needed to be with his wife. Their love was that strong. They thought this was the only way to prove to Daisy that she mattered to them, and now they were gone, and now she would never have the chance to prove them wrong. She would never have the chance to learn how to cook from Mary, or patch bugs in AIMI's system with Flint. She wouldn't be able to experience the love they'd tried to give her... and she'd been too damaged to accept.

She sniffed, unable to stop the overwhelming wave of despair coursing through her body. Like standing on the shore and watching a tidal wave come for her, she knew but was unable to stop it.

Despair. Thick. Black. Cold.

Daisy's siblings wouldn't see it the same way. But Daisy knew what it felt like to be left behind, how the sting would burn for years and fester like an open wound. This loss would hurt them more deeply than it had ever hurt Daisy.

Despair. Thick. Black. Cold.

Her fingers clenched around the hilt of her sword. She glanced at her siblings now dispensing with the respect that allowed the Sinners to keep them at bay. She glanced at Raven, half passed out and slumped. And knew what she had to do: end Julius, once and for all.

Her siblings would only get in the way. Before despair completely took hold of her, she had the sense to deposit Raven in the lab. Then she went back into the sewer, stepped deep into it, and ran toward Julius, welcoming the blackout that came with her sin, and the ruthless hunter she became.

As her vision crowded, she vaguely registered the sewer tunnel collapsing behind her, knowing that she must have used telekinesis to bring it down, knowing that she didn't consciously do it, knowing—

AXEL WAS ALREADY REROUTING the firetruck he'd commandeered when his cell phone rang. He'd heard multiple explosions coming from the south side of the Quadrant. The earth had shaken beneath their feet—all around the city. After Daisy's call, he'd tried to stay focused, tried to keep his mind on the civilians he helped rescue. But as the beast of a vehicle bumped over debris in the road caused by powered replicates, he knew the situation was more dire than Daisy had let on.

More than any of them had let on.

The closer he got to ground zero, the more damage and dead bodies he found. Some of the wounded were innocent people. It took everything he had to keep going after Daisy. Something in his heart said not to stop, for anything.

Some people jumped out from hiding spaces to flag him down, but with guilt wrenching his gut tight, he planted his foot on the gas and hurtled down the street to where a big dust cloud bloomed. Syndicate Tower.

His cell rang again. He hit the call button, swerving to narrowly miss an upside down vehicle.

"Alvares," he clipped.

"Daisy's gone dark," the deep voice clipped—*Parker?*

Axel's heart stopped. Spots swam over his vision. He shook his head and then beeped the truck horn at people in his way.

"What do you need me to do?" he asked tightly.

"I'm sending you GPS coordinates via text."

"Got it." He cut the call, then said aloud to give him courage. "I'm coming, Daze. Everything's going to be fine."

He hoped.

thirty-five
DAISY LAZARUS

DAISY'S CONSCIOUSNESS came back to her as she ran ankle deep in waste water. She stumbled with the sudden awareness, but quickly regained her footing when she realized she wasn't far from where she'd blacked out.

Still in the underground city sewer tunnels. Her sharpened eyesight held out, making her journey easier. Still with the sense of Julius's despair sharp in her gut, driving her to obsession. He was close. Somehow, she'd managed to fight off her own despair. Maybe it was the foreign blood in her system. She almost choked up thinking her siblings still had her back, even though they weren't here.

Maybe she'd overreacted after Mary's and Flint's sacrifice. Maybe her family would understand and forgive her. Maybe there was nothing to forgive.

With heaving breaths, she tried to fill her lungs but coughed on the miasma of sewer stench. She had the sense to hit her panic button on her Deadly Seven watch. If anything happened to her, they'd know where to find her.

Calm down. Take stock.

She focused on her body.

Sword still in hand. Heart pounding in chest. That sense of being connected through her gifts to the world around her was still present.

Once she focused on her connection, Parker's borrowed hearing sharpened and sounds surrounding her came into focus.

Traffic overhead. Water trickling underfoot. A stifling breeze blew on her wet ankles. The water drained away somewhere as though a sluice gate had opened. Metallic scraping ahead in the dark tunnel alerted her to the presence of someone. Griffin's borrowed sixth sense went haywire and shouted at her. *Metal. Heavy. Up ahead.* She felt the pull of it still simmering in her system. It wasn't as strong as before, but it was there along with a sin signature she'd recognize anywhere.

Julius.

But he wasn't alone.

Something else was in the darkness... watching... assessing... waiting. She felt company in the air. In her gut. Before she could uncover it, two beams of light hit her face. She winced, shielding her eyes with her free hand. When her vision adjusted, and she stepped out of the direct beam, her suspicions were confirmed.

The madman himself buckled into a powered mech suit that hardly fit into the tunnel space. He must have stashed it here for his escape. The man had backup plans to his eyeballs. She wished she could say she was surprised, but there were squadrons of these suits developed in the black site base. Some had full robotics built into them. It was where Parker's arm initially came from.

Julius sat in the cockpit, each leg inside a metal one, each hand fitting inside the exoskeleton arm of the robot. A cage door protecting his torso in the open cockpit. Vulnerable. She should stab there while she had the chance. But wild eyes latched onto her and he pulled it down with a clank. The beams came from spotlights on his shoulders. Without preamble, he lifted the mech-robot hands to point at her.

LANA PECHERCZYK

Attached to each arm was a gatling gun.

Julius roared his fury, vein popping in his forehead, and pulled his trigger.

They say when you stare death in the face, your life flashes before your eyes. You freeze and relive moments of note. From first loves to first kills. Some say these intense moments are ones you missed out on, or moments you regret, or simply times you feel deeply about. But Daisy had spent a lifetime wallowing in feelings, and the only voice she heard now, was Mary's. *Family first.*

Those had been her last words to Daisy. Those were the Lazarus family motto. And those would be the words Daisy honored.

Julius had to go, or he would never stop coming for her family. With the full force of this realization, her palms slammed outward. On instinct, she channeled Griffin's power through her body and connected with metal in the vicinity just like she did with her telekinesis. She sensed bullets hit air, compact space between atoms, and fly toward her, but she also felt the metal itself.

Stop, she commanded.

The kinetic explosion of two forces colliding sent her careening backward as though hit by a truck. Julius stumbled and the mech suit smashed into the wall. Daisy shook stars from her vision and picked up her sword, knowing she had to get him out of the suit.

She didn't have Griffin's expertise. Wasn't sure if instinct would help her further. So far, any time she'd used his gift, she'd fumbled and flung like a child. But maybe that was all she needed. There were other gifts in her arsenal. Electrocuting someone took zero finesse. She plunged her hands into the shallow murky water and squeezed her eyes shut until sweat dappled her upper lip. She gathered electricity. She unleashed, and within seconds, her lightning zipped through the water and up the metal mech suit to fry Julius in his cage. The smell of burning flesh filled the tunnel as he contorted and seized.

Tingles rattled her teeth and skipped over her skin, but she kept unleashing until eventually she had to let go, or pass out.

Gasping, Julius ejected himself from the contraption.

Scorch marks covered his body in the places that had touched the metal suit. There was something poetic about seeing him reach for her, seeing the red welts down the side of his face that had leaned against the cockpit cage—the same side of the face her own burn marks were on.

Breathing slowly, Daisy tightened her grip around the katana's hilt and prowled closer, trying not to puke from both overexertion and the disgusting air.

"Give it up, Julius. Apologize, proclaim your regrets, and maybe I'll let you live."

"My only regret was not leaving you to burn in that fire," he spat as he searched around the fallen mech suit's skeleton for something.

"Nothing can help you now," she said, incredulous. "It's over."

"It's not over until one of us is dead, and you're too weak to make the kill shot."

"Liar."

"Sad little girl," he crooned. "Where are your loved ones now? Or have they deserted you like I did?"

"Shut up." She booted him across the shoulder, rolling him back. He splashed and hit the fallen suit behind him. She wanted to smash his face into the water, to watch him struggle and drown beneath her, but his words were hitting too close to home. They were reaching into her heart and squeezing, reminding her of decades of failure.

"No one wants you," he laughed through a cough. "From the day you were born."

"I hate you," she screamed, and kicked him again. What was wrong with him? Why couldn't he accept defeat? Her attack only knocked him into the mech suit again. He groaned as he rolled to face it, head down, buttocks in the air. Dirty water soaked into his underwear, and all she could think was how pitiful he looked. Half clothed, half cut up, dirty.

He had always been half a man, but he'd hidden it behind a godlike visage.

She couldn't believe she'd let him bait her. She forced herself to take a few deep breaths and gather her composure. Fear and despair caused mistakes. She reminded herself of what happened last time she decided to go it alone. She'd almost died and her family was angry. Because they'd cared. Axel, in particular. They wanted to be included, to make mistakes together with Daisy.

The very thought of her mate brought a rush of warmth to her body and she smiled. She had something Julius never did. True love. His was only ever an illusion. It wasn't strong enough to bring his wife and daughter back. They were happy in their other place. Daisy knew she'd never be happy without Axel.

"You can't hurt me anymore, Julius." She lifted her chin. "You might have broken me, but I was not destroyed. My family helped put my pieces back together, and now I am stronger. And do you know what the best part of all this is? Knowing that if you had simply been half the father I needed, loved me instead of manipulated me, then none of this would have happened. Can't you see that you brought this on yourself? You are the very filth you want eradicated from this world, and you—" She laughed at the irony of it. "You are the reason your wife's and daughter's eternal souls no longer live in an afterlife filled with joy. They don't exist at all. Because of *your greedy actions.*"

When he refused to speak, she pointed the tip of her blade at his throat, but hesitated. Again. Something held her back and she thought, maybe she was weak like he'd said. But maybe she was okay with that. Because the alternative was becoming like him.

Her hesitation cost her. Julius found what he was hunting for. A syringe. He aimed the needle point at his neck, depressed and filled himself with what she guessed was the greed serum, but froze before he finished. Petrified as though locked in time.

The presence she'd felt earlier made itself known. Black vines slithered up Julius's legs from the water. They writhed around his body, amassing like bandages on a mummy. The paralytic agent in the plant had petrified him, despite the power enhancing serum feeding into his veins. His mouth moved as he tried to unleash a shout for help. But it was too late. Eyes filled with terror were the last part of him to disappear as the plant swallowed him whole.

All that stood before her was a tall, writhing mass of vines reaching for the ceiling. The plant kept feeding from the sewer. Water drained as it grew and swelled. Vines shot out from the humanoid mummy and embedded into the concrete and brick around them, like a spider making its web... or cocoon. It didn't come for Daisy. It simply became Julius's prison.

And then something strange happened. Parts of his face became visible again. It was as though the plant wanted him to see, too. As though it wanted to flaunt that hope of escape before its eyes like Julius had relentlessly done to his victims. When the writhing vines finally slowed, creaking and stress cracking filled the air, Daisy heard the faint sound of a heartbeat coming from within. His eyes blinked open.

"Julius?" she whispered, unsteady.

A flicker of hope emanated from his core. She supposed she could cut him out, but somehow, knowing he would be locked in that plant with only his misery for company felt fitting. Maybe the plant wanted him to suffer, so she should leave them to it. The plant Tony had destroyed felt despair and sadness. It had asked Tony to end its life.

Maybe this one had feelings too. Who was she to take its vengeance from it?

But unlike her siblings, she wasn't concerned for redemption. Julius had his chance. This was his own doing.

She turned her back and walked away, happy in the knowledge that he'd be down here, possibly for days, and had no one to blame but himself... at least until the plant finished feeding on him. But that was a problem for future Daisy. Right now, all she wanted to do was get out of there, shower, and find Axel and feel his arms around her until the sun came up. Maybe she'd even—

Danger.

Something hit her back, knocking her forward to the concrete culvert, now muddy from loss of fluid. Her katana skidded from her hands and wedged in sludge. Tentacles slid along her back, searching, trying to get to her skin so it could paralyze her, too.

She scrambled on her hands and knees to pick up her sword, twisted, and sliced. Limb after limb of vine severed as it came for her. But more came.

She'd been wrong. The plant hadn't wanted to make Julius suffer. It had only been evolving, and it had done it at warp speed thanks to the greed serum in his system. Every cut she made in the dark, more came at her. The sword grew heavy in her arms. Her lungs burned and her legs turned to lead. She barely had enough energy left. She spotted a manhole ladder, ten feet away.

If she could get to it and climb out, she could get to safety. She could get to her family. She made a run for it, but the moment her fingers closed around the first ladder rung, a vine wrapped around her ankle. Julius's sickening cackle echoed through the tunnel as he dragged her to him.

Her fingers clawed the muddy ground. *I can't believe this is how it ends.* As the slimy vines slithered up her legs and wrapped around her body, as its tendrils hunted for her flesh, she knew there was one last thing she could do. She'd been reluctant to use Tony's gift because of her fear of fire. But if the plant fed on her, and evolved to take on her traits—it would become unstoppable.

She had to stop it, no matter the cost.

A Lazarus never quits.

Parker's voice rang clear and loud in her mind. She'd heard her other siblings say that more than once. And then she heard Axel's voice, *So long as you're alive, there is hope.*

"Are you a Lazarus?" she growled at herself.

Yes, goddammit, she was.

"So, don't quit."

Her eyes snapped open. She gritted her teeth and formulated a plan. Unleashing Tony's fire in this small enclosed space meant she'd likely burn herself alive with it. Maybe the electricity would work. Possibly Liza's poison, but considering the animal had a toxin in its system, she wasn't convinced. She didn't think she had the energy for using more than one gift. Fire it was, then. But for it to work, she had to get as close to the plant's heart as she could. She had to allow herself to be taken.

She stopped struggling.

She closed her eyes. Held her breath. And waited until she felt its slithering embrace enclose around her middle. Then she burrowed deep within her soul, found that kindling spark inside her, and she fed it everything she had. She tried not to think about healing this time, if she lived. She tried not to think about Axel, and how he'd feel betrayed when she died over this. She tried not to think about how she should be there with her family, softening the blow of Mary's and Flint's loss.

She trusted her instincts.

She let the fire out. But she didn't stop there. When the plant monster—Julius—screeched in agony, she turned the tables and embraced *him*. She clung onto his withering and smoldering body as he tried to escape. She pushed the fire into his heart until it became all consuming.

For both of them.

Heat flared around her. Light blinded. But she wouldn't let go. Even when the body she clung to became ash in her hands, she fell with it to the floor. The pain of the fire was too great. She feared her skin would melt off, but she clung to her consciousness.

Time seemed to slow as flames sizzled, crackled, and flared around her. She must be dead because she was still here, existing despite the torrid inferno and heat. Black smoke choked her and she coughed. Her lungs burned on the inside.

Suddenly her courage didn't feel so invincible.

Suddenly she didn't want to die.

She wanted to live, damn it.

She wanted to see Axel's gorgeous eyes again. Wanted to hear him croon to her in his parent's language. Wanted to cuddle. Everyone.

It started to rain. *Weird.* How could it rain when she was inside a sewage tunnel? The rain thickened and soon the smoke increased. She coughed and suffocated, wheezed as she tried to find air. Her lungs burned as though she'd inhaled the fire. A vague thought that she could perhaps push the smoke out with her gift entered her mind but it was too late. She was losing consciousness.

As her mind shut down she felt strong, expert hands fit a mask over her face. Clean air rushed in to bathe her abused lungs in freedom. The rush of straight oxygen made her feel giddy like she was flying. She was a bird.

No. Not flying. Being carried in strong arms.

"I got you, Daze," Axel said, his rough voice distant through his fireman's breathing apparatus. "I'm not letting you go."

thirty-six

AXEL ALVARES

AXEL PACED along Daisy's bedside. He couldn't believe he was here again, waiting for her to wake up, hoping to the heavens that she would. He'd cleaned her up as best he could, but she still needed a shower. They'd given her oxygen. Fed her two IV bags of fluid. Grace had checked Daisy out and said she should be fine, but she was still asleep. He wasn't sure if he could take being the support person to a hero like this. It messed with his heart.

After he'd taken the call from Parker, and raced to the coordinates given, Axel had arrived at a deserted street. He'd immediately called the man to find out what the fuck was going on, but couldn't get though. Alarm bells went off in his head. Explosions in the distance caused the ground to shake beneath his feet. Smoke had plumed from Syndicate Tower, where Daisy had originally gone.

He'd been desperate to avoid thinking about her being in trouble, but that was the sole reason he'd been called. She'd blacked out, Parker had said.

Just as he had been about to get back in the truck and head to the tower, he'd smelled smoke. It came from a manhole in the middle of the road. He'd found Daisy at the bottom, in the dried out sewer, surrounded by smoldering charcoal and smoke. Her family were waiting up top on the street when he carried her out. They explained what had happened.

Daisy had saved everyone.

First, she'd somehow closed a rift into other dimensions expanding and devouring them, then she'd chased down Julius and stopped him for good. There was nothing left of him now but charred robotic remains, and the ashes of a plant.

To occupy his mind, he arranged the potted plants Elena had brought from their old apartment. The one with daisies the elderly lady had given him sat closest to Daisy by her bedside.

Daisy moaned.

"Daze?" He rushed to her side and kissed the back of her hand.

Despite finding her in the center of what had looked like a burned out fire pit, she had barely a mark on her. Wyatt's borrowed gift must have kept her safe, but the damage was inside her lungs and body. She'd driven herself to the extreme and had almost paid the consequence.

Her violet eyes fluttered open and he almost cried.

"Hey," he spluttered, blinking rapidly. Goddammit. *Porra!* There went the tears. He hastily wiped his eyes.

"Hey," she rasped with a frown. "What's wrong?"

A sharp laugh barked out of him and he pressed his forehead to hers. "Nothing, *minha margarida.* Everything is perfect."

Of course she would be more concerned with his sadness than her own fate. She rubbed her thumb along his cheek, wiping the tear away.

"Is everyone okay?" she asked, her voice a wobble.

"Sort of." He cleared his throat and pulled back to look into her eyes. "Your brothers and sisters are back and unharmed. There are no more replicates in the streets, the Faithful are all behind bars and the Mayor is singing the Deadly Seven's praise. Even said he wants to give Parker the key to the city."

"Elena?"

"Fine."

"Raven?"

"Everyone's fine. Except…" He shook his head, still unable to believe what Parker had told him only hours earlier. Mary and Flint were gone. For good. Raven had told them the full story.

Daisy's eyes turned sad and she looked away.

"I'm sorry, Daze," he said. "I wish it could have been any other way."

"It should have been me who made the sacrifice, but they wouldn't let me." She gulped in air as her emotions overwhelmed her. "They said they did it to prove they loved me."

"And for that I am eternally grateful. I told you, Daze, if I lose you, I don't know what I would do with myself."

He took her face between his hands and planted his lips on hers. His kiss started as a hard press, but from the moment their tongues clashed, her taste overpowered his restraint. Her fingers clenched tight in his hair and their kiss turned passionate, needy, as if they both needed this to know the other was real. Safe. He groaned into her mouth.

"Did you hear what I said when I found you?" he mumbled against her lips.

Her eyes glazed with desire. She whimpered and tried to tug him back to her. He guessed she was feeling better, but first…

"I'm serious, Daze. Did you hear what I said?"

"That you found me, or something." Her tone softened.

He growled, "I said I was never letting you go."

Their eyes clashed. Hers watered, then she bit her lip and answered, "I'd like that, Axel. I'm so glad you came back for me."

"Always." He claimed her lips again. Kissed her deeply. "Glad we got that cleared up."

He pushed onto the bed and flattened himself over her. She didn't complain. Their make-out session continued and he thought, he could die happy like this. Didn't care about anything but her lips. Things were getting hot and heavy when AIMI's voice came over the ceiling speaker.

"Mr. Axel Alvares, you asked me to warn you when someone was approaching," she said.

He scrunched up his face and forced his heart rate to calm, forced his hormones to slow down. He took a breath before answering. Daisy's hands made their way down his torso and dug into his jeans.

"Who is it?" he gasped to the air.

A pause, then AIMI's answer: *"Evan and Tony Lazarus are in the living room speaking with your sister."*

"Thanks, AIMI," he said. "You're a doll."

He could have sworn he heard a digital giggle before she replied, *"Stop it, you're making me blush."*

"No, you stop it." He grinned. "Thanks, AIMI."

Daisy's fingers paused on his belt. She raised her brow at him. "Did you just flirt with a computer?"

"She started it," he replied, then elaborated. "While I was waiting for you to wake up, we started chatting."

Her brows lifted higher.

"Shut up," he frowned and then shrugged. "I have this effect on women. I can't help it. You should see the receptionist at the station."

She chuckled as he slid off the bed and onto the more appropriate chair, then she said under her breath, "She better know who the girlfriend is in this relationship, or I'll have to have words."

Next he looked at her, the humor was gone.

"You okay?" he asked, concerned at her sudden change in temperament.

"I don't know if everyone will feel the same way as you about Mary's and Flint's sacrifice."

"You're here," he replied. "You're safe and I'm not going anywhere."

The door opened. Evan and Tony pushed their muscular bodies through. Like Axel, they'd both showered and patched up their injuries. Evan had a bandage on his tattooed neck. Tony limped but otherwise looked unharmed. Their eyes went immediately to their sister and softened with relief.

"I had a feeling you'd be awake," Evan said.

She tensed and squeezed Axel's hand painfully hard.

"I'm sorry," she blurted to them. "I couldn't stop them."

Both brothers shared a glance before Evan said, "We know. Raven filled us in, and—" He rubbed the back of his neck. "Even though some of us are pissed at the Sinners for what they kept from us, we can't argue with the fact that this was Mary's and Flint's choice."

"So... you're not angry at me?"

Tony scowled and folded his arms. "Why the fuck would we be angry at you for saving the world?"

"Because I could have saved them too."

Silence descended, and then Evan said, "You need to come down to the shared apartment. There's something we need to do. As a family."

Axel narrowed his eyes. He opened his mouth to warn them to not hurt his girl, but then Evan pulled a crumpled envelope from his pocket and waved it before them.

"She wrote us all letters," he explained. "We thought now that you're awake, we could read all of them together before we all turn in for the night."

"Okay," Daisy said. "Give me five minutes, and we'll be down."

"Thirty," Axel countered, and gave his gorgeous mate a meaningful look. He needed some uninterrupted alone time with her first.

"Ew," Evan said, his eyes ping-ponging between them.

"You kids be safe." Tony smirked before grabbing Evan by the scruff and forcing his brother out the door. "And don't keep us waiting long."

"She needs a proper shower," Axel tried to explain, but they were already gone.

He stared at the closed door for a moment before shrugging and locking it. He supposed their minds had already gone there, so why not visit too. He turned around with a smirk. "Now, where were we?"

thirty-seven
DAISY LAZARUS

DAISY CLENCHED the blanket as Axel stalked toward her with wicked intent in his eyes. Tall, dark and virile, she fell in love with him all over again. He'd saved her when she'd thought all else was lost. If he hadn't found her, the smoke would have killed her in that sewer.

He came for her.

And she wanted to spend the rest of her life appreciating him. Heat rose in her cheeks and she blurted, "You're right. I need a shower." Then she added when he didn't stop coming, when his eyes darkened on her. "I'm all gross. You should stay away."

"Daze," his voice deepened. "You could be covered in shit and I wouldn't care."

More heat flushed her cheeks and she had to look away. "Technically, I *am* covered in shit."

"Are you blushing?" he teased as he slid his hands under her legs and lifted her off the bed.

"I can walk," she murmured. "I feel fine."

"I think we've already been through this before. You're *minha margarida*. That means I take care of you."

"What does that mean, *min-ha...* ?" she asked as he brought them to the ensuite, turned the shower on, and undressed her.

"It means *my daisy*." His lips curved slowly.

"But you called me that from the beginning."

"I know," he said. "I've always known you were mine."

For some stupid reason, tears flooded her eyes and blurred her vision.

"Hey." He touched her cheek. "What's this for?"

"I don't deserve you," she blubbered. "You're too good to me."

"Daze, if you haven't figured it out yet, I'm going to tell you again. It's us who don't deserve you."

He undressed himself and then carried her into the shower. The moment her feet hit the tiles, she rushed into his arms and held tight. She squeezed until he grunted.

"This, Axel," she said, her face smooshed against his chest, feeling his heartbeat beneath her lips. "Another thing I know for sure."

He grabbed her hair and yanked down so she looked up at him. His eyes were full of so much emotion that she felt it echo in her heart.

"Show me," he said darkly. "Show me how you feel. I need to be close to you. I'm not sure how much of you on death's door I can take."

"I'm not doing it again, I promise."

He grinned. "Sure."

Her brows slammed down. "Are you mocking me?"

"I'd rather fu—"

She brought his lips down to hers and speared her tongue in. He gave a long, strangled groan into her mouth and then deepened their kiss. There was no other place she felt safer than in the arms of this burly fireman. He'd walked through flames to rescue her. She'd burn the world down for him.

Within seconds they were panting and pawing at each other. He pushed her against the wall, kneaded her breasts with his hands, and then she took his long, hard cock into her fist and stroked, pleased when a string of Portuguese curses fell from his lips.

Perfect.

He tried to take control of their lovemaking, but she wrenched it back, loving their dynamic, loving that he didn't treat her like a wilting flower. She bit his lip and he growled. He lifted her by the thighs and pushed her hard against the tiled wall. But despite his rough and ready actions, he held her gaze captive and entered her in a slow, torturous slide that shuddered sensation through Daisy's entire body.

Her eyes rolled at the bliss.

"Faster," she demanded.

"No."

"Yes," she growled, and pulled his hair.

He chuckled, "There's my girl."

Then without a word, he increased his pace. He pounded into her like a desperate beast, and she was there for it. She met him thrust for thrust, bit him, scratched him, kissed him. It all meant they were alive.

"Daze…" he choked out, eyes turning desperate.

"I'm not there yet," she panted, grabbed one of his hands from beneath her thigh and directed it between her legs.

When his finger pressed down on her sensitive nub, she almost screamed his praise. "Yes, more."

He pulled out suddenly and dropped to his knees. Her leg went over his shoulder and he replaced his fingers with his tongue. The magic he created with that mouth would go down in history. He brought her to climax within seconds, kept working her as she shuddered around him, then thrust back in and finished while she blissfully rode out the last of her throes.

When they were done, as she leaned against his chest under the stream of warm water, he pointed out that this time she'd not flooded the bathroom.

"There's always tomorrow," she patted his chest.

"Promise?" he laughed.

"Absolutely."

THE ENTIRE LAZARUS family waited in Mary's and Flint's living room. After making love in the shower, Daisy felt better emotionally. She thought she had the courage to face her siblings, but the moment she stepped into the apartment, and sensed despair, she chickened out. She turned to leave, but Axel put a firm arm around her shoulders.

"Take a breath. I'm not going anywhere," he promised.

It was one thing to see Mary and Flint leave. It was another to relive it. And they might ask her to explain. Despair was not a fun sin to have, but then again, she supposed none of them were. She had to be strong for her siblings. They would be looking to her to lead the way forward, to show them how to keep the faith, as Flint had put it.

She lifted her chin, patted Axel on the rear and they walked in together.

Everyone gathered around the living room sectional and adjacent dining table. Her siblings were injured. Split lips, black eyes, bandages, but nothing too critical. Relief washed through her at that.

Griffin sat with his heavily pregnant wife on his lap, his chin on her shoulder, his arms protectively around her belly.

Misha sat next to them with her baby girl in her arms. Wyatt was in the kitchen with Sloan and Tony, preparing cakes and tea. Liza, Joe, Bailey and Max were at the dining table, looking at a collection of white envelopes—unopened. Parker spoke with Evan at the sectional, and Grace and Alice stood to the side near the television, pretending to flick through channels.

Alice's body language was hunched. She had minor scrapes on her face but Daisy didn't think that was why she stayed separate from the group. It might have to do with the Sinners knowing about Mary's and Flint's final sacrifice play, but keeping the family from stopping it. From the protective way Parker kept his eye on her, Daisy guessed some sharp words had been exchanged between his siblings and Alice.

Everyone looked up when Daisy and Axel stepped further into the room. For a second, her nerves went haywire, but then Parker unfolded his immense form from the couch and stood. His bearded jaw clenched. And he started slow clapping.

One by one, everyone in the room stood and joined him until the sound of their somber applause filled the room. Was this a joke?

She met each of her brother's and sister's eyes and, no, they were deadly serious.

"You did it, Daisy," Parker said, coming over.

The applause died down, but they remained standing.

Parker stopped before her. "Julius is gone. The gates are closed. The Syndicate is gone. It's over."

Her jaw dropped. Axel squeezed her shoulder.

"I didn't do it alone," she choked out, blinking hard to hold the emotion at bay. "And…" She glanced at the letters on the dining table. "You're not upset?"

"I think I can speak for everyone when I say, yes, we're upset."

Parker's voice softened. "But not at you. And now that we've all cooled down, not at the Sinners."

That last bit was punctuated with a warning look cast at Liza and Wyatt. They must have been the ones who'd taken their grief out at the Sinners.

"I tried to stop them," Daisy blurted. "They said they wanted to prove to me that I was loved. I'm sorry. It's my fault."

"It's not your fault. They'd been planning this for a while." Parker gestured at the unopened letters. "We got back and found a letter on each of our pillows. Mary's handwriting was on the envelopes."

Daisy frowned. "I never got one."

Axel pulled it out of his pocket and handed it to her. "I wanted to wait until we were here."

As Daisy's fingers wrapped around the seemingly innocuous white paper, her heart rate spiked.

"What does it say?" she whispered.

"We don't know," Parker replied. "We all wanted to open our letters together. You don't have to read it aloud, but... if anyone does want to, we're here too. Come on."

Wyatt, Sloan and Tony carried the tray of tea and cake to the living room. Parker and Axel started walking to join them, but Daisy couldn't move.

"Wait!" she said. "There's something you all should know before we open the letters."

When all eyes were on her, she moved closer so they could see and hear her better.

"Unlike you all, I can also sense my sin's opposing virtue," she said. "For me, that meant any time someone felt hope or joy, I felt a tickle of butterflies in my stomach. Two gates opened. In one, I sensed only sin. But in the other, in the gate Mary and Flint walked into, I sensed only joy and hope." She wiped her eyes and took a deep breath. "I think it's important you should all know they're in a good place."

Sniffles and nods were her answer, but no words. She felt the same way. Liza distributed the envelopes back to their original owners. Once Daisy sat on the floor with Axel at her back, and everyone else was settled, they all began opening their letters.

thirty-eight

EVAN WAS grateful for Grace's steady hand at his nape as he ripped open the letter from Mary.

My dearest Evan,

You were the last to arrive, but the first to truly value the meaning of family. Out of all your siblings, I think you'll understand the most why Flint and I are leaving you.

You're ready.

To love. To save.

Keep using that big heart of yours. Keep reminding your brothers and sisters to not be so serious. Keep being their conscience.

Love,

Mary & Flint.

GRIFFIN, *our dear sweet boy.*

We are devastated we won't be around to see your son enter this world

—

Griffin hid the letter from Lilo.

"She knows," he said, eyes wide.

"Well," Lilo replied with a soft smile and rub of her belly. "I suppose it's not a secret anymore."

He went back to reading the letter.

We are so proud of you, Mary continued.

In some ways, you've come the furthest out of all your siblings. Remember to be patient, and to have an open mind.

And this in Flint's writing, *And if things get a little crazy after bub arrives, always remember happy wife, happy life.*

Love Mary and Flint.

WYATT, *our dear son. They call you the angriest, the quickest to temper, but we've always known the reason why. You feel the deepest. It matters to you.*

I left the recipe for my Jerk Chicken in the third drawer down in your kitchen. You're welcome. Don't ever quit your passions—and remind the rest to do the same.

Kiss Amari for us, and when she's old enough, I left my antique shuriken set for her to train.

Love, Mary and Flint.

SLOAN, *mija. Keep smiling. Keep your brothers and sisters smiling. And when the time comes, also know it's okay to feel sad sometimes. It's okay to rest. You don't have to take the world's emotions on your shoulders.*

Love Mary and Flint.

P.S. (in Flint's handwriting)

Do NOT let Parker forget we had a hand in creating AIMI. And don't let his head get any bigger or I will come back to prank you as a ghost.

TONY.

If there's one thing Flint and I both agree on, it's that we'll miss it when you return to the big screen. We know you won't stay away forever, but we also know your big heart will use that celebrity for a good cause.

Happy and safe travels. Don't forget to come back to your family.

Call.

Love always, Mary and Flint.

LIZA,

Daisy will need help to grow into the Lazarus we all know she is. The same woman you are—the one we are incredibly proud of and know will go far. The women in this family are stronger than the men...

Scribble over her words, followed by an arrow to Flint's footnote —*This is still up for debate.*

Liza chuckled to herself and then continued reading.

Keep being the champion for truth. The world, and this family, needs to hear it as it is. We love you.

Mary and Flint.

PARKER, *mijo, let Daisy share the load.*

You have to know by now that she is the leader not because you did a bad job—but because you've done your job well. It's time for a break. It's time to throw away the rule book. Stop caring what others think of you and go and spend some quality time with Alice.

Don't blame yourself for not seeing this coming.

We did.

We planned for it. One day, when you're a father, you will understand why.

We love you,

Mary and Flint.

P.S. (in Flint's handwriting)

Take care of my workshop. I'm giving her over to your capable hands. Hug Alice for me. Tell her... tell her I wished we had more time but am glad she's with someone who will take care of her forever.

DAISY STARED at her unopened envelope and considered leaving it that way.

Did she need to hear what Mary had to say? Would it only make matters worse?

But as her brothers and sisters all read their short notes, she decided to open her letter. She scanned the words and then stood up, cleared her throat and waited for everyone to finish reading their own letters.

"I thought I would read mine aloud," she announced. "I know none of you have, but I think I should."

She inhaled then exhaled slowly and began.

"Daisy, last but certainly not least. I don't think there's much more I can say to you about my feelings. You know I love you. You know the guilt over leaving you has occupied a constant space in my heart—in all of our

hearts. But if you need to hear it one last time why we did what we did, here goes.

You deserve more.

I want you to know I am sorry.

I want you to know I believe in you. I have faith in you. So much, that I don't need to be here to see you fill the empty space we leave in everyone's hearts. There's no one else more suited than you to occupy it.

Flint and I are in a good place, but we suspect you know that too.

We hope to one day see you all again.

But not too soon.

Live. Fly. Follow your heart.

What you want matters.

There is something I say often to your siblings. Something it took losing you to understand the importance of—family first, mija, and you can't go wrong.

Love Mary and Flint.

P.S.

(In Flint's handwriting.)

Give everyone a goodbye hug for us.

So Daisy put down the letter and went, one by one, to embrace her siblings. She closed her eyes and inhaled their unique scent. Tears were shed. Then she went back and sat on the floor. They were silent for a while, then Daisy spoke.

"I'm a little sad I won't get to learn some of these things Mary taught you all."

Wyatt waved his letter. "I can teach you to cook her Jerk Chicken."

"I'll teach you how to fight like her," Liza added.

One by one they all offered to share something they'd learned from Mary—and Flint—and it warmed Daisy's heart.

After it was all said and done, Sloan asked Daisy. "So what now?"

Daisy looked at Parker, but he waited patiently for her to speak. Right. This was her thing now. She stood up, cleared her throat and said in all seriousness, "I hear the Mayor has pardoned us."

"That's right," Liza added with a shrug. "He's even officially extended an offer for us to work with the city to keep crime at bay."

"Well then," Daisy said. "I guess it's time to go and live our lives. However we feel they should be lived. If you want to keep fighting, keep fighting. Or..." She glanced down at her letter. "Follow your heart."

epilogue

ABOUT FIVE YEARS LATER

"SIT STILL, FLINT," Griffin grumbled to his son as they sat in the bleachers of his first baseball game. It was too loud. Too smelly. And dirty. If it was up to him, they'd be home doing normal four-year-old things. They wouldn't be here at all. But he promised Lilo that their kid would receive a normal, American upbringing. And apparently that included baseball games, despite him feeling contrary to it.

Plus, Flint's cousin Amari wanted to come. And Daisy, who'd fast become as obsessed with the sport as Liza and Joe, had also wanted to come.

"Hotdog, hotdog!" Flint cried, making grabby hands at Daisy and Axel walking their way up the steps to their seats.

As he watched his eldest sister approach, he had to remark on how different she looked to when she'd first come to live with them. Her long, silver hair was as eye-catching as her violet eyes. She'd taken a shine to Wyatt's cooking and had convinced the man to start back in Heaven a few days a week. Misha was expecting their second child, so he hadn't wanted to commit to full time.

Axel and his sister Elena cooked a lot, too. Daisy had a plump glow to her body and he couldn't entirely blame her physique on giving up the crime-fighting life. He could neither blame her for taking over full time babysitting duties for the second generation of the Lazarus brood. She kept herself fit in the gym, just like the rest of them… just not fighting fit.

As she preferred it.

She arrived at their seats, she leaned across Griffin's front to hand Flint and Amari their hotdogs. On their other side, blocking them in from escaping into the crowd sat Wyatt with his arms folded, scanning their surroundings warily from beneath the peak of his baseball cap.

Since the Mayor had pardoned the Seven, and officially included them in the city's law enforcement roster, they were minor celebrities. Okay, minor was a regrettable understatement.

Elena now worked at Parker's company with Alice while Parker turned his genius mind to more philanthropic pursuits. He and Alice had occasionally disappeared on secret missions helping the Sinners, but that was a story for another time. Elena now spearheaded Lazarus Tech public relations department. She'd taken over official branding opportunities for the Seven, and had even worked with Evan to custom make a selection of bio-indicated tattoos that responded to emotional changes, like mood rings but in tattoo form. She was making a bucket load of cash. Daisy even sported one of her tattoos on her left forearm.

Elena was a bright kid.

But Griffin couldn't say he was happy with how she'd turned her homemade Deadly Seven collector cards into something flashy and professional. Lilo loved them, of course. She'd pinned Griffin's "Greed" character card proudly on her partition wall at work. She'd even pinned it to her chest once or twice and had pointed at it while in the office break room, chatting with her friends.

"My husband," she would blurt proudly to anyone nearby.

He couldn't turn up at the bakery without someone asking him for a selfie. They always touched him when getting close for the camera. He shuddered at the unpleasant thought.

When Daisy leaned back into her seat, she ruffled Griffin's hair, messing it up.

"That's from Liza," she said with a smirk, then took a bite of her corndog.

Griffin scowled at her. "How many times do I have to tell you, I'm too old for that, Daisy."

"I have decades of annoying my younger brothers to catch up on." She shrugged. "And with Liza and Joe getting busy making their own family, I have to make up for her not being here. So deal."

His brows lifted. "I don't think she would appreciate you announcing to the public her bedroom activities."

"Yes, she would."

He wanted to roll his eyes. Liza probably would. "So I'll be fifty and you'll still be ruffling my hair?"

"Probably."

He caught Axel's chuckle from Daisy's other side as he settled into his seat. This was a rare day off for Axel. He was on a fast track to becoming the next Captain at the Cardinal City Fire Department. It was nice to see him here.

Wyatt hid his smile too. Griffin's scowl deepened as he realized he was the butt of the joke. As usual. He straightened his hair and spectacles before wiping mustard from Flint's chin with a napkin. It must feel terrible. He pocketed the napkin then asked Daisy quietly, "What did you get Amari for her birthday?"

It wasn't for another week, yet he needed to be organized. Lilo wasn't that good at thinking ahead for these things.

"Well," Daisy smirked. "Since she's been exhibiting signs of her daddy's gifts, I've been working with Parker to refit the training room. He spent a fortune on some new experimental jungle gym equipment."

"He has?" His brow lifted. He supposed his kids' abacus, and math books would be boring in comparison.

Thinking on Daisy's words, he had to admit this was a cause of concern for himself and Lilo. Flint was almost four, and Amari had accidentally crushed things she shouldn't have a few weeks ago. Her skin was becoming impenetrable. They'd all figured that their children could receive the same gifts as their parents, but hoped it would be without any of the unpleasant sin-sensing side effects. So far so good. He still woke up in night sweats thinking about Flint moving metal around with his mind.

Daisy nodded. "In fact, we'll go and check it out after the game. Tony put in some cash for it too, but since he and Bailey are still on location in Hawaii, they won't be here to give it. They'll make a video call though... oh, *shh*. Amari's listening."

He glanced over at his perceptive little niece and then darted a glance to her father who still glared at the people around them.

"You didn't hear anything," Griffin said to her with a wink.

"But I want dress up costumes for my birthday," she whined.

"You're getting a little old to play dress up, Mari," Wyatt said absently.

"You let Mommy play dress up with you," she countered.

Wyatt's eyes widened and his cheeks turned pink. "No, we don't."

"*Yes*, you do! I heard you and Mommy pretending to be—"

Wyatt covered his daughter's mouth with his hand and whispered something into her ear. Probably a bribe. He was such a push over when it came to his little princess.

Daisy rescued him from further embarrassment and pointed down to the field. "Look, kids. The game is about to start."

The organ played loudly, the crowd cheered, and a person walked up to the pitcher's plate where a microphone stood. Griffin considered getting his earplugs out of his pocket to help block the anthem noise, but the person didn't sing. They announced the stadium had special guests in the crowd. Immediately Wyatt growled, tugged on his baseball cap and tried to shrink, but it was no use. Amari and Flint jumped onto their seats and pointed at the big screen, camera now focused directly on them.

"Dad, Dad. Look. It's us! We're famous!" Flint exclaimed.

The cousins squealed together as though this was a big game, but Griffin clenched his jaw and waved politely as camera bulbs around them started flashing.

Daisy was still shy with the attention, especially considering she'd given up the crime-fighting part of it. Everyone else in the family still put on a suit, so they were still the Seven. But things were more casual now. Crime in the city was under control.

Flint and Amari kept jumping on their seats. Flint slipped and almost tumbled forward, but Daisy's hand went out and caught him with her gift. He hovered mid air, half tipped over until Griffin nabbed him and sat him back down with a mumbled thanks to Daisy. He was grateful she still had her telekinesis. They still didn't know if she carried other gifts in her system. Any time one of them would ask, she'd just smile mysteriously and shrug. But they all respected her choice. Unlike them, who'd had a fairly normal upbringing, Daisy never had. This was her time to fly.

Daisy smiled, and he asked her why.

"I just realized something," she said, and nodded to the people still cheering them on. "Julius once told me it was us against the world, but he couldn't have been more wrong. They're not against us. We're all in this together."

He wanted to tell her that he preferred anonymity. But looking at her fitting herself snuggly under Axel's arm, Griffin was happy for her. He held his tongue. She deserved happiness too.

They all did.

Somewhere in the Afterlife

FLINT POURED STEAMING black coffee into a mug just as his wife walked into the kitchen. He smiled at her, hardly able to believe his luck in marrying the love of his life.

"Movie's about to start," she reminded him, her eyes crinkling as she smiled back.

Instant hard-on. He didn't care how old he got, he would always respond to her smiles like that. When she looked back at him with feminine appreciation, he tugged her close for a kiss. She melted into him with a sigh that ticked all his right boxes. She always had. Only for him did her tough as nails personality soften. Only for him did she put down her sword and relax.

Speaking of relaxing, it was Date Night. Movie time.

He handed her the coffee, then collected the popcorn and his own mug.

"Let's go," he said.

They sat down next to each other on the sofa. She fit under his arm and he tugged her close as she clicked the remote to turn the giant flat screen on. While she managed the TV, he covered their legs with a blanket and then handed her the mug from the coffee table.

Mary patted his chest affectionately as she sipped from her mug, her eyes alight with excitement.

"What's the movie called?" he asked.

"The Deadly Seven," she answered.

His brows winged up. "Cool name. What's it about?"

"Well," she said, taking a sip of her coffee. "It's about genetically modified vigilantes who sense deadly sin, but it's a little different than a normal superhero movie."

"How so?"

She met his eyes and smiled again. "It's also about love and family."

"Perfect."

The End.

afterword

Thank you ARC Angels for being on this Deadly journey with me.

I can't believe it's coming to an end after four years. I hope you enjoyed the ride.

Thank you to everyone who helped along the way. I can't publish without you.

Yes... there will be a spinoff. Hunter Nuns is coming soon. It will be a 5 book series. The covers are made. I just need to find time to write it.

Soon, my precious, soon.

P.S. Yes, you will get some small cameos from the Deadly Seven.

Artwork of Daisy and Axel by @dani.mdarts on Instagram

acknowledgments

It takes a village to write a book. Being independent is a tough gig, but I have a solid crew of angels who help me wrangle the crazy together.

Thank you to my developmental editor Ann Harth. These books are nothing without her.

Thank you, in no particular order of significance (y'all are so good to me), Sacha Galloway, Traci Burch, Cheryl Herrman, Crystal Wheat, Trish Dodge, Robbin Howard, Nic Page, Haydee Otero, LeAnn Whitley, Shelby Jones, Hanna Sanders, Tischa Sharp, Tracey Liermann, Cindy Bartimus, Krystal Barton, Colleen Dennis, Sahar Husseini, Helen Walton, Kathy Marie Arrington Beeson, Kellie Mills, Teresa Bruno Woodard, Ashley Yates, Sarah Wakefield, Caitlin Palmer, Terri Jo McAllister, Danyal Vierheller, Renae Brien and the entirety of the Lana's Arc Angels team. If I missed your name, it's not intended, but thank you as well.

Special thank you to reader Natália Fidelis and translator Erika Robles for their help with Axel's Portuguese words.

And all the other angels who've helped over the past four years during the writing of this series, thank you from the bottom of my deadly heart.

Love,

Lana

need to talk to other readers?

BOOKS ARE OUR LIFE!

Join Lana's Angels Facebook Group for fun chats, giveaways, and exclusive content. https://www.facebook.com/groups/lanasangels

also by lana pecherczyk

The Deadly Seven

(Paranormal/Sci-Fi Romance)

The Deadly Seven Box Set Books 1-3

Sinner

Envy

Greed

Wrath

Sloth

Gluttony

Lust

Pride

Despair

Fae Guardians

(Fantasy/Paranormal Romance)

Season of the Wolf Trilogy

The Longing of Lone Wolves

The Solace of Sharp Claws

Of Kisses & Wishes Novella (free for subscribers)

The Dreams of Broken Kings

Season of the Vampire Trilogy

The Secrets in Shadow and Blood

A Labyrinth of Fangs and Thorns

A Symphony of Savage Hearts

Game of Gods

(Romantic Urban Fantasy)

Soul Thing

The Devil Inside

Playing God

Game Over

Game of Gods Box Set

about the author

OMG! How do you say my name?

Lana (straight forward enough - Lah-nah) **Pecherczyk** (this is where it gets tricky - Pe-her-chick).

I've been called Lana Price-Check, Lana Pera-Chickywack, Lana Pressed-Chicken, Lana Pech…*that girl!* You name it, they said it. So if it's so hard to spell, why on earth would I use this name instead of an easy pen name?

To put it simply, it belonged to my mother. And she was my dream champion.

For most of my life, I've been good at one thing – art. The world around me saw my work, and said I should do more of it, so I did.

But, when at the age of eight, I said I wanted to write stories, and even though we were poor, my mother came home with a blank notebook and a pencil saying I should follow my dreams, no matter where they take me for they will make me happy. I wasn't very good at it, but it didn't matter because I had her support and I liked it.

She died when I was thirteen, and left her four daughters orphaned. Suddenly, I had lost my dream champion, I was split from my youngest two sisters and had no one to talk to about the challenge of life.

So, I wrote in secret. I poured my heart out daily to a diary and sometimes imagined that she would listen. At the end of the day, even if she couldn't hear, writing kept that dream alive.

Eventually, after having my own children (two firecrackers in the guise of little boys) and ignoring my inner voice for too long, I decided to lead by example. How could I teach my children to follow their dreams if I wasn't? I became my own dream champion and the rest is history, here I am.

When I'm not writing the next great action-packed romantic novel, or wrangling the rug rats, or rescuing GI Joe from the jaws of my Kelpie, I fight evil by moonlight, win love by daylight and never run from a real fight.

I live in Australia, but I'm up for a chat anytime online. Come and find me.

Subscribe & Follow

subscribe.lanapecherczyk.com

lp@lanapecherczyk.com

facebook.com/lanapecherczykauthor

instagram.com/lana_p_author

amazon.com/-/e/B00V2TP0HG

bookbub.com/profile/lana-pecherczyk

tiktok.com/@lanapauthor

goodreads.com/lana_p_author

www.ingramcontent.com/pod-product-compliance
Lightning Source LLC
Chambersburg PA
CBHW030419120726
47904CB00007B/2350